SOME DATES

THIS ON

He was a handsome devil.

Stacy stopped, mentally erasing the word "devil" from her vocabulary. A handsome specimen.

Specimen of what? Ectoplasm?

She shook her head. She couldn't think about this now. Things were already weird enough. She'd left reality behind a long time ago. Her new reality was simply what she could hear, see . . .

"And touch," he said.

She turned, catching the full brunt of Chance's devastatingly attractive smile.

"I wish you wouldn't keep reading my mind," she said.

He shrugged. "I can't help it. Half the time, I'm not sure the thoughts are my own to begin with. We seem to be thinking the same sort of things. Uh, Stacy, about last night . . ."

"Yes?"

"It was special. Unbelievably special."

"I'll agree with that. Especially with the unbelievable part," she said.

"So you're upset, eh?"

She nodded, biting her lip.

"Upset because you . . . made it with a ghost?"

The absurdity of the statement hit her in the face like a wet sponge. A single giggle started in the center of her chest and bubbled over in a cascade of laughter.

Some things just couldn't be explained in words. They had to be experienced.

RAVES FOR THIS AUTHOR—

"Laura Hayden will set a new standard for the genre!"
—*Romantic Times*

"Laura Hayden's *A Margin in Time* reads like a combination of a John Wayne movie, an episode of *I Love Lucy,* and the last and best Indiana Jones flick . . . Clever, witty, with endearing characters and a town peopled by genuine eccentrics, it's no surprise this book won RWA's Golden Heart award. Laura Hayden is bound for stardom."
—*Romex Review*

CHANCE of a LIFETIME

LAURA HAYDEN

PINNACLE BOOKS
KENSINGTON PUBLISHING CORP.

PINNACLE BOOKS are published by

Kensington Publishing Corp.
850 Third Avenue
New York, NY 10022

First Printing: July, 1996
10 9 8 7 6 5 4 3 2 1

Printed in the United States of America

In loving memory of my mother, Kenner Furman Beard
(1924–1996)
Thanks for teaching me to dream, Mom.

To: Brooke Hill School Class of 1974—
". . . and as we go our separate ways,
we'll have our memories, still . . ."
Let's not wait another twenty years!

and, as always, to the Wyrd Sisters—
Deb, Pam, Karen, Von and Paula.

Chapter One

A taker of souls on beauty relies;
To gather the lost, the foolish, the wise.

Pavlachek Strylezewski (1882–)

I hate mimes.

Stacy Reardon glanced out from behind the mannequin display and watched the performer juggle invisible balls. Every once in a while, he'd break away from his juggling act and mimic the hurried stride of a single-minded shopper or pretend to drape his arm around a couple walking hand in hand. The adults in the mall all ignored him, but the children always seemed to respond to his crazy antics.

Each day, he adopted a new entertaining disguise, drawing a crowd in front of her store. Today, he was a mime, complete with pasty makeup and a black leotard which certainly highlighted his . . . assets much better than the rabbit suit he wore the day before.

During his performance, the parents gossiped while the children snickered, crowded and, quite frankly, made sweet little nuisances of themselves. Their noise sliced right into the soft, inviting soundtrack Stacy had painstakingly created to amplify the ambiance of her store. Soothing violins suited Victorian lace and satin gowns, not the sound of babbling two-year olds clamoring for "More!"

Customers seemed unwilling to brave a gauntlet of giggles to enter her store, Lacy Lady. The elegant atmosphere she'd cultivated was dribbling away like air from a leaky balloon. In fact, she'd just spent the slow morning examining the previous week's sales figures. She could mark the very day he showed up to bring smiles to the children and drain the dollars right out of her cash drawer.

Stacy broke a nail punching in the telephone number for the mall business office. Her complaints fell on unresponsive secretarial ears; the woman informed her the mall did not "have any performers currently under contract."

The second nail cracked when Stacy's grip tightened on the phone. *A two-nail day!* Was there no justice? She cleared her throat. "What about soliciting? Don't you have a rule against solicitors?"

The secretary grew a bit more interested. "Have you seen him collect money? Hand out flyers?"

Stacy glared at the man who had hopped up onto a bench to catch a wayward balloon before it could reach the ceiling. He scuffed his feet as if running in place, snatched the balloon's string then jumped off with a flourish. Bending down, he handed it to a crying toddler in a stroller.

"Uh, no, I haven't seen him accept money. And I haven't noticed any flyers."

He reached out to give the little girl a pat on the head, but withdrew his hand before touching her. Stacy noticed the mother made no effort to thank him and merely pushed along her way.

Serves him right . . .

The voice on the telephone intruded into her thoughts. "If

he's blocking the entrance to your store, the best I can do is send a security guard to ask him to move."

The phone buzzed dead in Stacy's ear. *Now what?*

She hung up and glanced out again, spotting the mime in a rare moment of inactivity, seated on the bench. If she wanted to confront this man and suggest he take his act elsewhere, now was the time. She stepped to the door of her store, noted no potential customers in the immediate area, then approached him.

"Excuse me?"

He continued to look over the railing down at the shoppers on the level below, either ignoring her or unaware she was addressing him.

"Uh, sir? Mr. Mime? May I talk to you for a moment?"

When he turned around, he wore a look of absolute and honest shock. *Me?* he gestured.

Stacy had already prepared her argument about demographics and about how she paid big bucks every month to conduct business in an expensive mall setting. But when she looked into his dark soulful eyes and watched his silent shock turn to something which looked like sheer elation, she couldn't remember what she was going to say.

After a moment's hesitation, she rallied, regaining a grip on her anger. "Yes. You. You're causing me big problems."

He stared at her, wearing what she could only describe as a sappy, almost dumbfounded grin.

"As much as I appreciate your attempts to amuse the children, could you please be a good little Pied Piper and lead them somewhere else? Like the toy store?"

His elated smile dimmed a few watts. His gestures were easy to read. *You don't like children?*

She balanced her hands on her hips. "Of course I do. I have a gaggle of nieces and nephews who'd swear to it. It's just that I don't sell things for children."

His gestures provided his side of the conversation. *Children have parents. Parents buy things.*

"I'm aware of that. However, when parents come into my store to buy lingerie, they don't usually bring their kids."

He nodded, then pointed to the mannequin in the window, indicating the silk boxer shorts and the see-through black lace teddy. He gave her an exaggerated wink which made her blush.

"Look at it this way; how would you like to explain to a five-year-old why you're buying slinky lingerie for Mommy? Of course, you do realize he'll repeat the entire conversation to his friends hanging around the sandbox."

She expected another game of charades, but the man stunned her by dropping his posture and giving her an honest grin. "I can see your problem."

His voice sounded clogged, rusty, as if he hadn't said anything to anybody in a while. She supposed it was an occupational hazard with silent performers.

He cleared his throat. "Maybe you're the reason why the kids are here in the first place. Silk and lace are conducive to seduction, and we all know what can happen nine months after a close encounter of the silk kind."

"Hey wait, you can't blame me for—" She broke off her protest, but before she could return to the subject, he raised his hands in surrender.

"If I'm bothering you, I'm sorry. I'll . . . I'll move over there." He pointed to an empty store across from Lacy Lady. "Okay?"

"Well . . ." It was a small concession, but it did succeed in moving his antics some twenty feet away where the herd of noisy children wouldn't be so close. "Thanks." She stuck out her hand. "No hard feelings?"

He hesitated, then reached out tentatively to grasp her hand. The moment he touched Stacy, her fingers tingled, then grew numb. A cool breeze shimmered around her face, then dipped to her shoulders, making her shiver. She stared at his hand, then lifted her glance, noticing for the first time that his eyes were brown. Deep, rich brown.

Concern creased his face and he pulled away. "I . . . I have to go." He pivoted and stumbled into a young couple.

The teenage boy braced his date and turned a scowl in the man's direction. "Hey! Watch where you're going, mister!"

Stacy watched the mime give the boy a stunned look, then stammer an apology. Shooting her a wan smile, the costumed man dashed off.

"Strange guy," the teenager commented. "Was he hassling you or something?"

Stacy shook her head. "N-no."

Rufus Bryant, one of the mall security guards, sauntered up. He wrapped a beefy hand around the teenager's upper arm while giving Stacy a grandfatherly smile. "Is this the young man who's been causing a disturbance?"

"Hey, let go of me." The boy attempted to escape from Rufus's iron grasp. "I didn't do nothin'!"

"Yeah, let go of him. We weren't doin' anything wrong," the girl protested.

Rufus shook his head. "Now son, you don't—"

Stacy placed a hand on the guard's shoulder. "Hold it, Rufus. He's not the one. In fact—" She bestowed a grateful, if not slightly embarrassed smile on the teenager and his girl, "—this young man was offering to come to my rescue."

A dark furrow formed between Rufus's bushy gray eyebrows. "You needed rescuing?"

"Well, not really. However, he was certainly willing to jump in and help when he thought I needed it." Now, she was *really* pouring it on thick!

Rufus reddened, loosening his grip then brushed an imaginary piece of lint from the boy's sleeve. "Then I'll apologize for jumpin' the gun, young feller. I was just concerned someone was bothering one of my favorite ladies." He gave the young couple a smart salute. "You have a nice day and thank you for shopping Chapel Valley Mall."

The teens hurried off, acknowledging Stacy's added thanks with a wave.

"So where's the guy who's been bothering you?" Rufus asked, looking around.

Stacy scanned the immediate area. So where *was* the mime? "I don't see him now, but I did talk to him and I'm pretty sure we came to a mutually satisfying compromise. It's not like he was deliberately bothering me." She shrugged.

"Well if anybody does, you let ol' Rufus know." His time-worn face twinkled when he grinned. "I take care of all my mall ladies!"

His radio chirped, the tinny voice belonging to the mall secretary. "Security number three—west parking lot. Unauthorized use of a 'reserved for handicapped' parking spot."

"Ten-four, HQ." He rubbed his hands together in glee. "Now those are the tickets I like to write! Call me if this guy shows up again." He trotted off toward the west mall exit, pausing to call over one shoulder, "Take care, Lacy Stacy."

She winced at the nickname. Rufus obviously thought he'd been the first person to think up the name.

So had the postman, the Federal Express delivery man, the window cleaner, the head of maintenance, and practically every other male in the mall. Some of them said it with slightly more lascivious smiles than others. No matter the level of intent, they all suffered from making that one automatic assumption. You Are What You Sell.

And after all, the sporting goods store was staffed by jocks, the bookstore by devout readers, the health food store by vitamin groupies . . . Why shouldn't the lingerie shop be staffed by a passionate woman who understood and appreciated the true allure of lace and satin? Perhaps someone who frequently field-tested her merchandise?

Stacy ran a forefinger down the lace of a camisole which was hanging on the edge of the sale table. She could suffer the nickname from impersonal sources, as long as no one tried to make it more personal. Straightening and refolding the display of tops, she returned to the counter to work on the books.

When the door chimed, Stacy looked up with a ready smile which faltered when she saw her "customer."

"Mornin', Lacy." Chuck Canton obliged her with the same hard appraisal he always gave the scantily clad mannequins in the window. "You look . . . nice."

She buttoned her jacket, wishing it were made of thicker material. "Thanks. What can I do for you today?" She winced. To anyone else, those words constituted a pleasant greeting. To Chuck, it was an invitation.

He leaned over her counter, tracing smeary circles on the glass top. "I need a present."

She knew the drill. Chuck would search for a gift for his latest conquest and have difficulty remembering her exact size. He would make unflattering comparisons between Stacy's figure and that of his momentary—and most likely imaginary—paramour in hopes of determining what size to buy. Stacy knew she wouldn't be tall enough, leggy enough, and certainly not busty enough to measure up to Chuck's high standards.

Talk about suffering from an overdeveloped imagination!

But unfortunately, he had a wallet to match, so in order to satisfy a steady, although unbearable customer, she played along.

He wandered around the store, asking inane questions about fabrics and making ridiculous comments about style. Stacy followed behind, playing her role of the obedient merchandiser. As he babbled about his fictitious girlfriend's elegant taste, Stacy tuned him out. Glancing out the window, she spotted the mime holding court across the way.

The man commanded the rapt attention of a pair of prekindergarten types whose mothers were deep in conversation. The mime pretended to fall, which made the two children giggle. As he repeated his gag, he glanced up, suddenly aware of Stacy's attention. At the moment he was supposed to recover his balance, he sprawled awkwardly on the floor, causing the children to break out in peals of laughter.

Stacy tried to cover her own laughter with her hand, but she failed. When Chuck turned around, she fought to regain her composure, but his look of confusion made her laugh even harder.

"What's wrong?" He scanned the mall, looking past the children. "What's so funny?"

The mime struggled to his feet and brushed off his knees, giving Stacy a rueful smile. He waved to her, then silently urged the children to wave as well.

Stacy kept a straight face as she reached beyond Chuck and shifted the mannequin's arm so it waved back. The two mothers looked up in shock at Stacy, then down at their children who were waving enthusiastically. The ladies broke into identically indulgent smiles.

"—paying any attention to me?" Chuck asked in a whiny voice.

"Huh . . . what?" Stacy turned around, reading the man's pout and hearing the echoes of his complaint. "I'm sorry. What were you saying, Chuck?"

He propped his fists on his hips. "I think you're more interested in those . . . those children than you are me." He glared at her for a moment, then pivoted and stalked toward the door.

Stacy came within a hair's breadth of stopping him. Chuck was always good for at least fifty dollars a week in sales. Fifty bucks might not make her or break her, but it was steady income. And over the year it came to . . .

Over twenty-five hundred dollars . . .

By the time her sense of commerce kicked in, Chuck was halfway back to the Electro Shack store he managed. Before Stacy could berate herself over lost revenue, one of the mothers walked into the store.

Twenty minutes, one robe and two nightshirts later, Stacy decided she wouldn't miss Chuck or his wad of damp, crumpled five-dollar bills. After a slow morning, the sale marked the beginnings of a busier afternoon. Stacy didn't even have a chance to look for the mime until near closing time, but he was nowhere around.

After locking the doors, she counted out the cash drawer and tallied the register. Even without Chuck's contribution, the day had ended profitably. Once she finished all the paperwork, she ducked into the storeroom to get her coat and purse. As she entered the area, the overhead light blinked, then faded, leaving her in darkness.

I thought the maintenance guy said he'd fixed that switch.

A sufficient amount of light poured through the door from the sales floor to illuminate her trip back to the switch which she jiggled in a time honored tradition. The naked bulb in the ceiling flickered, then died again.

"Oh great . . ." she muttered.

A voice, a distinctly male voice, penetrated the darkness. "You ought to get that fixed."

Her first reaction was to turn around and see who had slipped into the store without her knowledge, but the voice didn't come from behind her.

It came from inside the storeroom.

A shadow disentangled itself from the darkness. The figure shuffled forward, clutching her coat and purse in one hand. "Are these what you're looking for?"

She screamed.

Chapter Two

Before the intruder could make a move toward her, Stacy slammed the storeroom door and locked it from the outside. She punched the silent alarm button beneath the cash register, then ran toward the front of the store. Her hands shook as she fumbled with the key, first from inside the store, unlocking the door, then, after she escaped, from outside, locking it back again. If the man was going to try to get her, he'd have to battle his way through *two* bolted doors to do it!

Stacy stepped out into the mall and was drawing a deep breath in order to scream for help when she saw Rufus and another guard charging in her direction.

"We got the alarm. What's wrong?" Rufus managed between gasps of air. His companion was equally winded.

"A m-man," she stuttered, pointing through the window. "In my back room."

"Is he armed?" the second guard wheezed.

"I don't think so. He popped out of nowhere, scaring me."

Rufus's face tightened. "Did he threaten you?"

"No. Just frightened me."

Rufus gave his cohort a resolute nod and took the keys from her. As he unlocked the door, the other man drew his gun. They performed just like the cops on television, pressing their backs against the wall and counting to three before they burst into the store. Their maneuver would have been more impressive had they not taken cover behind a wall of glass.

"I locked him in the storeroom," she whispered, pointing to the back of the store.

Rufus nodded and motioned for her to stay behind as the pair of guards inched their way across the store. She split her attention between the two men and the closed door, half expecting it to burst open.

A damp hand touched her arm. "What's going on?"

She jumped, pivoting to face her second unwanted companion of the night. "Damn it, Chuck. Can't you see something's wrong?" She turned back to watch the two guards take forever to reach the storeroom door.

Chuck peered through the window. "Well, golly gee! Do Andy and Barney have a crook cornered or somethin'?" His put-on accent grated on her ears.

She batted away his hand. "Sssh! Someone was hiding in my storeroom and it scared me."

Chuck's voice dropped to a irritating purr. "Poor baby. You're shaking." He reached out, this time with two moist hands. "Let me hold—"

She elbowed him away, stepping into the store. Anything. A mad intruder—even Rufus's dubious aim—would be better than being pawed by Chuck Canton. To her relief, her "hero" made no effort to follow her into the combat arena.

The coward . . .

Rufus and his assistant took positions on either side of the storeroom door. "I'll count to three," the older man instructed, "then kick the door in."

"Oh no, you won't!" Stacy grabbed the keys, pushing her way between the guards. "No one's kicking or breaking anything around here!" she said as she unlocked the door. "I can't afford the repair bills. Just go in there and get him out." She noticed the sweat forming on the second guard's forehead. "And *no* guns!"

Rufus motioned for her to move back, then shouldered open the door on *three.* "All right," he shouted. "Come out with your hands up."

No one answered.

Rufus waited for a moment. "If you come out now, things'll be a lot easier on you."

Still no answer. No movements, no rustling sounds in the darkness.

Stacy tiptoed closer to peer from behind the safety of Rufus's broad back. "No one's going to hurt you," she added in a shaky voice. "Just give yourself up."

Rufus released a sigh. "Don't make me come in and get you, son."

Silence.

"Damn . . ." Rufus turned to his assistant. "You'll have to go get him."

"Me?" The uniformed man paled. "Why me?"

Rufus gave him a tight-lipped smile and uttered the one word which seemed to cut through all the arguments and protests: "Seniority."

The second guard grimaced, hitched up his pants with one hand and took a hesitant step into the darkness. A few seconds later, his plaintive voice echoed through the room. "I can't see any—wait! Hold it." They heard scuffling noise in the dark. "I think I—I got him! Lights—turn on the lights!"

Stacy and Rufus slapped at the wall switch at the same time. Their combined force must have reconnected a loose wire because the room was suddenly flooded with light.

The second guard stood in the middle of the floor, performing a perfect, textbook chokehold. Unfortunately, his victim wasn't a masked intruder; it was a naked mannequin. The man looked at his quarry, blushed, and released his grip.

Rufus stepped forward and scanned the room. ''Where's the perp?''

The two men began to search behind the boxes of merchandise, methodically inspecting every inch of the area. Somewhere during the course of the search, they discovered that the rear door was bolted shut from the inside, which meant the intruder couldn't have used it to escape into the service hallway.

Finally, Rufus tugged off his hat and ran his hand through the gray fringe ringing his bald spot. ''Stacy, are you sure you saw a man in here?''

She scanned the room in a futile search for the one hiding place they'd must have missed. ''There's no way he could have escaped, Rufus.'' Her throat tightened in either fear or wounded pride. She couldn't tell which. ''He has to be here. Somewhere. There's no way out.''

''Is it safe, gentlemen?'' Chuck took a tentative step into the storeroom. ''Did you catch the crook in mid-burgle?''

''Rufus says there's no one in the storeroom.'' Stacy crossed her arms, trying to prevent a shiver from dancing across her shoulders. What sort of smarmy gesture would Chuck make if he thought she was actually scared?

To her relief, Chuck paled. ''He's loose?'' He scanned the area with a look of sheer panic. ''Is it safe?'' He took two steps backward, flinching when he ran into the door frame. ''I . . . better go check my store, too.'' He made a hasty retreat.

Rufus shot Stacy a patronizing smile, dripping with paternal condescension. ''No need to worry. I don't think there's any real danger. I 'spect our favorite lady simply saw her mannequin in the shadows and thought it was an intruder.''

''Me? I didn't imagine anything of the sort.'' Stacy clenched her hands into fists. ''There was a man here. He stepped out of the shadows and spoke to me.''

Rufus shook his head. ''Honey, everybody knows mannequins don't talk.''

She turned her narrowed gaze toward him. "That's exactly my point."

Mannequins don't talk.

She continued to repeat the phrase to herself several times as she drove home. That night, her dreams were of stiff, faceless bodies with blank spots where their painted mouths should be.

The images continued to haunt her on her trip back to work the next day. When she arrived, she was surprised to find Rufus standing outside of her store, evidently waiting for her.

"Morning, ma'am." He doffed his hat.

"Good morning, Rufus. Is there some reason why you're here?" She took a furtive look through the display window. looking for signs of another intruder. "Nothing happened last night, did it?"

He jammed his hat back on his head and shook his head. "Nope, it was as quiet as a church, last night. I just thought you'd feel a mite better if I was here when you opened up. Just to make sure there were no bogeymen hiding in the back room."

He followed her into the store and made a great show of checking behind the counter and exploring every nook and cranny of the back room. While she readied the store for business, he even opened up the malfunctioning switch box and showed her the loose ground wire. He pulled a Swiss Army knife out of this pocket, extracted an efficient-looking screwdriver blade and went to work.

A few minutes later, he dusted his hands in completion. "There. That light switch shouldn't give you any more trouble."

"Thanks, Rufus." She opened the cash drawer and drew out a five-dollar bill.

He shook his head. "Now you put that back, young lady. As I always say; if you can't do a friend a favor, then what good are you?" He shot her a snappy salute, then looked past her out the window. His smile grew from fatherly to something slightly less paternal. "Well, I'm off to watch the jog club make their laps. If you'll excuse me . . ." He exited and caught up with three gray-haired ladies who were trotting along the mall at an ambitious pace.

Stacy turned toward the storeroom, feeling a familiar sense of dread. Although Rufus had assured her that it was safe, she still hesitated before entering the room. The light glowed brightly, minimizing the shadows. The mannequin stood in frozen repose.

"There's no one here," she told herself. "No one at all." She hung her purse and coat on the rack and turned around.

Charlie Chaplin stood in the doorway leading from the sales floor.

She bit back her scream.

He offered her a sweet Chaplinesque smile. "Don't be scared . . . it's just me."

She recognized the voice; it was the Great American Mall Entertainer. Her sudden stab of fear congealed into anger. She shouldered him out of the way as she escaped the storeroom. "Don't you *dare* scare me again like that!"

He ducked his head. "I'm sorry. I came to apologize."

"For what?"

"For yesterday."

"You moved when I asked you to, so I don't see why you should—wait a minute!" Her mind caught up with her thundering heart. "You were the one . . . last night . . ."

He nodded, then hung his head.

Her congealed anger liquefied under the heat of a new accusation. "You scared the crap out of me, mister!"

He hung his head even further. "I didn't mean to. I'm sorry."

"Of all the stupid, inconsiderate things to do!" Stacy slapped the glass countertop with her open hand, making a loud noise. "To jump out of the shadows at a woman! What if I'd had a gun? I might . . . I might have *shot* you!"

He reached up and pulled his crumpled black hat from his head and toyed with its brim. "I didn't consider how it would appear from your point of view, that it would be so frightening. I'm sorry." He scuffed his battered shoe on the carpet like a guilty schoolboy. "I really am sorry, Stacy. That's why I brought you these." He put on his hat, reached behind his back and produced a dozen roses which he placed gently on the countertop.

Stacy stared at the perfect blossoms, wrapped in green tissue paper. She suddenly caught a whiff of their delicate fragrance. "They're . . . beautiful."

Just as Superman had kryptonite, Stacy had her own weakness: roses. Somewhere in the deep recesses of her mind, she'd learned to equate flowers with love. Maybe she'd simply fallen for the commercial rhetoric presented by countless florists. Maybe she'd watched too much television where the hero presented the heroine with a dozen roses and a heated smile, then carried her off-screen as it conveniently faded to black.

No matter what the reason, Stacy's anger dissipated as she inhaled the roses' intoxicating scent. She picked up the bouquet and buried her nose in them for a sweet aromatic moment. "Th-thank you."

"Forgive me?"

She looked up and watched him fiddle with the top of his curved-top cane. Pain and honesty washed across his features. His lips quirked into a tentative smile beneath his greasepaint mustache. "I never meant to scare you."

She closed her eyes and drew in another deep, fragrant breath. "Yes," she muttered. "I'll forgive—" She stopped as logic struggled to the surface of her attention. "Wait a minute. First, tell me how you got out the back—" She opened one eye.

He was gone.

Lord, that man's fast. Placing the roses on the counter, she moved quickly toward the store entrance. When she reached the doorknob, she tried to turn it.

The door was still locked.

* * *

Everything went wrong that day.

Someone stole the roses before she could get them into a vase.

The cash register miscalculated the tax on seven transactions before she caught the error.

The door chime, which was supposed to announce anyone entering or exiting the store, stopped functioning.

Twice, she looked up and spotted someone dressed in black, walking past her store. Neither one was her elusive Chaplin, but it spooked her nonetheless.

Worst of all, Chuck oozed into the store on three separate occasions, trying to commandeer her attention while she had real customers to tend to. For some reason he was in high-whine mode.

''Stac-cee . . . don't you have anything in plum?'' He rooted through a table of sale items, destroying her carefully folded display for the third time that day. ''Dominique just adores plum.''

Dominique. Another one of Chuck's invisible girlfriends. Why did they always have inexplicably French-sounding names? The closest he'd ever gotten to Paris was the Air France poster at the travel agency downstairs.

Oh, brother . . .

Stacy smiled at her female customer, excused herself and skidded around the counter. Keeping an artificial smile plastered on her face, Stacy leaned toward Chuck, praying he wouldn't confuse her need for confidentiality with his desire for intimacy. ''Listen, I don't have time for this right now. Can you come back later?''

''What about apricot?'' he asked in an unnaturally loud voice while dangling a silk teddy from his forefinger. ''Do you have this in apricot? In a medium petite?''

She spoke through clenched teeth. ''No, I'm sorry. What you

see on the table is all we have left. I don't believe that particular style came in apricot to begin with."

"Oh, miss," the woman called over her shoulder, "Do you have this gown in royal blue?"

Stacy nodded, gladly abandoning Chuck to return to her other customer. She searched through a second rack and produced the garment. "Here it is, ma'am. Royal blue. You know, we also have a robe—"

"Oh, miss . . ." Chuck feigned an innocent smile. "What size would you say you'd wear in this style?" He held up a pair of sheer lace panties.

Stacy's spine as well as her voice turned to steel at the same moment. "I wouldn't." When she faced the woman, Stacy tried to present a cool, professional facade. "As I was saying, we also have a robe to match the—"

"You wouldn't wear your own merchandise?" Chuck was baiting her. He wore an unctuous grin which he probably intended as lascivious, but it made him look more like a jack-o'-lantern.

Stacy gripped the plastic hanger so hard it broke. She considered the action merely a precursor to the grip she wanted to place on his neck. "No. What I won't do is discuss with *you* what size underwear I wear."

The older woman grinned, then winked at her. "You tell 'im, honey."

"Yeah, Stace." He shot her a repellent grin. "Tell me a thing or two."

She squeezed her eyes shut and began to count. *One, two, three—I'm going to throw him out . . .*

Four, five, six, seven—I don't care how much he spends each week . . .

Eight, nine, te—

"Yowl-ouch!"

Stacy opened her eyes to discover Chuck sprawled across the carpet. For some unfathomable reason, he had a pair of pink lacy French-cut briefs pulled over his head.

The woman beside her pointed at him and hiccuped in laughter. "I can't . . . believe this. It was . . . just perfect!"

"What?" Stacy demanded. "What happened?" She turned to Chuck who was struggling to pick himself up off the floor. "Would you get up from there, Chuck, please?" she hissed. "You look . . . silly."

He groaned and rubbed his shin. "Something, somebody tripped me." He reached up, pulled the panties off his head and stared at them with a dumbfounded look. "How th' hell did this get here?"

"It's the closest you'll ever get to France . . ."

Stacy glanced at the woman beside her, who giggled helplessly. Had the woman said that? Or did Stacy merely think it—really loudly? She turned toward the red-faced Chuck who was using the panties to brush off the knees of his slacks. Self-remonstrance wasn't his style.

So who said it?

Suddenly, Chuck stiffened, then reached into his suit jacket. He pulled out red-stained fingers and stared blankly at them. "I'm bleeding . . ." He sagged toward the sales table, bracing himself. When he pulled back his jacket, he revealed a growing red blossom discoloring his shirt. "I've b-been hit," he stuttered.

Stacy glared at his shirt pocket, spotting the red-capped pen. *You idiot* . . . The woman beside her muttered something about calling a doctor.

"World's s-spinning . . ." He sank to his knees. "Turning black."

"Can the theatrics, Chuck." She crossed her arms and glared at him.

He squinted in her direction, drawing in a raspy breath. "But, Stacy, this may be the last time—"

"This may be the last time I ever let you into my store." She pointed to his stained shirt pocket. "You broke your pen, stupid."

He reached into his pocket and withdrew one half of a shattered ballpoint pen. His face rapidly stained to match his ruined shirt. "I—I . . ."

"Get out, Chuck." She pointed toward the door. "And don't you *ever* come back again!"

The other customer remained quiet until Chuck left. The moment he stepped out into the mall, the woman exploded in laughter, again.

Stacy tried to find something to smile about, but being generally humiliated—before lunch—didn't exactly make her day. She attempted damage control and turned to her customer. "I'm sorry you had to witness that. He works here in the mall and he's a . . . real pain, sometimes." She hesitated. "All the time." Then curiosity proved to be too strong to handle. She leaned forward and lowered her voice. "What—how . . . why did he fall? What happened?"

The woman dabbed at her eyes with a tissue. "I can't believe you missed it! It was *so* wonderful. So fitting!" She paused as her laughter resurfaced once more. "While you had your eyes closed, he started to walk over here. I was afraid he was going to try to kiss you or something like that. Then suddenly, he tripped over absolutely nothing." The lady muffled another giggle with her hand. "He still had the panties in his hand and for some strange reason, as he fell, his arm jerked up and he pulled them over his own head. He looked *so* silly!"

She wiped away one last tear, then leaned forward with a conspiratorial gleam in her eyes. "And he deserved just such a comeuppance. It proves there *is* justice in this world."

Stacy shrugged. "I suppose . . . I agree." She paused, trying to imagine the scene the woman described. "Considering what happened . . ."

The woman beamed. "Now about this nightgown and robe. Do you gift-wrap?"

After Stacy rang up, then wrapped the purchase, she attempted to apologize once more for the incident, but the woman cut her off. "Are you kidding? That's the most fun

I've had all week. Don't let him worry you. I bet he won't be back anytime soon."

The woman walked toward the door, pausing to stoop over and pick up something from the floor near the sales table. "Funny. I wonder how this got here?" She straightened and held up her discovery: A single rose.

Stacy stared at the blossom. "That can't be one of mine. Someone stole them—" The sight of a brimming vase full of blooms on her counter stopped her cold. *Where did those come from?*

"Then this *is* yours." The woman handed the rose to her. "How in the world did it ever get over there?"

"I . . . I don't know." Stacy glanced out the display window and spotted a comical figure doing a silent-move pratfall routine in the mall. As if instinctively knowing he had her attention, the man performed a magnificent maneuver disguised as a drunken stumble. He ended it by springing to his feet, bowing to her, then pretending to trip. He ended up sprawled on the floor in an eerily familiar position with his hat pulled down over his eyes.

Stacy suppressed a giggle. "He must have seen it happen."

The woman turned to the window. "Who?"

"Him." She pointed to the entertainer.

He jumped to his feet, mimicking Chuck's search for a nonexistent wound, then, instead of a pen, he pulled another rose from his rumpled jacket. He sniffed it grandly, then fell backwards in a dead faint.

"Who?" the woman prompted. "The little boy in the stroller?"

Stacy noticed the child gleefully applauding the man.

"No, not him. Charlie Chaplin."

The woman lifted an eyebrow. "Charlie Chaplin? The silent movie actor?"

Stacy was growing a bit annoyed. "Not the *real* Chaplin, the guy out there—" she pointed to the man, "—*dressed* like the Little Tramp, making the little boy laugh."

The woman gave her a quizzical look. "I don't understand who you're looking at. I don't see anyone out there, dressed like that."

Excusing herself, the woman exited, leaving Stacy alone at the window to stare blankly at the performer. He continued to entertain, oblivious to her growing apprehension. After a few moments, he stiffened, then pivoted slowly to face her. Their gazes locked for a fleeting moment until Stacy closed her eyes, unwilling to continue such an intense contact. Seconds later, she heard the door-chime tinkle as someone crossed the threshold.

Now it works . . . She opened her eyes.

It was him.

Something akin to panic flashed across his face. "What's wrong?"

She took an involuntary step backward as he approached.

"Are you all right?" he continued. "You're not worried that Canton guy is going to come back and try something, are you? You won't have to wor—" He broke off abruptly, his concern turning into something more hauntingly personal. "Stacy, why are you looking at me like that?"

Her skin began to prickle. "She didn't see you."

"What?"

"The woman." Stacy pointed to the door. "The woman who just left—she looked out this window directly at you, but she didn't see you."

"Uh . . . maybe there was a glare on the window and—"

Stacy waved aside his feeble explanation. "She saw the two mothers and the little boy in the stroller, but when I mentioned the man in the Charlie Chaplin costume, standing right beside the kids, she acted as if I was crazy."

"You're not crazy." He took off his battered hat and ran his hand through his dark hair. "But you have to realize I can't really explain much."

"Can't or won't?" Her confusion transformed into anger, and she reached forward and grabbed his sleeve. "I don't like being played for a fool, Mr.—"

"My name's Chance. Just Chance." And I'm not trying to fool you." He gave her a pained grin. "I wish I, myself, understood what's going on, but I don't."

She felt the muscles in his arm begin to tighten, bulging against her electrified grasp. "Look you, I—"

"Excuse me?" A matronly type stood in the doorway, glancing with obvious discomfort at the scantily clad display models. "I don't mean to interrupt you, especially if you're with another customer, but do you carry support hose?"

Still clutching his sleeve in her white-knuckled hand, Stacy turned around and gave the woman a quickly formulated smile of apology. "No ma'am. I'm afraid we don't. You might try Barstow's at the end of the mall. They carry several varieties and sizes in their ladies' wear department."

"Thank you." The woman paused, then gave Chance a small smile. "I always liked Chaplin."

As soon as the woman left, Stacy jerked away from him, releasing his arm. She rubbed her tingling palm against her leg. "Hold on! I don't understand any of this. The first woman didn't see you, but that other lady just did! What's going on here?" She watched guilt spread across his face. "So this *is* some sort of crazy trick you're playing on me. Let me tell you—"

"Would you calm down?" He looked out the window, anxiously scanning the area in front of her store. "People'll think you're crazy!"

"C-crazy?" she sputtered. "Because I don't like discovering I'm the brunt of what appears to be a particularly sick joke? Let me tell you what you're going to do, Mr. Chance . . . just Chance," she mimicked. "First, you'll explain to me and then to the security guard exactly how you got into my—"

"Would you shut up, please!" he thundered.

The echo of his voice settled like a dense fog to blanket her anger. She stood in shock, wondering if she'd miscalculated the situation. Maybe he wasn't as harmless as he appeared. Maybe he had a more sinister agenda. Maybe—

''Look.'' He pointed to the three-piece mirror on the store's wall. ''What do you see?''

She turned to glance reluctantly at her reflection. Her cheeks were red, her hair a bit mussed. She looked hot, tired, and frustrated.

And alone.

Stacy leaned forward and squinted, examining the reflected image. She could see herself clearly as well as seeing the racks and tables behind her. Everything was as it should be in reverse. Except that he was not there.

''Where did you—'' She turned around, discovering him still standing behind her. The world took a drunken tilt to the right, and she fought to reclaim her mental footing. ''I-I don't underst-stand.''

''Watch.'' He pointed to the mirror. When he placed his hand on her shoulder, it felt cool yet unmistakably solid. Glancing in the mirror, she still saw no one behind her.

The familiar stinging sensation radiated from her shoulder down her arm. A shiver danced down her back, making her stiffen in response. She glared at the mirror, empty except for her. She swallowed hard. ''I'm not *going* crazy. I *am* crazy!''

''No, you're not,'' he admonished. ''Just give me a minute.''

When her reflection began to dim a bit, she raised her hand and rubbed one eye. In the mirror, a faint image began to form behind her. She squinted harder.

Once, long ago, she'd attended a carnival sideshow where angled mirrors had been used to make an image appear out of nowhere. Like that carny trick, the figure of a man slowly materialized into view, vague at first, then sharpening as if someone was adjusting the focus on a projector.

Her ears buzzed and she grew noticeably light-headed. A few seconds later, she saw the complete image of two people in the mirror. Herself and the not-so-little Tramp.

When she turned around, her stare centered on the broad expanse of his chest, then followed his narrow tie like a pathway to his face. For the first time, she realized he had a red handkerchief stuffed in his jacket pocket. Tipping up her head, she became instantly captivated by the twinkle in his smile, by the matching gleam in his deep brown eyes. Somewhere in the back of her mind, she'd assumed his hair was black, but now realized it was brown, woven with golden and red highlight. *He needs a haircut,* she thought to herself before the disparity of the situation hit her in the solar plexus. She drew in a uneven breath. "Who . . . what are you?"

The twinkled grin faded and he cleared his throat. "The best I can figure out . . . I'm a ghost."

Stacy lifted a shaky hand to touch his cheek. She expected something cold, unyielding. But his skin was smooth, clean-shaven.

And warm.

"A g-ghost?"

He nodded. "No one can see me except you and small kids."

Her numbed mind stumbled over the glaring inconsistencies. "But that woman . . . she saw you. She even made a remark about your costume. And the teenager yesterday. He saw you, too!"

Chance's smile returned, lacking the devilish glint. "That's because we—you and I—were in physical contact each time. When I touch you, for some reason I can't possibly explain, I become real. Solid. When you aren't touching me, no one can see me except for the kiddies."

It was more than she could fathom. The logical side of her intellect drew the blinds and closed shop for the day. She stared blankly at him. "Huh?"

He gently turned her so she faced the mirror again. "Watch."

The slight pressure lifted from her shoulder as he removed his hand. A few seconds later, his image started to blur, growing indistinct around the edges, then his reflection slowly faded away.

"See?"

She whirled about, surprised to see him still standing behind her—the Little Tramp in all his black and white celluloid splendor. "I thought—you faded—you're still here." The words sounded silly to her the moment she spoke them.

He shrugged. "I can't leave."

"Can't?"

He shook his head. "When I try to exit the mall, it's like walking into an invisible brick wall. Something's keeping me here, making me stay."

"But why?"

He ran a hand along the back of his neck and shrugged again. "I guess it might have something to do with the fact I died here."

Stacy watched his image start to fade away. "Wait . . ." She held out her hand, surprised at how leaden it felt. Her knees grew watery and the world started to twist to one side.

"Don't go . . ." she managed to say before her own world turned black and collapsed with her.

Chapter Three

As Stacy woke up, she grew aware of several voices, all speaking at the same time. A sharp odor penetrated the haze numbing her consciousness.

"See there? She's coming around. Stacy?"

"Get that . . . thing away from me," she muttered, batting away the ammonia capsule someone held under her nose. She focused and recognized the woman kneeling beside her. "Gwen, what happened?"

The woman helped her to a sitting position. "I was hoping you could tell me. This lady came running into my store and said she found you on your floor. I called mall security and came over here to help you."

Another woman moved closer, helping to brace Stacy. "My daughter said she saw you 'fall down.' I didn't know what she was talking about, but she insisted we come in and I found you on the floor."

Stacy looked over and saw a wistful little girl standing beside the sales table. "Thanks, honey."

The child merely stared at her, then reached up to wipe her

nose on her sleeve. "The man with the funny hat and stick told me to tell you he was sorry. And he'd be back later to explain."

Stacy's heart clogged her windpipe, and she had to fight to draw in a breath. "He d-did?" she managed to stutter.

The child nodded.

The mother shook her head. "She's been spouting some sort of nonsense about a 'funny man' who told her you were sick and to get help. I don't know what's gotten into her, but I'm glad she was able to alert us."

Stacy spent the next few minutes convincing everyone she'd been dieting, and that basic food deprivation accounted for her ungainly collapse. Left with no recourse, she promised to close the shop for a long lunch hour during which she would eat, then rest. To her great relief, her part-time employee, Peg Sullivan, walked in on the whole mess and was able to throw everybody out with a solemn promise to take over.

Once the gawkers, well-wishers and helpers had left, Peg turned to Stacy. "You go home. Now!" the woman ordered, clucking like a mother hen. "You know I can handle closing up without you."

Stacy shrugged. "It's nice to know I can be so easily replaced."

Peg shot her a knowing smile. "Oh, be quiet! You know that's not what I mean. You work too hard, and God knows, I can use the hours."

Stacy looked up in surprise. "You do? I thought Danny didn't want you working any more than you have to."

Peg's face darkened. "Danny decided to dabble in the market. We now need a steadier income to cover his losses."

Stacy winced. "Sorry. Then you wouldn't mind working a few more hours a week?"

The women's faced lightened. "Are you kidding? I was hoping you'd offer. We'll discuss this when you're steadier on your feet. Wait here." Peg marched into the storeroom and returned, carrying out Stacy's coat and purse.

For a moment, Stacy mentally flashed back to the image of her surprise visitor, holding her belongings in very much the same manner. "I don't really feel bad . . . just . . ." She searched for the right word. "Just hungry."

"Then why don't you get some lunch?" Peg asked, oblivious to Stacy's moment of discomfort. "Then if you feel better, you can take it easy, go shopping. If not, go home, put up your feet and read a good book. Or even better yet, take a nap. You work too hard, anyway."

With a sigh of defeat, Stacy reached for her purse. "I'll come back later for my coat. I think I'll go get something to eat, then wander around and see who . . . er, what I can find."

Stacy hadn't taken a half-dozen steps into the mall when she suddenly had the overwhelming impression she was no longer alone. Battling rampant fear, she scanned the area, cautiously at first, then growing bolder as her search proved fruitless.

She could still feel his presence.

She took a half-dozen more steps before she stopped. "I know you're here. You might as well make yourself . . . visible."

A silken voice buzzed in her ear. "You look silly, talking to yourself."

She closed her eyes and fought the shiver of electricity that draped a cold, hasty web of sensation across her skin. When she opened her eyes, to her surprise she didn't find him touching her. If she didn't know better, Stacy would have said the reaction felt like one of . . . of basic attraction?

She drew a deep breath. "Then what *is* the etiquette for talking to a ghost without looking like you're crazy?"

He began to waver into sight like a cheap special effect from a science-fiction television show. "I don't know . . . pretend you're talking into a tape recorder or into your lapel like a Secret Service man."

"Secret Service?" She blurted out the words just as a trio of young women walked by. They openly stared at her, then hid their giggles behind their hands as they walked off.

Stacy stalked off without saying a word.

Chance stared at her. Maybe he'd pushed her too far After all, he could hardly blame her if she tuned him out. Everybody else had—with the possible exception of the kids.

And they weren't what he'd call stunning conversationalists.

"Stacy, wait!" He hurried after her, his feet barely skimming the carpeted floor. He'd learned that even a ghost could build up enough static charge from the carpet to occasionally generate enough power to make himself visible for a second or two.

And it hurt like holy hell! Of course, then there was always the possibility of scaring someone with his inadvertent appearances. He certainly didn't want to be guilty of causing someone to have a heart attack because he couldn't learn to pick up his feet.

He caught up with Stacy as she reached the bank of pay telephones located in a side hall. She snatched a receiver, pretended to jam a coin in the slot and pivoted to face him. "Okay. Now only *I* think I'm crazy. The world is safe in its ignorance. Who th' hell are you and why are you haunting me?"

Chance sat down on nothing in particular. "First, I'm not haunting you. Second, I don't know why you can see me and no one else can. It's as much a mystery to me as it is to you. If I concentrate really hard, I can—" he searched for the right word, "—shift myself so you can't see me, but it takes a whole helluva lot of energy and after a while, I get tired."

She looked dubious. "Ghosts get tired?"

He nodded. "I guess. I . . . sort of fade to nowhere until I get my energy back." He offered her a smile in apology. "And like I said, I'm not haunting you. I suppose you could say I'm . . . haunting the mall."

"The m-mall . . ." She shivered. "Why? Because, you said, you d-died here?"

"I think I did. I don't really remember how or when it happened." Chance peeled off his Chaplin hat then made it vanish back to wherever. He'd stopped asking "how" and "where" after the sixth or seventh time he'd made things occur by merely willing it. "But isn't this the way ghosts have been doing it for years in movies and books? They haunt the place where they died.''

''But this isn't fiction. It's real life—'' She broke off, her face growing distinctly flushed.

''Real *death,* you mean.'' Chance uncrossed his legs and stood, jamming his hands in his pockets. ''It's a bitch, you know. Stuck here, not knowing what I'm supposed to do other than entertain the kids around here. I'm not even certain why I'm doing that, other than keeping myself from becoming excruciatingly bored.'' He knew his words sounded almost emotion-filled, but there was a curious hole in him where he'd once had feelings, sensations.

Memories.

He looked up and wondered if she was entranced by his story or if it was pure fright that riveted her attention to him. Her grip on the phone appeared distinctly white-knuckled.

He sighed in a pseudohuman fashion. It was hard to leave behind physical reactions like sighing, fearing fire, hesitating before stepping into midair, sidestepping people as they barreled along, ignorant of his nonexistence.

But Stacy knew he existed.

He tried to smile. ''I know my name is Chance.''

''Chance who?''

''Johnson, I think, but that's about all I remember. I assume I died here, but I don't know if this is supposed to be my heaven. Or my hell.''

''Hell?'' Stacy sent a surreptitious glance around at the bustling shoppers and the fern-draped mall decor.

Chance wondered if she was trying to liken the trendy surroundings to something out of Dante's *Inferno.* He made a silent gesture to the receiver which she'd allowed to dangle from her hands.

''This could be hell?'' she repeated, pulling the phone back into position.

He shrugged. ''I suppose it could be if you hated the mall.

Or shopping or people or—" He stopped, feeling a momentary twinge of confusion, "—or kids."

"Kids? You hate kids?"

Did he? He searched inward for an answer, finding emptiness where insight should be. "I . . . I don't think so. Maybe I used to and this is why I'm forced to stay here."

She gave him a look of open astonishment. "You don't know?"

He shook his head. "Hey, I'm lucky to be able to recall my name and I'm not too sure about that. All I *do* know is one day, I simply appeared here. I don't remember anything else before that moment."

She ran her fingers through her dark blond bangs, pushing them out of the way. Gray-green eyes bore a hole right through him. "And you'll stay here? Forever?"

He struggled to draw in a shaky breath, then realized he didn't need to breathe. *Old habits* . . . "How do I know? There's no convenient *Book of the Dead* with the official guidelines for being a ghost. I guess I'm supposed to stay here . . ." He paused for a moment as an incomplete thought hovered on the edge of his mind. "That is . . . unless there's something I have to do here in order to go on to somewhere else."

"You mean the mall could be a . . . a way station?"

She looked too wide-eyed, too believing, too caught up in what even he considered absolutely absurd. If he didn't break her intense stare, he was going to need a cold shower, ghost or no ghost. He offered her a grin. "Maybe. Or perhaps, instead of following the white light, I simply followed a blue one. You know . . . *Attention K-Mart Shoppers* . . ."

It took a while for the giggle to bubble out. But once it did, the floodgates opened. She smothered her sudden laughter with her free hand. "I can't believe I'm doing this," she managed between giggly sniffs. "I'm talking to a ghost."

"You think *you* find it hard to believe? What about me? I'm running out of ideas!" He indicated his Charlie Chaplin costume. "There's only so much you can do with basic black and white."

She stared at his costume, realization dawning across her features after a moment. "Black and white . . . of course! The white rabbit suit, the black mime costume and now this . . ." Her gaze narrowed. "But I remember your handkerchief as being red."

"Red?" He repositioned the dark-colored square of material jammed in his jacket pocket. "I wish!" Reaching into its depths, he pulled out an apple, a Valentine-shaped box of candy, a toy fire engine and a rose, each one redder than the one before. Yet, the handkerchief remained black. "These things . . ." He stared at the articles he clutched. "These I can colorize, but me?" He shrugged, then clamped the rose between his teeth and began to juggle the other three items. "Not a chance." He grimaced. "No pun intended."

"This is too much." She hung up the receiver and pressed a palm to her forehead as if she was measuring her rising temperature.

He made the objects freeze in midair so he could collect them one by one and stuff them back into his handkerchief. "You're telling me! I can hardly believe any of this is happening to me."

She muttered something, shook her head, then turned around, heading back toward the main part of the mall.

Her action took him by surprise. "No, wait ! I need your help."

She ignored him and quickened her pace.

"Stacy . . . please." Chance caught up with her and placed a hand on her shoulder.

She stopped abruptly, arching her head back with eyes closed, lips parted. For a split second, she looked like a woman caught in the throes of an erotic moment. Then as quickly as the expression flashed across her face, it faded.

A warmth poured into him, spreading from his hand down his arm and radiating through his body. Suddenly, he was no longer hovering a half inch above the floor. Gravity pulled him down until he could feel the nap of the carpet in the hole in his shoe.

It was a magnificent feeling, being real.

Smells, sensations, sights . . . everything grew sharper. Stronger. He drew in a breath, a real one, then expelled it slowly. "Oh God . . . this feels good." He shifted, reaching for her hand, savoring her warmth, her beauty and her vitality.

Now he *really* needed that cold shower!

"Why is this happening?" she asked in a strangled voice. "How?"

"I have no idea." He tightened his grasp on her hand. "I won't ask why or how. I'm just thankful it can happen."

"Look." She nodded toward his chest.

He glanced down, now discovering a bright red handkerchief jammed in his breast pocket. Flexing the fingers of his free hand, he reached up, tugging the material loose. "It's red." He drew a second breath, feeling an uncomfortable tightness in his chest. "I didn't notice before. I was so busy trying to show you what I was, I didn't think to look . . ." *At what* I *look like!* Realization made his heart lurch and spurred him into action. He jerked her off balance and headed for the main artery of the mall.

She dug in her heels, putting up an admirable amount of resistance. "Hold on. What . . . what are you doing? Where are we going?"

A dozen emotions washed over him at once. Curiosity, vanity, happiness, confusion. It had been so long since he had to deal with the physical side of emotion that he'd forgotten how to cope with a sudden influx of feelings and sensations. "A mirror . . ." he managed to croak in a hoarse voice. "I want to find a mirror."

"Why?"

He skidded to a stop, willing himself to calm down and to regain control of himself. He took a deep breath, reveling in the sensation of air rushing into his lungs. "Before, I was so involved in explaining my situation, my *self* to you, I didn't pay any attention to anything else. I don't even know what I look like." He rubbed his chin impatiently. "I never thought to look."

She gave him a strained smile. "You look like Charlie Chaplin."

The costume . . . "Oh damn. I want to see the real me. Not some stupid costume. Wait just a minute." He jerked her back toward the quiet, side hallway leading to the mall offices. Large advertising posters decorated the walls and they stopped under a men's clothing ad. Glancing around to make sure that no one was watching, he closed his eyes and began to concentrate. In times past, it took only a few seconds for him to will his image, his clothes to change. But this time, nothing happened. He opened his eyes to find her staring at him intently.

"So?"

He gave her a wincing smile. "Let me try it again. But first . . ." He released her hand.

Stacy watched the color slowly fade from him. His skin grew pale, his hair darkened to an indistinct color and his bright red handkerchief faded to black. His face tightened in concentration, then his clothing started to change. The dark jacket and white shirt slowly turned into a dark, short-sleeved polo shirt. The baggy pants transformed into well-worn, grayed jeans.

Stacy glanced up at the poster beside them, and realized where Chance had received his inspiration.

"Better," she admitted. "A little less colorful than the poster, but definitely better than before."

"Now . . . an acid test for acid-washed jeans." He reached for her hand.

Although she anticipated his touch, she still couldn't put words to the sudden feeling which enveloped her as his hand slipped into hers. She didn't feel drained. Or tired.

She felt . . . shared.

He blossomed into color, his jeans still faded but now with

a tinge of blue, the polo shirt turning bright red. He looked down at his shirt front, then shot her a twinkling grin.

"Better?"

She nodded toward the wall poster. "Better than the original."

"Now, about that mirror . . ."

As they made their way back to the main mall corridor, Stacy glanced up and spotted a Calvin Klein ad. For a fleeting moment, she wondered what she would have done if Chance had taken his inspiration from an underwear ad.

As if reading her thoughts, he glanced at the poster, at her, then they both laughed. They didn't have to go far to find a mirrored panel flanking a display window. Chance skidded to a stop and stared at his reflection. His hand tightened on hers.

"T-that's me?"

She watched herself nod in the mirror.

He was handsome—not in a male-model way with chiseled features and a perfect smile, but in a real-world way, with a slightly crooked nose, laugh lines near his eyes . . . and a perfect smile.

But he wasn't smiling at the moment. He stared perplexed, mesmerized by the sight of himself. As he gaped at his own reflection, Stacy realized that vanity wasn't galvanizing his attention but pure, unbridled curiosity.

How could she blame him?

He ran his free hand over his cheeks, probing the skin gently. "I-I wonder how old I am? Where I'm from?" He paled visibly. "How I died . . ." He managed a half smile as he flexed his neck and spread his fingers across his midsection. "There don't seem to be any extraneous holes." His gaze strayed further down. "Or anything . . . missing."

She swallowed hard. "Thank heavens." As soon as she spoke, she flushed, realizing how true her apt words might be.

He lifted her hands to his lips. "Maybe you're right. I have a Higher Cause to thank for this. Maybe, this *is* heaven and you're my guardian angel."

Her empty stomach chose that moment to growl in hunger.

He grinned. "An angel with an appetite. Come on!" He pulled her in the direction of the food court. "Let's get you something to eat." He stopped in midstep, making Stacy run into him. His grin deepened. "Let's get *me* something to eat, too! I haven't done that in . . . I don't know how long!"

Chance acted like a hungry child turned loose in a candy store, unable to make up his mind. He ended up with an eclectic assortment of fast foods which would have made a normal adult cringe in fear and reach for the antacids. Evidently, he had a weakness for fried foods, the greasier the better. Stacy wondered if high cholesterol had been his weapon of choice and coronary blockage his method of dying.

She watched him sample everything on his tray before getting down to what her Great-aunt Marcelette would have called "some serious eatin'."

Stacy found it disconcerting to sit so close to him on the bench seat. He was an attractive man as a ghost, a devastatingly handsome one in "real" life. But she knew she had to continue to touch him if he was going to remain solid and enjoy his first meal in what may have been days, months, or even years. Once she got over the shock of the evident reality of his temporary hold on life, she began to enjoy watching him get such puerile satisfaction out of the simple act of eating. Great-aunt Marcelette also had a saying about a man who appreciated good food.

Of course, three types of French fries, a double order of onion rings, a malted milk shake, two burgers with everything, an egg roll and something called a Super Colossal Bellybuster Parfait Delight with whipped cream and nuts—none of it really qualified for the title of "good food."

"It might not be good for me, but it really *is* good food."

Stacy dropped her forkload of lettuce. "What?"

He reached for the salt. "You said none of this was good food. And you're so-o-o wrong." He jammed a fry in his mouth and savored it with his eyes closed. "Heck . . . who needs to worry whether it's any good for me or not." Chance shot her a crooked grin. "The cholesterol can't kill me; I'm already dead."

"But I didn't say anything."

"Sure you did. He snatched his shake and took a deep draw. Suddenly his eyes widened and he winced in pain.

Her heart wedged itself in her throat. "What's wrong? Are you okay?"

He continued to make a face as he nodded. "It's okay. Must have swallowed it too fast." He pointed to his head. "Brain freeze. Funny how you can forget about little things like that."

"Oh . . ." She remembered her initial objection and was about to speak when he interrupted her.

"You did too say it aloud."

She tossed her fork down, her hunger vanishing. "Chance! Stop it!"

He drank more shake and seemed to actually enjoy the painful sensation. "Stop what?"

"Reading my thoughts!"

"Reading your what? That's crazy."

She stared at him. *Are my lips moving?*

He grinned. "No, but have I told you they're very nice li—" Chance came to an abrupt stop and paled. "You . . . they . . ." He swallowed hard, reached for his shake, then put it down without drinking any. "Think something."

"What?"

"Think something," he repeated. "Anything."

Stacy concentrated hard on the words *I want a French fry,* but to her astonishment, they came out as *I want a kiss.*

His look of confusion melted away into something more personal. He leaned toward her, twined a hand behind her neck and pulled her forward for an electrifying kiss which made her toes curl.

He was real. Undeniably so. Real lips pressed against hers,

gentle at first, but then growing more forceful as her hands found the ridges of his broad back.

He was definitely real.

And her physical reaction was real in return.

I'm afraid.

He pulled back, keeping his leg pressed against hers for contact. ''Me, too. This is all so . . . real.'' He took a deep breath, then spread his palm across his chest, shooting her a goofy, adorable grin. ''I . . . have a heart.'' He glanced down. ''I can feel it beating. Thundering, even.''

She gulped and nodded. Her heart was doing its own furious flamenco. ''This is . . .'' Her mind betrayed her by replacing the word *crazy* with the word *love.*

''Love?'' He gave her an awe-filled stare. ''My goodness, you work fast.''

''Me?'' She sputtered. ''Now wait a minute! It doesn't count unless I say it aloud.''

He nodded. ''You have a point there. We shouldn't be held responsible for things we think but don't actually say.''

''But it's not fair. You can read my thoughts but I haven't been able to read yours.''

''Well . . .'' He flushed, his cheeks tinged red. ''I'll admit I found myself stumbling over the L-word, too. It seems a bit . . . premature to face something like that.''

Stacy leaned back in the plastic bench seat until it dug into her shoulders. ''Why is this happening to us?'' She nudged the uneaten salad away. ''After all, I don't even know you.''

He shrugged. ''Think about it from my point of view. Hell, I don't even know myself! One morning, I wake up to discover guess what? I'm dead.''

Stacy didn't have time to warn him before the couple in the next booth turned and stared at them. She offered them a weak smile. ''We're . . . we're w-writing a screenplay. It's a sequel . . . uh, to *Ghost.*''

Their curiosity satisfied, the couple turned back around.

Stacy lowered her voice. "We have to be careful talking about this. It makes us both sound—"

"Like screenwriters?" he supplied with a grin.

She sighed. "I was going to say *crazy.*"

"Ah ha!" He stabbed the air with his finger. "The last time you were going to say *crazy,* you said *love,* instead. I won't even mention the thing about the French kiss."

"I didn't say *French kiss.* I only said *kiss.*"

Chance wiggled an eyebrow at her, picked up a French fry and proceeded to make the gesture of offering it to her damn near erotic.

Stacy glared at him. "If you don't stop this, I'm going to walk away. Then all you'll be able to do is stare at this food. Not eat it."

Chance snatched his milk shake. "And deny a man who hasn't eaten in—who knows how long—a chance to drink himself into brain freeze-induced agony?"

She crossed her arms and glared at him, fighting to keep a straight face. "Yes."

He ducked his head. "I'll be good." He sipped his milk shake, shivered, then smiled. "I promise."

"Okay . . ." Stacy looked at her salad without enthusiasm. She snagged one of his fries, making a concerted effort to forget the erotic possibilities of food. "Chance . . . what's it like being a ghost?"

He shrugged as he rotated his shake and adjusted the straw. "Boring. My sheets keep getting dirty and my chains are leaving rust marks on my hands."

She nudged him with her leg. "No. Really."

"Like I said. Boring. That's why I entertain the kids. Nothing else better to do. I tried to talk to them, but three-year-olds aren't what I'd call really up on current world events. You can't sustain a long chat with a kid that young when your topic choices are limited to Barney, Power Rangers, and toilet training. That's why I was so shocked when I realized you could see me. Until then, I really had started to think this might be my own personal hell."

"And you don't have any idea how you died?"

He dragged a fry through the puddle of catsup on his paper tray. "Not one single memory. Of course, I suppose that's a mixed blessing. I'm not too sure I want to remember the actual act of dying, but I *would* like to know when, where, and especially *why.* I think I have the right."

Stacy nodded. "I agree. So what are we going to do?"

He pushed his tray away. "We?"

"Maybe that's why I can see you. Why you become real when I touch you. So I can help you find out how you died."

"Based on what we know, that's a mighty big leap in logic to make.

"It's no more difficult than believing you exist in the first place. Up to now, I never believed in ghosts, friendly or otherwise."

He shrugged. "Then what happens next? Instead of being Caspar the Friendly Ghost, do I become a vengeful spirit, out to vindicate my death?"

"Maybe. If your death was unjustified."

He stared blankly across the court toward the center of the mall. "I have this feeling that if I discover exactly how and why I died, I'll go on to the next level." He refocused his gaze on Stacy. "And at this moment, I'm not so sure I really want to leave."

Stacy looked into eyes that she might under any other circumstance call "haunted." She tried to smile, but found herself unable. The pressure of his leg against herself became suddenly unbearable. "I need"—she glanced down at her hands—"to go . . ." Her skin began to burn.

She started to inch away. Chance reached out and touched her arm a split second before she pulled her leg away from his.

"Please."

It was a simple word. Not a demand. Not a plea.

"I don't want to go back. Yet."

"Back? Where?"

"Back to not feeling. To the nothing place where my emotions ought to be." He glanced down at his empty milk shake cup. "It's hell being a ghost."

"How?"

His hand tightened on her arm. "How do you think? I don't belong here, not in this world. It's for the living." He sighed, shooting her a bittersweet smile. "And I'm afraid to find where the dead *do* belong."

She covered his hand with her own. "Chance . . ."

Their gazes locked and a hundred messages flashed between them. After a moment, he shook his head and sighed. "I know." He scanned the area. "I guess this is a good time. No one's looking."

When he released her arm, Stacy still felt an ineffable sense of belonging, of being shared. It began to fade only when the color drained from his clothes and features.

He surveyed the eating area. "Good. No one noticed." He lifted straight up, hovering about a foot above the table. "Listen . . . you've had a rough day. Why don't you go home and get some rest?"

"What are you going to do?"

He smiled. "Just hang around, juggle for the kids . . ." His expression faded for a moment. "Maybe try to remember just who the hell I am and . . ." His voice trailed off.

"And what?"

His pained grin returned as he pointed to the table littered with empty paper containers. "And be thankful I can't feel the heartburn I ought to be experiencing after eating all that."

He faded away to nothing, leaving his Cheshire-cat grin behind for a brief moment.

Her stomach somersaulted. Her thoughts stuttered.

Stacy in Wonderland?

Chapter Four

The next morning, Rufus wore a grim expression as he intercepted Stacy at the entrance to her store. He stood in the doorway and wagged a paternal finger at her.

"And just *what* do you think you're doing, Missy?"

"Me?" Stacy stifled a yawn which came out of nowhere. She'd slept hard the night before and it had taken almost an entire pot of double-strength coffee to rouse her that morning. "Just trying to make a living, Rufus." She reached around him and attempted to shove the key somewhere in the vicinity of the lock.

He took the key ring from her shaky hands and unlocked the door himself. "Well, I heard all about yesterday from Gwen and I must say I'm shocked to see you back." He held the door open for her, allowing her to reach in and input the alarm security code.

"All I did was faint."

"And it was all my fault."

Stacy spun around and spotted Chance hovering in a reclined position over her sales table.

He leaned up on one elbow and doffed his referee-striped ball cap. "Morning, Stace."

She came within a hair's breadth of returning his greeting, but snapped her mouth closed before saying a word.

"Aha!" His face split in a grin as he rolled over to a seated position in midair. "Now you understand. If you start talking to the invisible man, you just might be awarded a one-way ticket to the Looney Toons ward. . . ."

"I wouldn't speak so lightly about your health if I were you," Rufus continued, oblivious to their visitor.

Chance twirled the cap on one finger. "I—for one, sir—am glad she doesn't resemble you at all." He gave her a calculated once-over which raised her temperature a notch. When Chuck Canton made the same overture, the only things he raised were her hackles.

Stacy waited until Rufus ducked in the storeroom to perform his security check before she made a frantic gesture to Chance to be quiet.

"Why?" he challenged. "Rufus can't hear me."

She spoke between clenched teeth. "But *I* can."

Rufus returned from the store room. "You can what?"

Stacy swallowed hard as she searched for a fast answer. "I can . . . er . . . I can always rely on you to keep an eye out for me, Rufus. Thank you."

He reddened around the collar. "You know, me and Mrs. Bryant—God rest her soul—we never had any children, but you've always reminded me so much of my favorite niece, Mildred."

"Mildred?" Chance started laughing. "You remind him of someone named *Mildred?* Don't tell me, let me guess—six-foot even in her stocking feet, straight face, straight hair, straight body. Mil-dred . . . oh Mil-dread!" he called out in a falsetto voice.

Stacy tried to ignore Chance as he slowly rotated in midair, propelling himself in a circle by his spasms of laughter. She turned instead to Rufus. "That's very sweet of you to say so, but you don't have to waste any time worrying about me. I'm only going to work a half day. Peg's coming in at lunch and will stay until closing."

"That's good. You need the rest and Peg could sure use the money . . . what with Danny losing his shirt in the stock market and all that."

Stacy gaped at the security guard. "When did you find out about that?"

His collection of keys jangled as he adjusted his belt. "Lessee, I think she mentioned something about it last week. Or was it the week before?" He glanced at his watch. "Oops, almost time for the jog club." He eyed the mall corridor with a gleam of expectation. "There's this new lady who just joined and she has legs that would do Betty Grable proud." He winked then headed for the door. "Now you take care, Lacy Stacy. I'm going to be keeping an eye on you."

Chance rolled in a lazy circle as he shook with laughter. "First 'Mil-dread,' then 'Lacy Stacy'! Where in the world does Deputy Rufus come up with these names? Hey . . . wait a minute. Look." Chance pointed out the window at the group of gray-haired women speed walking down the mall. A group of men lagged behind them, apparently appreciating the rear viewpoint. Rufus fell in step beside a darkly dressed man.

"Good Lord, look at ol' Rufus move!" Chance called down from his bird's-eye perch. "Who would've thought he could get up a head of steam like that? I'm impressed!"

Stacy felt suddenly protective of her aged benefactor. "Leave him alone, Chance. He's a nice guy."

Chance slowly floated closer to the floor. "You're right. He's a pretty good rent-a-cop. A bit territorial, but basically an honest guy."

"I'm glad you approve," she stated with a bit more sarcasm than necessary. "At least he thought well enough to plan ahead and meet me at the door this morning and inquire as to my health."

Chance crossed his arms, bobbing slightly in the air. ''Whoa! And who got up on the wrong side of the bed this morning?''

''Me.'' She glared up at him, then winced in pain. ''Would you get down from there? You're giving me a crick in the neck.''

''Testy, testy,'' he clucked. ''I'm not sure I want to be within firing range of your temper.''

''Temper?'' Stacy scanned through the display windows and saw no one within view. Reaching up, she grabbed hold of his ankle.''

He started to smirk. ''You can't pull me . . .'' A moment after she touched him, he suddenly gained mass. And with the advent of mass came gravity. ''Yowl . . . ouch!'' Chance fell hard, barely missing her sales table, and landed in a crumpled heap on the floor. He pushed himself up, wearing a grimace. ''Why did you do that?''

She released her hold on his leg. ''Don't blame me. Blame gravity.''

He pushed his cap to the back of his head. ''I don't think Sir Isaac Newton had this in mind as he was formulating his theories.'' Chance stretched, then lumbered to his feet. ''I'm just glad that I don't feel any pain when I'm a ghost. I think I broke my ankle when I landed.''

''Broke your what? I didn't think . . .'' Stacy's face reddened in guilt. ''I'm so sorry, Chance.''

He waved a careless gesture in her direction. ''Don't give it a second thought. I don't feel a thing now.'' He stood and proved his point by hopping on what had been his injured foot. ''Listen, I heard what you said to Rufus about working only a half day. Is everything okay? Are you really all right?''

She shrugged as she walked over to the sales counter. ''I suppose it's nothing a little sleep wouldn't cure. Besides I can't very well explain to them I fainted because I saw a ghost. I don't mind taking a little time off, especially if Peg could use the extra hours.''

He nodded sagely. "Yeah . . . what with Danny's bad turn in the market."

Stacy braced two palms on the glass-topped counter. "Where have I been that I don't know about Peg and Danny's financial problems? You know about it. So does Rufus, the woman who works next door . . . Good Lord, I've known Peg and Danny forever and *I* didn't have a single glimmer that they were having any money problems."

"Maybe you've been working too hard to notice what's going on around you. I think you really need that time off." Chance pulled his hat off and ran his hand through his hair. "So what do you plan to do with your free time?"

She glanced around the store. Her store. It had been the center of her universe for six months. Every moment of her time, every thought that crossed her mind was totally devoted to Lacy Lady, to its upkeep, its success. She couldn't remember the last time she'd had a day off.

Free time. She shivered in spite of herself, then glanced up into his eager face. "I have no earthly idea what to do. You have any suggestions?"

He stuffed his hands in his pockets and shrugged. "You've spent almost as much time here as I have." His face darkened for a moment. "Of course, you can leave—I can't. But, if I had the freedom to escape this place, I'd go find a park where I could stretch out in the grass and watch the clouds go by." A strange look of longing passed over his face. "Only time I get to see the sun is when it shines through the skylights in the center court." He sighed as his expression of longing faded to one of sadness. "This is my world. Such as it is."

His world. Her world. Were they the same worlds? Stacy didn't think so. Although he glossed over one point, Stacy realized the crux of the differences between them wasn't the fact that he was dead and she was alive. The real difference was that she was free and he was bound to the mall.

"How many times have you tried to leave?" she asked in a soft voice.

"About a million times." His unfocused stare sharpened into something harsher. "I can make it out the first set of doors, but when I try the second set, it's like running headlong into an invisible concrete wall. I can feel it, blocking my way, preventing me from escaping." He pulled off his referee ball cap and dragged his fingers through his hair. "It's just so frustrating to see the real world out there but know I can't get to it. I'm stuck here. In an ugly little plastic microworld where money is the universal language."

His palpable pain filled her as if it was her own. "I'm . . . I'm sorry."

He shot her a strained smile. "About what? You haven't done anything wrong." His expression faded. "As far as that goes, I don't even know if *I* did something wrong to deserve this. If only I could remember . . ."

Stacy remembered.

She couldn't help remembering. His words stuck with her, haunting her morning. When Peg finally arrived at lunchtime, Stacy grabbed her purse and coat and headed out to find Chance. As soon as she exited her store, the magnitude of her task hit her. How do you find a single person, much less a ghost, in a mall that size?

The answer was simple.

"Mr. Johnson, paging Mr. Chance Johnson," intoned the mall announcer a few minutes later. "Please meet your party at the Information Desk."

Stacy propped up against the counter and waited, figuring it wouldn't take long. It didn't. A minute later, she saw Chance streaking toward the desk, dodging shoppers and hurdling strollers. He slowed when he saw who was waiting for him at the counter.

"Oh . . . it's you."

She pretended to pout. "Don't look so disappointed."

He graced her with a halfhearted smile. "I'm not disappointed, Stace. I thought . . . just for a second that maybe someone else knew I was here."

"Who?"

He shrugged. "I don't know. Maybe I thought you might be a guide sent to take me to my correct afterlife. Or to help me escape this place forever."

She felt a small spark of excitement grow inside of her. "Maybe that's just what I'm supposed to do. I know this might sound crazy—" Stacy glanced up in time to see the lady at the information desk give her a cautious stare.

"You're doomed. That's Tabloid Tess, the biggest gossip in the entire mall. I have a feeling you're likely to be her next headline: 'Another mall merchant snaps under the pressure and starts talking to herself.'" Chance thumbed his nose at the woman. "Get a life, lady."

Stacy pivoted and began to head toward a nearby bank of phones. Chance was trailing right behind her. "But I have an idea that I think could possibly work."

"What?"

"If you can't exit the mall because you're a ghost, then why don't I touch you, then—"

He zipped past her shoulder and planted himself in her path. "—then we try to go outside? Together?" A look of sudden animation flood his face. "It all makes sense. And maybe once I get free of this place, I will be totally free!"

"Exactly!" She checked the urge to grab his hand and bring him to life that very moment. After all, they were still in the middle of a busy mall and even if such a miracle could be overlooked by the teeming masses, the eagle-eyed mall gossip wouldn't miss a thing.

And what would the woman see?

A refugee from Monday Night Football?

Chance shook his head in mock sorrow. "It's not *refugee*—it's *referee*.

Stacy nodded toward Chance's striped outfit. "Actually you

looked more like a rouge athletic-shoe salesman than a reject from Monday Night Football."

"Thanks . . . loads." Moments later, he stood before her in the polo shirt and jeans he'd worn the day before. "This better?"

She nodded. "And now to find someplace where you can—" She stumbled over the words, "—become real."

They ducked into a service corridor but found a brown-shirted delivery man unloading a shipment. Stacy went down a staircase and by the time they reached the bottom tread, Chance was fully human. He stopped in the corridor, drew a deep breath and grinned, squeezing her hand.

"It smells wonderful."

Stacy glared at the overflowing trash can pushed out into the hallway. The stench was almost unbearable.

"You're kidding, right?" She dragged him toward the service door which she knew opened out to a loading dock. They both paused for a moment, her hand resting on the push bar that would release the door. "Are you ready, Chance?"

He nodded, then squeezed his eyes shut.

She opened the door and together, they stumbled onto the loading dock, hand in hand. A wave of heat hit her, almost knocking her off her feet. When she looked up at Chance, he still had his eyes closed.

"Are we . . . outside?" he said between clenched teeth.

She glanced around. "Not technically."

He opened his eyes.

They were standing on the covered dock which was part of the building inset. Luckily, there were no trucks waiting to unload, thus allowing them a clear view of the acres of parked cars shining in the noonday sun.

Chance gave her a nervous grin. "So close . . . yet so far away." He lifted her hand to his lips for a quick kiss. "Ready?"

Stacy nodded. The moment they stepped off the last stair and into the sunlight, she felt his body stiffen. She instinctively tightened her hold on him, preparing for the worst.

For one terrifying second, he imagined himself being torn from her grasp and hurled back to the mall. The mind's eye played out several scenarios during that one moment, including one unpleasant analogy about vampires disintegrating in the light of day.

But nothing happened.

"I'm out." He squinted toward the sun, lifting his face so the beams of light bathed him in gentle warmth. "I'm free." He started to breathe faster, almost panting, as his body adjusted to the miracle of life in great outdoors. A thousand sensations hit him at once.

The glare of the sun.

A cacophony of sounds. Horns, people, airplanes overhead.

The lingering smell of diesel exhaust riding a fresh breeze of summer air.

As they stepped toward a sidewalk, he felt his knees grow watery, his mind grow fuzzy. The sensations swirled as his ability to separate them vanished. He smelled heat. He tasted the sun. He saw the rainbow colors of the various noises around him.

If his control was vanishing, would he be the next thing to go? His stomach lurched. "Stacy . . . it's happening." He gripped her arm. "I'm starting to feel funny. I think I'm getting pulled back."

She shook her head, then reached up and brushed a curl of hair off his forehead. The tender gentleness of her gesture robbed him of all thought. "Everything's all right, Chance," she whispered. "You're not going anywhere." She gave him an encouraging smile. "You're just hyperventilating."

He held his breath and closed his eyes one more time.

One last time?

When he opened them again, he found himself still standing on the sidewalk. He was outside. Free.

He'd escaped!

Chance tightened his grip on her hand. "It worked. My God, Stacy! It worked!" He whirled her around, then pulled her into his arms. His simple kiss of celebration lasted only a split second before it transformed into something infinitely more personal.

Whether it was the intensity of the sensation which astounded him or merely the newness of it all, he couldn't be sure. Up to now, his "life" on Earth had been devoid of intensity, of passion, of any emotions, in general. When Stacy brought him reality, she brought a host of other concepts with her.

Like gravity.

Pleasure.

And pain.

When he had fallen earlier in the store, the brief moment before she broke contact, he had experienced excruciatingly real pain. The sensation was an exquisite oasis of reality in the midst of a barren existence.

But now, whether he was falling in love with Stacy or merely with life, he found himself reacting to the sheer, nearly unadulterated pleasure of the kiss they were sharing. His thoughts melted away as the physical intensity mounted between them.

When she finally pulled back, he felt almost as bereft as he did when he reverted to being a ghost. He glanced down at their hands, relieved to see her fingers still safely laced with his. He leaned forward for another kiss, wanting to satisfy the insatiable itch of newfound desire.

As their lips met again, a truck horn blasted, making them both jump. Chance pulled her closer, his sense of protection jumping to life.

A man leaned out of the cab of the truck which had pulled beside them. "Yo . . . lovebirds. Take it somewhere else. I got a delivery to make."

Chance led them to the sidewalk, then turned to the woman who fitted so very comfortably in his arms. "You okay?"

She nodded, then ducked her head, the tips of her ears reddening. "Why don't we . . . walk for a while?"

They wandered down the sidewalk which circled the building. Each time they passed a mirrored window, Chance marveled at their reflection. Together, they looked like a normal couple, not like a ghost and his girl out for a stroll around the ephemeral block.

"So . . . where do you want to go?" Stacy asked, nudging him away from the next window. "To a park?"

"Huh? Park?" He turned his attention from her reflection to the real thing. "Oh, uh—yeah. Definitely." He turned around, lifting his face toward the sun, thrilled by the warmth, even the glare of the sun. "Is there one close by?"

She nodded. "Just a couple of blocks north. Do we walk?" She paused, then shot him a conspiratorial smile. "Or ride?"

His heart lurched with one extra beat. "Ride? You mean like in a car?"

Her smile deepened. "I thought that might get your attention."

"I haven't been in a car in . . . I don't know *how* long!" The thrill of the prospect dimmed as he tried to imagine the logistics of such a task. "But how can you drive and maintain contact with me at the same time?"

She gave him a sidelong glance and grinned. "Teenagers have been doing it for years."

Chance stretched out on the blanket, careful to keep his leg pressed next to hers. They'd discovered they needed both hands to manage the burgers they'd gotten from a drive-through window. Although he'd eaten the day before, he hadn't had a chance to experience the sensation of feeling full. Now, although his stomach groaned in protest, he loved every caloric-carbohydrate-fat-laden minute of it.

"Stacy?"

"Hmm?"

He stared up at the clouds, trying to see objects in the ambiguous shapes. "Tell me about yourself."

"Me?" She sipped from her cup, then fitted it back into the cardboard drink carrier. "What's there to tell? I'm a struggling business owner trying to make a living by selling dreams to women."

"Dreams?" He sat up a little. "And here I thought you only sold lingerie. Is that what satin and lace really means to women? I always thought it was men who dreamed of things like that."

Stacy stretched out on the blanket beside him, paying attention to the task of maintaining contact as she turned over onto her stomach. "Some women buy lingerie to please their men. Some do it to please themselves. It's not a matter of increasing sex appeal. It's all about making a woman feel comfortable with herself."

He rolled over and shot her a dubious stare. "Aren't you placing a lot of importance on a simple piece of material? Even if it's sometimes a piece of incredibly skimpy, almost transparent material?"

She toyed with a blade of grass, tearing it into tiny strips. "Not really. If I were working in a sterile environment like a hospital, or a highly structured one where I had to wear power suits all the time, I might find it very comforting to know that beneath it all, I was wearing something decidedly feminine."

"Exerting a little individualism in a regimented world?"

"Something like that."

"Too bad men don't have the same option."

She shrugged. "I have male customers, too."

He released a snort of laughter. "I'll bet. There are always a couple of—"

"No . . . not like that. I sell men's wear, too."

He tried to bury his thoughts, fearing that Stacy might discover one of his lesser-known secrets. "Men buying lingerie? For themselves? Interesting concept."

"Silk boxer shorts are one of my biggest sellers in men's wear. Women find it very attractive to know that beneath a man's very staid business suit, he's wearing something daring. Provocative, even."

Chance felt heat rush up his neck to flood his face. *Damn!* He'd forgotten all about physical reactions like blushing.

She grinned at him. "You're blushing. Why?" Her gaze narrowed, then she clamped a hand over her mouth. "If all you have to do is imagine what you're wearing and it appears, then how hard would it be to imagine a pair of fancy silk boxer shorts rather than some old boring white briefs?"

He closed his eyes, knowing his face told all. He felt her fumble with his waistband.

"Let me see . . ."

He swatted away her hand. "Stacy . . . please! Have some decency."

"Aw, Chance, let me look, please? You've got me curious now. You copied one of the patterns from my store, didn't you? Which ones?"

He groaned and kept his eyes closed. "The paisley ones."

"Which paisley ones?"

He took a deep breath. "The blue ones on display in the window."

She clapped her hands in obvious approval. "Just perfect. They're exactly the ones I would have picked out for you."

"Oh joy . . ." he muttered. He opened his eyes and moved to sit up. Suddenly, he realized he'd broken contact with her. It started with a numbing sensation in the center of his chest. He pressed a hand to where he'd felt his own strong heartbeat earlier, but now, there was only an eerie stillness.

A deadly silence.

When he turned to Stacy, she stared at him dumbfounded. "What's wron—" She glanced down at the gap between their legs. "Oh no." Abject fear filled her face as she tried to grab his arm. Her fingers passed through him without touching any substance.

"Too late, I guess." He tried to smile at her. "It wasn't your fault, though. I moved. I just didn't . . . think." He hunched over as the pain increased, radiating through his body like jagged streaks of lightning. It made no sense to him; reverting to his previous ghostly status shouldn't hurt at all.

Should it?

Pain was for the living, not the dead.

As he struggled to hold himself together, literally, his senses blotted out one by one. Black dots filled his sight and a roaring sound clogged his ears.

As the area around him darkened, all he could make out was Stacy's terror-stricken face. Tears streamed down her cheeks. Her mouth moved, but he couldn't hear her words. She tried to throw her arms around him, but he couldn't feel her.

No warmth. No satisfaction. No nothing.

He read her lips: "I'm sorry."

Chance lifted a leaden arm and tried to caress her face. "N-not your f-fault."

The world collapsed onto itself.

He existed no more.

Chapter Five

The final moment of pain on Chance's face was more than Stacy could bear. After he disappeared, the image continued to flash in her brain, burning accusations of her guilt with each distorted repetition.

She prayed for him, for his soul. And then she prayed for forgiveness. In her heart, she knew she'd just watched a man die. And it was all her fault.

Stacy sat in numbed shock in the middle of the park for an indeterminate length of time. Finally, dark clouds collected, blotting out the sun, and a building wind forced her to take retreating action. Not knowing whether to blame her shivers on the dropping temperatures or on the last vestiges of trauma, she gathered up the blanket and their trash and made her way slowly back to the car.

She drove back to the mall, out of habit more than anything else. She remained in the parking lot for a while. How long? She didn't know. It would require a vast amount of courage for her to enter and confirm the fact that Chance was indeed gone. She discovered that what she lacked in courage, she could replace with hope.

Hope whispered weakly to her, *Maybe. Just maybe.*

Bracing herself against the rain which had begun to lash the car, Stacy got out and dashed through the parking lot toward the mall entrance.

When she made a soggy arrival at the store, Peg merely lifted a critical eyebrow. "I wondered how long you could stay away." She glanced at her watch. "Four hours. I think that's a record."

"Is everything . . . okay?" Stacy asked tentatively.

"Here." Peg reached under the counter and pulled out a wad of Kleenex which Stacy used to mop the water out of her eyes. "Everything's fine and dandy. We've had a couple of good sales plus several piddly ones, but you know how those add up. By the way, we need to order more black silk boxer shorts. I sold the last pair." A haze floated over Peg's eyes. "He was dark and dreamy and I bet he'll look—" she released a theatrical sigh, "—marvelous in just the boxers."

Stacy tried to smile but couldn't. "Remember what Danny says: look but don't touch." As soon as she spoke, she realized how true her words were. She should have never touched Chance.

Never taken a chance.

Taken a *Chance.*

Oblivious to Stacy's inner turmoil, Peg glanced at the puddle forming at Stacy's feet and grinned. "If it's raining that hard, I guess we can't expect much more in sales for today." She patted her own chest, her hand imitating a beating heart. "No more Mr. Tall, Dark, and Handsome Heartthrobs."

Stacy found herself nodding too quickly. "I-I t-think I'll just hang out in the back room and catch up on some paperwork."

Peg looked at her with open concern. "Are you sure you're all right? You look worse than when you left."

She pulled off her damp jacket and shot her assistant the most sarcastic smile she could muster under the circumstances.

"Thanks. Loads. You just . . . just sell some dreams. I'll go handle the books."

Stacy closed the storeroom door behind her. Settling herself at the desk, she pulled out the inventory sheets and began to tally the sales against the current inventory. After fifteen minutes, her eyes blurred and the tears made big wet splotches on the ledger paper. Her tenuous control splintered, and she lowered her head and began to cry.

After she got the bigger sobs out of her system, she was left with the small hiccuppy ones. Between sniffs, she heard a noise in the back of the storeroom. She wiped her eyes on her sleeve. "Is someone there?"

She heard what sounded like a groan.

"Chance?" she whispered into the shadows.

"S-Stace?"

She sprang to her feet, her heart rumbling like an earthquake. She squinted into the darkness. "Where are you?"

"Over here."

She followed the sound of his faint voice, spotting a dark form on the floor behind some boxes. Her heart threatened to stop entirely when she realized it was indeed Chance, lying on the floor. She fell to her knees beside him and reached for his cheek. "Oh, Chance . . . you're aliv—"

"No," he croaked, flinching away from her. "Don't touch me."

She withdrew her hand, feeling a sudden emptiness within. "I w-won't. What's wrong?"

"Can't touch you. I'm not completely formed. If I become real now, I won't be able to stand the pain."

She stared at him, slowly realizing she could peer through his vague shape and see the cracks in the concrete floor beneath him. "What happened?"

He pushed himself up to a seated position. "When I left the park, it was like every atom in my body was being torn apart. Then, boom. I came back here. To the mall. That's where the real nightmare began."

He turned a pale anguish-ridden face toward her. "Stacy, I saw how I died. It *was* here . . . in the mall. I fell." He pointed toward the front of her store. "I was by the railing one minute. The next, I was falling over it. I landed . . ." His voice trailed off. "Whatever it was that pulled me back from the park, it forced me to experience my death all over again." His image faded for a moment, then reformed. "I relived it all . . . the rush of the air, the sound of breaking bones. The echoes of my scream as I fell." A shudder racked his body, making his image waver like a rippling pond.

Tears clouded her vision. "What can I do, Chance? How can I help?"

"Stay here. Talk to me. I don't want to be by myself."

She offered him a bleary smile. "Of course." She looked around for something to sit on rather than the cold concrete floor. She spotted a large bag of Styrofoam packing peanuts and dragged the bag over. "Just like a big beanbag chair," she offered with a weak smile.

Chance managed a nod in return.

She pushed her makeshift chair as close to him as possible and positioned herself so her face was only inches from his. "What do you want to talk about?" she whispered.

He looked straight at the ceiling. "I want to know why I'm here."

She swallowed hard. "I think everybody's asked that question of themselves at least once in their life."

"But should they have to ask it in their death, too?" He remained quiet for a minute, then turned to face her. "Who am I, Stacy? Why did I fall? Why am I here?"

It took all the control she could manage to keep herself from reaching out and stroking his cheek. "Oh, Chance . . . if I knew any of the answers, I'd tell you."

He nodded. "I know you would."

"But we could go looking for the answers," she offered.

"How?"

"If you died here, then there must be some record of it. The mall office must be required to fill out all sorts of paperwork if there's an accident. Insurance companies are notorious for insisting on things like that."

He seemed to rally a bit. "You think so? Then maybe we can find out something about me. And find out how I died."

A sudden wave of fatigue washed over her. She snuggled down into her makeshift beanbag, feeling her warmth reflected by the plastic peanuts. "I bet so," she said, fighting a yawn.

"Sleepy, eh?"

She nodded, forcing herself to keep her eyes open.

"Why don't you catch a nap?"

"I thought you wanted to talk."

He gave her a stronger smile. "Having you here is good enough. Who knows? Maybe it'll be the first time we *sleep* together."

"Good grief, Chance." Her eyes fluttered closed. "Everybody knows ghosts don't sleep . . ." Her voice trailed away.

He watched her face relax as she drifted asleep. "Don't I know . . ." he whispered.

"Stacy? Stacy, wake up. Time to rise and shine, Sleeping Beauty."

She rolled over, finding her face adhering to the plastic bag. "Uh . . . what?" She blinked. "Where am I?"

Peg squatted down beside her. "Evidently, you decided paperwork was boring and decided to take a little nap."

Stacy forced her sluggish mind to stir into action. She focused on Peg, then belatedly realized the woman stood exactly where Chance had been stretched out. "You're standing on him! Move," she commanded in a sleep-clogged voice. She batted at Peg, hoping to make the woman shift to a different spot.

Peg complied with a smile. "Him? Oh, one of *those* dreams. No wonder you were so hard to wake. Look, Stacy, there's no one here but you and me. Prince Charming has ridden back to the castle."

"Don't believe a word she says." The voice came from behind Peg. "Prince Charming has rallied and is ready for a little action."

Stacy scrambled to sit up and tried to see around her assistant. She spotted Chance standing by her desk. He stood with his arms crossed, wearing black jeans, a black turtleneck shirt and a dark stocking cap pulled on his head.

Her heart raced. When last she saw him, he looked horrible. And now here he stood, as if nothing had happened. He looked energetic, vital . . . so damn alive!

He shot her a crooked, sexy grin. "I'm ready to do a little reconnaissance work at the mall office. How about you?"

"Yes," she answered without thinking. She glanced up at Peg and blinked. "Uh, yes . . . you're right. My dream . . . it seemed so real."

"Ah . . . to be young, single, and have an active imagination. I miss those days." She glanced at her watch. "Jeez, do you realize it's ten-fifteen, already? Once I finished closing the store, I waited around for a bit to see if you'd wake up on your own. But you didn't. I'm going to have to head on home and I didn't want you to wake up here in the middle of the night and think I'd forgotten all about you."

Chance stepped forward and shook his head. "C'mon, tell her you want to stay late and work on the books or something. Tell her anything and let's get this show on the road."

Stacy gave Peg a forced smile. "You go on. I'm so sleepy right now, I'd probably be a hazard on the road. I want to nap awhile longer, then I might work on the books."

The woman gave her a dubious stare, then shrugged. "Seems to me you'd be happier if you got out of this place and tried to have some sort of social life." She pulled on her coat. "You have to promise me you won't go traipsing around the mall by yourself. You call one of the security guards and have him escort you to your car. In fact, you ought to call and let them know you're here, working late."

"I promise, Auntie Peg. I'll—" she glanced past the woman

at her impatient second-story man, "—make sure someone's with me, okay?"

"Well . . . don't stay too late, okay? I'll worry about you."

"Go, Peg." She shooed the woman toward the door. "I'll be fine."

Peg complied but paused in the doorway, balancing her fists on her hips. "I'm setting the perimeter alarm on the way out. At least, *I'll* feel more secure that way."

Stacy waited until she heard the front door lock click before she said anything. "I take it you're feeling better."

Chance gave her a wide grin. "Like nothing ever happened."

She shook her head. "You've got to be kidding. When I found you here, you looked like . . ." She paused, in search of an appropriate comparison.

"Death warmed over?" he supplied.

She winced. "I wasn't going to be so graphic, but yes. That's an accurate description of just how bad you looked. What happened?"

"It wasn't the trip from the park that screwed me up. Once I realized I had to stop fighting the urge to return, it wasn't as bad as it could have been. Although it hurt like the dickens to get pulled back, I pretty much landed here unscathed." He tugged off his black watch cap and ran his hand through his hair. "My big mistake was thinking if I tried hard enough, I could get back to you."

"What do you mean?"

He wadded up his hat, then smoothed it flat again. "I kept trying to go through the double doors. Every time I'd hit the second set, I'd get thrown back. I guess I tried two or three . . . dozen times."

"Dozen?" she repeated in shock.

He nodded, paying an inordinate amount of attention to his hat and not looking up at her. "I guess you could say I did the ghostly equivalent of beating my head against a brick wall. I made it to your storeroom before I collapsed or passed out or whatever the non-living equivalent is."

"So what's with the cat burglar outfit?"

He smiled, pulling the cap back on. "Like it? I thought it was appropriate for a little midnight raid. So, how are we going to get in there?"

"Where?"

"The mall office. Where they keep their files, their accident reports."

She rubbed the sleep from her eyes. "We need a plan? How difficult can it be for you? You walk through the wall and *voilà,* you're in."

"And what do I do then? I can't open the file drawers or turn on their computer. I need you to go in with me."

"Me?"

He nodded. "I have to be real to search through the office. I can't very well do it like this." He reached for the phone sitting on her desk and his hand passed through the instrument. "See?"

She stretched sore muscles as she shifted to her feet. "Remind me—ow—never to try to sleep on plastic peanuts again." She winced as she flexed her neck.

"May I?" Chance stepped closer. "Maybe I was a masseuse in my former life."

She gave him a scathing once-over. "Somehow I don't think so but . . ." She lifted one shoulder and wrinkled her nose in discomfort. "Be my guest."

As soon as his fingers touched her, a pleasant shiver danced across her shoulders. He kneaded her knotted muscles, working out the kinks her stopgap bed had caused. As he continued massaging her neck and back, the sensation started to build, triumphing over her aches and pains and becoming something more personal, more intimate.

"Better?" he asked in a husky voice.

She didn't trust herself to speak, and answered with a nod instead. His hands stopped their luxurious torture and she felt him press against her, his hot breath scorching her neck.

"You know . . ." He traced the edge of her collar. "What

you're wearing is nice, but I'd like to see you in something . . . different."

Her mind jumped ahead to an outfit similar to the mannequin in the window. A merry widow? *What color?* Her heart betrayed her with an extra beat. Was she honestly thinking about seducing a ghost? Her next thought supplied her answer. *Black.*

He leaned down and rested his chin on her shoulder. "You got anything in—let's say—basic black?"

A thrill of anticipation shot through her with such force that she thought she'd have to forego lingerie all together. "What d-did you have in m-mind?" she managed to stutter.

"Something that covers you from here—" he touched her nose, "—to the tips of your toes."

She tried to translate his request in terms of available lingerie. A cat suit? Something stretchy and lacy? She cocked her head. *Could be fun.*

"Fun?" He stiffened against her and drew in a shaky breath. "Don't think things like that, lady. I don't think I can resist such a mental picture."

She pulled away from him, severing their physical connection. "You read my mind? How dare you! What I was thinking was personal—"

"And so damned erotic that I could barely concentrate." He glanced down at his spectral loins and his smile dimmed a notch. "It was so nice while it lasted."

She didn't dare ask what. She knew exactly what he meant.

He continued. "As I was saying before you rained cold water on my parade, if we're going to sneak into the mall office, you need to wear something so you blend in the shadows. Got anything like that around here?"

Stacy forced herself to center her attention on his request. He failed to realize that she might have doused *his* libidinal thoughts by breaking contact with him, but it hadn't affected *hers* at all. She tore her mind from that damned lace cat suit and tried to imagine a more utilitarian outfit. "How about a black leotard and tights?"

He shook his head. ''Too unusual. If you do run into a guard, how could you explain yourself? Heading for a midnight aerobics session?''

''How about a black jumpsuit? It has a rather plunging neckline but if I wore a leotard underneath, it wouldn't appear too odd.''

''Good.''

She made him wait outside with a promise not to sneak through the wall and take a peek as she changed. Before she emerged from the storeroom, she turned off the lights inside, then she stepped out into the dark store. ''Well?''

''I can hardly see you. Great.'' Chance materialized at her elbow. ''Ready?''

She swallowed hard. ''As I'll ever be.''

''Let me go first and check to see if the coast is clear.'' He passed through the display window and was gone for a few minutes. By the time he returned, Stacy's eyes had adjusted to the darkness.

''Okay, here's the deal: three men on duty tonight. One's evidently outside, patrolling the parking lot, one's walking an inside beat and the other one's in the booth, manning the security cameras. So all we have to watch out for is the inside man and the cameras.''

''You make it sound so simple.''

He pointed to himself with a look of smug pride. ''With an invisible advance scout like me, it's going to be a piece of cake.''

''I hope so.''

Stacy disarmed the store's perimeter alarm and they exited into the empty mall corridor. Stacy started to hug the walls in order to stay in the shadows, but she realized how absurd it looked. She walked those corridors almost every night on her way home, often that late or later. Even if she took a detour down the hallway leading past the mall office, no one would think anything odd about it. As a mall merchant, she had a perfect right to be there.

Just before she reached the hallway, Chance rushed back from his scouting position, gesturing for her to stop. "Big problem. There's a camera down there, sweeping past the doorway."

Stacy tiptoed toward the junction, staring at the video camera mounted above her head. As it swung her direction, she backed away quickly. "What do we do now?" she whispered. "We can't just break in. They'll see us."

"Not *us*. You. I don't show up on cameras."

She glared at him. "Are you sure?"

He nodded. "I messed around in the electronics store one day and discovered that if I stay still for a real long time, you see a very faint, blurred image where I am. But otherwise, if I move around normally, you can't see me at all."

"Then you can get in the office without anyone seeing you."

"Sure, but there's not much I can do by myself once I get inside."

Stacy closed her eyes to think, picturing the door in her mind. Suddenly the answer came to her in a flash. "I know exactly how to get in there. Go ahead and get in the office. I'll be right there."

"Huh?"

"Just go!"

Chapter Six

After Chance disappeared through the wall, Stacy snagged a piece of paper from a nearby trash can and sauntered down the hallway, hoping she appeared normal. She stopped in front of the office door and knocked loudly. "Anybody there?"

"Nobody but us ghosts," Chance answered.

She swallowed her smile and turned to face the camera. "Uh, excuse me, you . . . up there. Who's on duty tonight? Rufus? Derrick?"

A disembodied voice came out of the speaker grill next to the camera. "It's Derrick Bains, Miss Reardon. Anything wrong?"

"No, I was just checking to see if the office personnel have left already." She pictured the guard consulting his log book.

"I'm afraid everybody went home hours ago."

"Hours? What time is it?"

"Almost eleven."

She feigned shock. "That late? I must have lost track of time."

"Is there a problem, ma'am?"

She held up the piece of paper, now an important communiqué in her little theatrical presentation. ''No, I'll just drop this letter through their mail slot.'' She stopped down and made a grand show of shoving the missive through the rectangular slot in the door. ''Oh dear . . .'' She made an equally pretentious act of trying to extract her hand from letter slot. ''Damn it.''

''You okay, Miss Reardon?'' the guard asked.

Chance partially materialized, sticking only his head through the glass panel of the door. ''What are you doing, Stacy?''

''My sleeve has snagged on something,'' she called over her shoulder to the camera. ''Just a minute.'' Stacy turned back to the door and glared at Chance. ''Get back in there,'' she whispered between clenched teeth, ''and touch my hand. Then you can become real and unlock the door.''

An animated grin lit his face. ''How devious of you! This is a new side of your personality, Stace. I must say . . . I like it.''

''Just hurry, please!'' she hissed.

Chance disappeared and a second later, she felt him touch her hand. A tingle enveloped her fingers, then she heard the door's lock click.

''Miss Reardon, do you need me to send some help? I can contact the patrol and have him help—''

''No!'' she said a bit too quickly. ''Uh, that's not necessary.'' She pulled her hand out and stood. ''Thank goodness. I didn't think I'd be able to get free without tearing my sleeve.'' She smiled toward the camera. ''But I really appreciate your offer of help. Well . . .'' she faltered, not knowing how to make a graceful exit. ''See you tomorrow, Derrick.''

''Good night, Miss Reardon.''

Stacy started down the hallway, keeping watch on the camera out of the corner of her eye. When the camera made its slow arc, sweeping past the office entrance, she doubled back, and slipped in, easing the door closed behind her.

Chance met her with an anxious grin. ''You are positively brilliant!'' He leaned forward, his lips becoming real the moment they grazed her cheek. The resulting surge of sensation made the hairs rise on the back of her neck. He laced his fingers in hers, then pulled her closer for a long, hard kiss. When he finally broke away, he kept his hand in hers and turned toward the desk.

"Now let's see—"

She jerked him back, wrapping her arms around him. It was time for someone to take control of this crazy situation and she figured it was up to her. At her instigation, the second kiss was longer, definitely harder and made her lose her breath with its explosive intensity. To her utter delight, the kiss seemed to evoke a similar reaction in him. When they finally pulled away, both gasping for air, he stared at her wearing a dumbfounded look.

"W-wow . . ."

She smiled at him, savoring the sweet rewards of being the instigator. "Time to get to work."

Once they worked out the logistics of maintaining contact, they got into the rhythm of searching the file cabinets. As he held the flashlight, Chance continued to sneak looks at her when he thought she didn't notice. She ignored him, searching instead through her assigned drawer. It wouldn't do to let him know how fast her heart was beating or how she savored the memory of his lips on hers.

After a few moments, he held up a file. "Eureka!"

She flinched. "Keep your voice down," she whispered. "Remember, you're real at the moment."

He proved the fact by blushing. "Sorry," he whispered. "I forgot . . . sort of."

They spread the contents of the thick file across the nearest desk. Chance drew up a second chair and they sat down. Stacy hooked her foot around his and released his hand. They split the papers into two piles and began to go through each report.

After a few minutes, Chance sighed.

"What?" After a few seconds with no response, she looked

up to find him totally captivated by the page he held. "Did you find something?"

He shook his head. "No. It just amazes me how stupid people can be. Here's one where a kid put his fist through a plate-glass window because he wanted to steal a baseball card. Apparently, his parents are trying to sue the mall for his medical and legal bills because the mall 'enticed their son to perform a criminal act.' How convenient of them to forget he broke into the mall after hours and was trying to take something that didn't belong to him in the first place."

She nodded. "I know what you mean." She slid the paper closer to the flashlight which spilled its light across the desk. "Here's one where a kid tried to skateboard down the escalator. He's lucky all he did was break his leg, not his neck. You wanna bet someone's trying to sue the mall for not having up signs which say No Skateboarding on the Escalators?"

He held up the next sheet of paper and squinted at it. "Here's one where a poor schmuck actually committed suicide by jumping . . ." His voice trailed away.

Stacy glanced up from the report she was reading. "How did he—" The expression on Chance's face told her something was terribly wrong. "What is it?"

He said nothing as he handed her the sheet of paper, but his gray face and shaking fingers spoke volumes.

She scanned the sheet, her attention instantly riveted to the name of the victim, *Johnson, Chance.* Her heart thundered, the blood rushed through her ears, drowning out all thought. It was all she could do to pick out the key words. *Jumped. Suicide. Despondent.*

She pressed a hand to her mouth. "Oh my God . . ."

"It must be true," Chance said in a leaden voice. "It explains everything—why I'm a ghost, why I'm stuck here and haven't gone on to some sort of reward."

Stacy felt a sudden emptiness sweep through her as he withdrew, both physically and mentally. "Don't go, Chance." She held out her hand, hoping to reestablish contact.

"I . . . can't. Not right now." He stood, walking through the desk without disturbing a single piece of paper. "It's easier to take the bad news like this, like a ghost." He faced away from her, his posture clearly reflecting his sense of defeat.

"Why, Chance?"

He pivoted to face her. "Why in the hell do you think? This way it doesn't hurt as much. This way I can't savor the shame of knowing I was a coward." A cold hatred filled his expression, belying his very words. "Remember, ghosts can't feel. We're dead."

"You're not a coward," she whispered.

"Sure I am," he thundered. "Isn't that what suicides are? People too scared to face life? People so frightened by the consequences of their own actions that they'd rather die than face them? As far as that goes, isn't that what I just did a minute ago? Retreated from life because I knew I couldn't stand the pain? Looks like I just proved that history repeats itself."

"But Chance I don't think—"

He dismissed her with the wave of his hand. "It doesn't matter what you think. Or what I think, for that matter. I'm probably here for one reason, and one reason alone—to prove the old saying was right."

"W-what saying?"

"A coward dies a thousand deaths."

Although he tried to mask his pain with an ugly sneer, she saw through his efforts, even when he turned his back to her, signifying the end of their conversation. Undaunted, Stacy glared at the report through her tears. She'd force herself to read every word of it, to search it for details, find the proof to refute its claims.

Suicide, indeed.

Even though he was in a ghost-state, she'd never met a man more alive, more vibrant than Chance Johnson. He would never have done anything as stupid as throw his life away. Just the fact that he could come to life with her help proved that he was different from any old ordinary chain-rattling, mall-haunting specter.

She wiped her tears on her jumpsuit sleeve, stood and stalked over to the copy machine. She found its switch and turned it on.

"What are you doing?" he asked in a dull voice.

"Making a copy of the report."

"Why in the hell are you doing that?"

"Why in the hell do you think?" she asked, throwing his words back at him. "It's nothing but a bunch of baloney and I intend to prove it." She tapped her foot impatiently, waiting for the machine to warm up. When the indicator light flashed, she proceeded to punch in an order to make three copies. As the last page slid out of the machine, she heard a noise in the hallway.

Chance came to life, streaking through the wall and returning a moment later. "Kill the light!" he ordered. "It's a security guard."

She stood, rooted in the middle of the room, unable to move.

"Stacy, c'mon. Quick!"

She fumbled with the flashlight, trying to make her quivering hands operate. Chance made a face, grabbed her arms, and the moment he became solid, pulled her down behind the desk. Huddling together in the cramped kneehole, she became aware of his undeniable, almost uncomfortable proximity. His pain still existed in palpable waves, but he'd faced it, even survived it in order to rescue her from detection.

Stacy tried to inch away from him—to break contact so he could transform back to a ghost and escape the harsh constraints of the living. In addition to being free, he would also be able to observe the situation without being seen. When she tried to explain her plan, Chance placed a finger on her lips, gesturing for silence.

They heard someone rattle the doorknob, then the lock clicked and light from the hallway spilled into the office. Echoes of the heavy footsteps bounced all around the room. Stacy couldn't tell if the guard was approaching their hiding place or not. She curled into a tight ball, trying to take up the least amount of space. As long as she touched Chance, he was in as much danger as she of being discovered. Finally he understood, and together they created enough distance between them to break contact. Chance reverted to his vaporous state. She watched in awe as he stood, passing right through the desk and out of view.

"He's doing a premise check," Chance reported in a steady voice. "Now he's checking the inner office . . . nothing interesting there. He's back in this office, now—hold it. He's walking around the desk. Stace, keep still. Keep absolutely still."

She held her breath. Part of her wanted to be reassured that the mall security force was a crackerjack team of professionals there to protect her business interests. The other part of her prayed the man had the prowess of Deputy Fife and couldn't possibly find her even if she stood up and sang "The Star-Spangled Banner." The contrary nature of her wishes made adrenaline surge through her body and buzz in her ears. She saw the khaki pants and scuffed shoes loom into view then stop by the chair. The man stood only inches away from her.

"Don't move, Stace," Chance instructed. "He's reaching for the drawer . . . just hold it, hold it . . ."

Stacy watched a rough hand pull open the desk drawer and reach in. It took all her control not to scream, tumble from her hiding place and beg for mercy.

Chance released an expletive along with a sudden blast of harsh laughter. "It's okay. He's sneaking some candy from the secretary's drawer. Nothing more sinister than that."

The drawer scraped as it closed, and a discarded candy-bar wrapper landed in the vicinity of the trash can. A moment later, the door swung shut, plunging the room back into darkness. After a jangle of keys, a solitary click rang out and the footsteps faded into the hallway.

"Stay there," Chance cautioned. "Let me check and make

sure he's gone." After a minute, his voice rang through the room with an empty echo. "You can come out, now. It's safe."

She crawled out from beneath the desk and rose stiffly to her feet. She wrapped her arms around herself, trying to combat the sudden chill that made her shoulders shake. "I don't think I'd make a very good burglar. I was ready to throw myself at the man and plead for leniency."

Chance said nothing.

She felt the chill change into a deep freeze. "Chance?"

He made no effort to answer her. He was staring in her general direction with what she could only describe as a lifeless expression.

"Chance?" she repeated. She stepped closer to him and reached out to touch him.

He blinked and neatly sidestepped her, avoiding contact. "No . . . we don't have time for that. You can't stay here."

She tried to supply the humor which he lacked. "Yeah, the guard might get hungry for another candy bar."

"Wait here," he ordered. He passed through the door. "When I say Go," he called out from the hallway, "you be ready to open the door and get out of here. Fast."

Stacy realized this wasn't the time to argue. She grabbed the copies, rolled them into a tight tube and switched off the copy machine. "Ready when you are."

"Three, two, one . . . Go!"

She slipped out the door and ducked into the hallway. The door swung closed and locked behind her. Before she stepped from the small hallway into the main mall corridor, Chance scouted ahead, informing her of the clear passage. When she got to her store, he seemed reluctant to follow her in.

"C'mon, Chance."

He'd lost his earlier look of angered despair and in its place, was distraction. Stacy's stomach twisted in a tighter knot. Apathy was a strong enemy to overpower. "Maybe later."

"Later?" Stacy fought to keep her voice low. "No way, mister. We talk—now." She stabbed the alarm code with a savage forefinger and strode into the store. "My back room. Now!"

He followed her to the rear of the store and passed with obvious reluctance through the door which she held open. When she switched on the lights, it almost seemed as if she could see through parts of him, as if he hadn't completely formed. It was a disturbing sight.

She unrolled the papers clutched in her hand and smoothed them out across the desk. "I no more believe you committed suicide than I believe in the man in the moon."

He stood in the middle of the room, his posture reflecting his sense of defeat. He said nothing.

"After all, this report was filled out by a security guard, not a professional investigator. I mean . . . look at Rufus; he's a good man, an honest man, but he's not a trained policeman. He deals with things like shoplifters and store security, not violent deaths. Or murder."

Chance remained silent, appearing even more vaporous than before.

His lack of solidity upset Stacy the most. It was becoming eerie evidence of his lack of belief in himself. She balanced her fists on her hips. "So you're just going to accept this suicide theory without a fight?"

"Fight?" he repeated in a distracted voice.

"Yes, fight, damn it! What are you going to do? Lay down and die? Again?"

He shrugged.

She took a calculated risk, rushing him and wrapping her fingers around his arm before he could move away. To her surprise, he pulled out of her grasp. She tried again, discovering it was like trying to grab a handful of smoke. He backed toward a corner. For a moment Stacy feared he would simply turn and pass through the wall, disappearing . . . perhaps, forever. She reached for him again.

"No . . . don't," he ordered in a strangled voice. A look of quiet desperation slowly filled the emptiness in his eyes. It was his first open show of emotion since they'd exited the mall office, and it was scaring Stacy to death.

She seized her fear and molded it into anger, wishing he would do the same. "How dare you! How dare you give up when you face the first moment of opposition."

"Maybe that's what I do." He crossed his arms and backed away from her. "Maybe that's why I committed suicide. It's the ultimate escape from responsibility."

"No. That's not how you operate."

"How do you know? You don't know me. Hell, I don't even know *me*. What I am now—" he gestured to himself with a terse wave, "—may have nothing to do with what I was."

"Is that the problem?"

"What?"

"You're afraid to find out who you were? Afraid to discover the sequence of events which led up to your death?" Her voice rose with each question. "Afraid to find out the truth?"

"Yes," he shouted.

For the first time, the reality of the situation hit Stacy. She was arguing with a ghost. Someone who didn't live on the same plane of existence as herself. Someone who was . . . dead.

Her world spun for a moment and she steadied herself by bracing her palm against the stack of boxes. "This is—" she allowed herself to fall to her knees, "—just too much for me."

For the first time, he moved toward her. "Stacy . . . are you all right?"

Stacy looked up at him and released a laugh mixed with a sob. "Oh sure. I'm arguing with a ghost. I'm in tiptop shape. Some of my friends said I was crazy to try to open a lingerie store in the mall. Maybe I'm just proving them right."

Chance slipped silently toward her, his feet never touching the carpeted floor. He hovered over her for a moment, then mimicked her stance, lowering to his knees. He stared at her, face to face, trying to find the details about her which had captivated his imagination during their sojourn to the park.

He had to look hard to find the small scar above her right

eye, the sprinkle of faint freckles across her nose, the small strand of reddish hair feathered through her darker hair.

For some reason, it reminded him of their stroll on the beach . . . They'd rolled their pants' legs up and carried their shoes and socks as they waded through the surf. She grew cold and her teeth began to chatter and—

No, the inner man screamed. *It wasn't Stacy. It was someone else. Someone from that other life. The life you threw away . . .*

"Chance?"

The angst in her voice roused him from his memories. When he looked at her, the image wavered and blurred. It was becoming increasingly difficult to maintain his grip on her world, a task which had been so easy before.

"Don't go," she pleaded. "Don't give up."

"Why not?" he slurred. Even his words seemed imperfectly formed.

She held out her hand. "Because I don't want you to go. I believe in you. I believe you didn't jump."

He contemplated her outstretched palm, holding his own out for comparison. Gentle lines creased her skin, the sort of lines a Gypsy would read to tell her she would have a long happy life . . .

Life.

Life lines.

He had no lines in the palm of his hand. No indicator to tell where life began and where it ended.

She misinterpreted his gesture, slipping her warm hand into his lifeless one. The shock of reality filled him, flowing through his nonexistent veins like needles riding a tidal wave of hot wax. All the other times, the process of becoming real was pleasurable, almost indulgently satisfying. This time, it hurt, like a million tiny bolts of electricity spreading through his body, clawing at him from inside.

When he could open his eyes, he stared at Stacy with a renewed clarity. He memorized her features, seeing a woman caught in the throes of something almost passionate in nature.

His first act as a real man was to get the undeniable, physical feeling of desire.

But a greater emotion suffocated his burgeoning lust.

Guilt raised its ugly head.

You had life. You had the opportunity to meet someone wonderful, someone like Stacy, to live out a life with love . . . but you threw it all away.

He tried to escape the accusations, to pull away from her and back into the inexplicable void where the pain slipped away. A cradle of nothingness was preferable to the harsh realities awaiting him. He tried to jerk his hand out of hers, but she held on tight.

"Stacy . . . no—"

She muffled his protests with a soul-shattering kiss.

Vaporous thoughts and concepts solidified, strengthened by her kiss. The concept of desire became overwhelming, accelerated by her enchanting proximity. He steeled himself not to respond, not to enjoy the sweetness of her lips pressed against his, the warmth of her hands spread across his chest, the urgent, near-frantic rhythm of her heart which led his in a merry chase.

He had no right to feel, to want, to love. He'd tossed away that right when he'd thrown away his life.

Yet, he experienced those very feelings.

God, he wanted her.

He reached for her, showing her exactly how he reflected the reality she bestowed on him. A hard reality, but not a harsh one. Her hands slid down to anchor at his waist, then after a moment, to inch his shirttail out of his pants.

Given bold permission, he trailed his kisses from her mouth, down her throat, until he encountered the zipper of her jumpsuit. It took all the control he possessed to lower the tab slowly, revealing the clingy leotard beneath. It hugged curves that took his breath away. Still clutching her hand, he backed away from her to take an admiring look. A fine blush colored her skin from her cheeks to her modest neckline. He felt an unbridled response course through his body, reaffirming his new lease on life.

Moments later, they had collapsed to the makeshift beanbag chair, frantically working out the logistics of removing their clothes while maintaining contact.

It wasn't difficult.

He pressed a knee between her legs as he stripped off his shirt, tossing it away with abandon bordering on gleeful. She surged against him, her fingers clawing at her own restricting clothes. When she peeled off the leotard, he discovered she wore an enticing garment of peach-colored silk beneath. He never got his pants completely off before their combined restraint dissipated.

She was perfect.

A demure temptress.

A wanton innocent.

She writhed beneath him, responding with an unbridled enthusiasm which took his breath away. They made love with a ferocity which made his mind explode along with his body.

Afterward, she lay limp in his arms, breathing heavily, out of exhaustion rather than desire. A light sheen of perspiration clung to her skin. He trailed a finger down her cheek to the valley between her breasts.

"I do believe you worked up a sweat, m'dear."

She nodded, arching her back and releasing a languid yawn. "Hmmm . . ."

Chance wrapped a strand of her dark blond hair around his thumb, then lifted it to his nose to inhale the fresh aroma of her shampoo.

"I love this."

"What?" She burrowed against his bare chest him, starting a whole new wave of hunger to flow through him.

"The sensations of being alive."

"How so?" she asked in a sleepy voice.

Chance tugged playfully at her hair. "The smell of shampoo . . ." He nibbled at her ear. "Taste . . ." He splayed his fingers over the soft mound of her breast. "Touch."

Her sharp intake of breath sliced through his control.

"S-sound."

She turned around, pinning him with gray-green eyes.

He took a deep breath. "Sight . . ."

Chapter Seven

After their second, and then their third lovemaking session, Chance knew the exact moment when Stacy fell asleep.

One minute, he was real, savoring the aftershocks of unsurpassable sexual satisfaction. The next, he was a ghost, inert, unfeeling.

Dead.

Although they were still holding hands when she finally drifted asleep, the lifeline between them was inexplicably broken, evidently unable to survive the rigors of sleep. It nearly broke his nonexistent heart when she shifted, reacting unconsciously to his sudden "departure" by curling in a tight ball and releasing a drowsy sigh. He resisted the temptation to wake her—he realized how tired she looked.

Sleep did nothing to erase the lines exhaustion had placed on her face. In his blunted state, even if he couldn't touch her, he could at least hear her, see her. He tried to find as much vague reassurance as he could in the soft rhythm of her breathing. But the spectacle of her—a sleeping woman wearing nothing but a lingering smile . . .

If he was real, the sight of her would have played havoc with his libido. But lucky for him . . .

Lucky?

He tried to sigh, then rolled his eyes in disgust. Life was so much easier when you actually *were* alive. A moment later, the emptiness inside of him expanded, reminding him of their latest revelation.

I killed myself.

Whether he was real or not, the words shook him to his core. He searched inwardly, looking for a glimpse of memory, a small snatch of recollection. All he knew was that Chance Johnson had plunged from a mall railing and died when he landed.

Why?

It was the $64,000 question—not that money meant too terribly much to a dead man. It was the lack of information, the unending questions that kept him wandering around the mall. He glanced over at Stacy, who burrowed deeper into her beanbag bed, evidently seeking warmth in her sleep. He could see the goose bumps on her arms and legs.

She needed a blanket or something. He zipped across the room, examining the wall of cardboard boxes and finally discovering a container marked Shawls. He reached into the box, discovering that he lacked whatever energy he needed to move solid objects. It was pretty simple to figure out; the longer he stayed "alive," the more difficult it was to reestablish his powers as a ghost.

Great. And what do I do, now? I can't open the box, much less cover her up. How do I . . .

Inspiration struck. *The static charge!* During the brief moment of discharge, he'd become real, albeit for only a split second. Perhaps, with a great deal of planning and split-second execution, he could actually get her covered. He had to try.

Chance lowered himself until his soles skimmed the small piece of carpet near the desk. Then he began to shuffle his feet. As the static electricity built up in him, a prickly sensation disturbed the dead pool of non-feeling in the center of his chest. As the condition built, he worked his way to the box, poising over it to take advantage of his brief moment of solidity. During the nanosecond discharge, he reached into the box and snatched out a shawl. It passed through his fingers and fluttered to the concrete floor as he reverted to his ghostly status.

Taking no time to celebrate his initial victory, he repeated the process several times until he inched the shawl across the floor, closer to her makeshift bed. His energy level decreased with each discharge, until it took almost fifteen minutes to build up enough static electricity to make the final push and drape the shawl partially over her nude body. He smiled when she roused long enough to pull the material over her and snuggle down for a warmer night's sleep.

He stared down at his own hand, watching it slowly fade from view. The last flash into reality had sapped whatever strength fueled his extended visits on a material plane. It was time to return to that nothing place where he hated to go. It robbed him of his last two senses, hearing and sight.

The worst part was sinking into the unknown, not knowing if or when he'd return.

Or how much time had passed since he left.

In the nothingness, there was light. Sunlight, fluorescent light, Christmas lights, candlelight, neon light . . .

Too much light.

He fought against its insidious attraction.

He didn't belong there. However, the moment the thought crossed his mind, its antithesis hit him with equal strength; he didn't belong in the mall, either.

Just where did he belong?

Perhaps that was his punishment for a lifetime of misdeeds. He was a man without a country. A soul without a home.

I must have been a real bastard to deserve this.

He expected an ominous voice to answer him. Something in

a thunderous, omnipresent bass to damn him for a string of unforgivable sins. Or perhaps a choir of heavenly hosts would strike up an overture on their harps, giving him a befitting accompaniment as they conducted him down the superhighway to heaven.

The lights flared for a moment as if to answer him. In the center of the brightest light, a small black spot began to grow, slowly blotting out the white glare.

The shadow twisted, forming a vague figure.

Chance squinted, trying to make out the silhouette against the radiant background. Just as he began to discern shape and size, the lights began to dim.

No! He leaned forward, trying to get a better glimpse of what looked to be a man dressed in a dark robe.

Lights exploded with a soundless roar.

The nothingness twisted around him, wrapping around him like a damp sheet.

A damp sheet?

His heart soared. *It's a dream! I'm having a dream. I'll wake up and find myself in my bed with the sheets knotted around me.*

It's a dream.

A dream.

A . . .

Chance felt himself falling, his molecules easily passing through the asphalt roof, the steel roof trusses, the insulation, the electrical conduits, the recessed ceiling grid. When he landed in an ungainly heap in the center of the fountain, he couldn't stop himself from emitting a groan of pain, even if he didn't feel anything.

He struggled to sit up, to shake some sense into a brain fogged by his clumsy free-fall. The water remained perfectly still, showing no signs of having been disturbed by his abrupt arrival. Elevating himself out of the fountain, he continued upward until he reached the second level of the mall. Pausing in front of the clock shop, he took only a moment to reorient his own internal clock. It was 5:30 in the morning; he'd been away for almost four hours. He streaked up toward Stacy's store.

Not too bad, this time. I—

A premonition of doom flashed across his consciousness, destroying his concentration and causing him to skid to a halt.

Stacy!

He doubled his speed, not even pausing to close his eyes when he plunged through the walls to get to her storeroom.

A dark shape hovered in a corner of the room, evidently watching Stacy. Chance didn't know what it was, why it was there, or what it intended to do, but he did know he had to chase it away.

A flash of sudden inspiration told Chance the shape wasn't a "what" but a "who."

He moved until he stood between the hooded figure and the sleeping woman. *"Get away from her,"* he shouted. He used both his voices, the physical one that Stacy could hear and the one which emanated from somewhere from within. He advanced toward the figure who kept his ground for a moment, then slowly retreated until he sifted through the back wall and disappeared.

Chance inched forward, splitting between standing watch over Stacy and following her mysterious visitor. He satisfied his curiosity by sticking his head through the wall and watching the dark figure disintegrate in the weak golden light of the dawning sun.

Once he pulled back into the storeroom, Chance gave Stacy a long, almost possessive glance. She remained safely snuggled in the shawl, blissfully unaware of the dangers of the night. He savored the memory of loving her, the intertwining of a physical desire with a mental one.

No one, no *thing* would get to her with him on guard. He took his station in the corner of the room, affording himself the best possible vantage point to survey his duties.

He crossed his arms.

And watched.

Where is he?

Stacy wrapped the shawl around herself as she wandered around the room, picking up the clothes which had been abandoned with such joyous disregard. She thanked God for an internal time clock which had awakened her only a half hour later than usual. She could just imagine how embarrassed she would have been if Peg stumbled in and found her boss asleep in on the storeroom floor.

Naked.

Stacy would never be able to explain that one.

As she tugged on her pants, she heard the front door unlock. "Peg? That you?" The last thing she wanted to do was pop out of nowhere and scare the daylights out of her employee.

"Stacy? You're here already? I thought *I* was supposed to open up this morning." Peg stuck her head through the open doorway. "Merciful heavens! Did you sleep here last night?"

Stacy winced as she stuffed her shirttail in her pants. "Uh . . . yeah. I guess I got too comfortable."

"Comfortable?" Peg pointed at the bag of packing material. "On that?"

Stacy shrugged. "I've slept on worse."

"Me, too." The voice originated as a whisper behind her ear.

She spun around out of surprise, expecting to find Chance peering over her shoulder. No one was there.

Peg nodded in sympathy. "I bet you're sore."

"Tell her you're hungry." Chance's voice buzzed in Stacy's ear like an annoying insect. "Then we can go talk."

An annoying but sexy pest.

A shiver sped up her arms. "Uh . . . I'm sore *and* hungry, Peg. If you don't mind I think I'll go scare up some breakfast in the food court."

''Coffee,'' Peg supplied with a sage nod. ''I prescribe lots and lots of coffee. It's the universal antidote for those slow, stiff mornings.''

''But it won't do this slow stiff any good,'' Chance said in a slightly stronger voice, punctuating his joke with a short bark of laughter, then a groan of pain.

Stacy grabbed her purse and made a beeline for the front door.

Peg followed her as far as the cash register. ''If it's not too much trouble, could you bring me back some coffee when you return?''

''Sure.'' Stacy moved as quickly as she could, wanting to get out of Peg's view before she stopped. She skidded to a halt in front of the banks of pay phones and snatched a receiver.

''Where are you?''

''You don't have to shout.'' Chance appeared as a wavering form, sitting cross-legged in the air and pressing a palm to his forehead.

''Something wrong?''

He didn't open his eyes. ''Not really. I just find it hard to concentrate.''

''Why?''

He shrugged and opened his eyes, giving her a faded grin. ''Because you knocked me off my feet, last night.''

She felt the blood rush to her face and the memory of their lovemaking filled her with sudden, reminiscent warmth. If anybody should be thanking someone, it should be her. She'd never had anybody pay such thrilling but tender attention to her before. She opened her mouth to speak but he shook his head.

''No . . . me first. I have a suspicion that what happened to us last night flies in the face of . . . the natural order of the world.''

''N-natural order?''

He nodded. ''After all, you're real and I'm not. Somehow I'm not too sure we were meant to . . . to get together.''

Her heart fluttered. "Get together? That's what we did? We simply got 'together?'"

Chance's bleary gaze suddenly sharpened. "You know that's not what I mean." One moment he sat in the air. The next, he was at her side, a whisper's length away. "Last night . . . was magnificent. It was unbelievable . . . *you* were unbelievable." He raised his hand as if to touch her cheek, but stopped short of touching her.

"I can't . . ." his voice trailed off. "Not now."

"Why?" She glanced around. "No one's here."

His sigh cut through her like a cold razor. "Because it's not right. These things aren't supposed to happen. Conventional logic says that—"

"Logic?" she sputtered. "You want to talk about logic? I can see you and hear you. When I touch you, you're real. What you made me feel last night—that was real, too." A snatch of corporeal memory made her shiver in reminiscent delight. "I think we left logic behind after the first time we met."

He shrugged. "I guess you're right."

"It's early. No one's around," she stated, glancing around.

His voice dropped to a husky murmur. "Right again."

Stacy raised her hand, holding it flat as if touching an invisible mirror. She gestured for him to match her stance. "I believe in what I can see and hear and touch. I believe . . . in you." She slowly laced her fingers in his, aware of their transition from nonexistence to warm life. She closed her eyes as a momentary rush of feeling took her breath away, reminding her of a similar sensation she'd experienced the night before.

But I killed myself.

"No, you didn't."

Chance stared at her. "Who's reading minds now?"

Her grip tightened on his. "Maybe I should be surprised, but I'm starting to get used to the unusual when I hang around with you."

He looked as if he wanted to grin but dark thoughts were short-circuiting the process.

"Chance, I do *not* believe you killed yourself."

"But—"

"And I intend to prove it."

The muscles in his arms flexed perceptibly. "How?"

"We investigate."

"We? How?"

She led him to a bench nestled in a bank of ferns. It was her favorite spot in the mall. The splashing sound of the water fountain beside the area muted the usual mall hubbub and sent a fine mist in the air. It was an oasis in the midst of a bustling civilization.

Chance looked around. "This reminds me of the park."

She nodded. "Me too. I guess that's why I like it here. I don't get to go to the park very often any more. Umm . . . about the park," she started.

"What about it?"

"Could you go through something like that again?"

"You mean go outside?"

She shook her head. "No, I mean what happened when we broke contact."

"You mean my return to the mall?" A small shudder betrayed his unspoken thoughts.

Stacy nodded.

He tried to gesture with a wave of indifference. "Like I told you before, it wasn't the return that really drained me. It was my efforts to go outside again. My . . . repeated efforts."

Her instincts flagged his careless courage as a lie, but she didn't say anything.

"What do you have in mind?" When she didn't answer, he crossed his arms and knitted his brows. "Stacy . . ."

She shrugged. "It's a stupid idea."

He paused for a moment, then shook his head. "No, it isn't. It's a good idea."

"How would you know? You don't know what I'm thinking."

"I can read your mind, remember? Let's do it."

"Are you sure?"

He nodded. "Yeah. Let's go for it."

Chance sat beside her in the car, tugging at the collar of his thousand-dollar suit and adjusting his red silk tie for the fourteenth time. Finally, he abandoned his tie only to reach up and turn the rear-view mirror in his direction. "How do I look? Honestly? You think I ought to keep the mustache?"

Stacy sighed, jerked the mirror back in place and gripped the steering wheel a little harder. "Would you stop that? You look fine. Anyway it's too late for you to change, now. We're almost there."

He shifted uncomfortably in his seat, keeping one arm around her shoulder. She told herself it was the easiest way to maintain contact while they drove. However she found the possessiveness of the gesture to be oddly reassuring.

Chance looked down at his impeccable attire. "I still wish I'd changed into that gray suit in the Sandori's Men's Wear window display."

Chance had run her around the mall that morning, transforming his clothes to match those displayed in a half-dozen store windows. Finally, he settled on his conservative black suit with a red power tie and matching handkerchief. It looked fine on him.

Stacy gulped. It looked *more* than fine on him.

He was a handsome devil.

She stopped, mentally erasing the word "devil" from her vocabulary. A handsome specimen.

Specimen of what? Ectoplasm?

She shook away her interruptive thoughts. She'd left reality behind long time ago. Her new reality was simply what she could hear, see . . .

"And touch."

She turned, catching the full brunt of Chance's devastatingly attractive smile. The skin itched across the top of her shoulders at the exact places where his arm rested against her.

"Quite frankly, I think both of us are handling this well, considering the situation."

The burning itch turned into an inferno as a flush crept up her neck. "I wish you wouldn't keep reading my mind."

He shrugged. "I can't help it. Half the time, I'm not sure the thoughts are my own to begin with. We seem to be—" He paused as a blush of color started above his own collar, "—thinking the same sort of things." He coughed, clearing his throat. "Uh, Stacy . . . about last night."

She signaled for a left turn, then quirked an eyebrow at him. "Yes?"

"Making love was . . . something special. Unbelievably special."

The car grew unbearably hot. "It was special for me, too. Special *and* unbelievable."

An uneasy silence floated around the interior of the car as she negotiated a sudden increase in traffic.

"So you're upset, eh?"

She nodded, biting her lip.

"Upset because you . . . made it with a ghost?"

The absurdity of the statement hit her in the face like a wet sponge. A single giggle started in the center of her chest and bubbled forth, turning into a cascade of laughter by the time it reached its exit.

Chance joined her as they laughed together. It seemed the safest reaction to an unreal situation. He nearly broke contact with her when he reached to wipe the tears of mirth out of his eyes.

But the sight of his damp fingers seemed to stun him into silence. After a few seconds, he reached over and dabbed the tear on Stacy's hand. The drop of water wavered, then disappeared like a soap bubble reaching the end of its fleeting life.

He stared at her hand and sighed. "Another great mystery of the universe—solved at last."

Stacy steered toward an empty parking space in front of their destination. "Which mystery is that?" she asked in a low voice.

He tried to smile. "Mind you, it's not a scientific experiment conducted in a controlled lab, but I think this—" He pointed to where the teardrop had existed only moments before, "—answers one important question."

"What question?"

His thoughts became as clear in her mind as his words had been in her ears. *Whether a ghost can get you pregnant or not.*

She stomped on the brake, bringing them to an abrupt stop. She gaped at him. "P-pregnant?"

He offered her a weak smile. "If you recall, we didn't use any protection. I don't want to be known as irresponsible as well as deceased."

"Irresponsi-"

Chance adopted a clinical manner. "However, I think we can conclude that outside of my body, my sperm has approximately the same life span as my tears."

"S-sperm?" she sputtered. "Ghost sperm?" She stared at him, her thoughts bouncing from one extreme to the other.

How could I have been so stupid not to think of birth control?

How can a ghost look so damn analytical? And so handsome?

I wonder what would our children look like . . .

Chance shot her a shy smile which made him appear even more sexy-looking. "Thank you."

"For what?"

"For thinking I'd make a good-looking, analytical-type father. I guess I need to keep the mustache." He shifted his contact, tugging at her hand. His air of insistence prevented her from feeling even more embarrassed. "C'mon. Let's get out on my side."

Once they exited and stood on the sidewalk, they gazed up at the stately red-brick building.

"You ever been here before?" Chance asked.

"Nope. You?"

He shrugged. "I wish I knew. Well . . ." He placed a protective arm across her shoulder. "Here goes nothing."

They walked into a lobby filled with an eclectic assortment of humanity, from gaudily dressed women to wizened old men clutching shopping bags in their wrinkled laps. Chance slid his arm from her shoulder and grasped her firmly by the hand.

"Ready?" he whispered.

She nodded.

He marched them to the officer manning the central desk. The sign read simply, Desk Sergeant.

"Excuse me, sir?"

The man looked up from his computer screen. "Can I help you?"

Chance cleared his throat, betraying his nervousness. "We need to speak to the officer in charge of investigating a suicide."

The sergeant turned his attention back to his keyboard. "A specific suicide or just suicide in general?"

Chance's grip tightened on hers. "One in particular."

"Case number?"

"Johns—" Chance turned and gave Stacy a blank look. "Case number?" he repeated.

She shrugged and turned to the policeman. "We don't have a case number."

The man sighed, shaking his head. "How about the date of the case and the victim's name?"

Chance opened his mouth, but nothing came out.

Stacy took up the slack when she realized he couldn't respond. "The date was April 23 of this year and his . . . er, the victim's name was Johnson, Chance Johnson."

"Johnson?" the man repeated with a scowl. "That's almost as bad as Smith or Jones. Lessee . . . Johnson" He typed the name and waited for a moment, then ran his finger down the monitor screen. "Johnson . . . John, Johns, Johnstons . . . here it is. Johnson, Chance. #HS6784806A. Hmm . . ." He rubbed his chin and gave them a quick glance. "The detective in charge of that case is Lieutenant Harrold."

Stacy pulled up her best professional smile. Pleasant without being too personal. "Is he in?"

The policeman punched his keyboard again and consulted the screen. "Probably." He reached over and picked up a telephone. "Yes. It's Brannigan, on the desk. I have a couple of people who'd like to speak to Lt. Harrold. He in? Yeah . . . about the Johnson suicide. #HS6784806A. Yeah, an alpha suffix. Yes sir."

The officer turned to them. "Lt. Harrold'll be down in a few minutes. Just take a seat and I'll send him your way when he comes down." He waved them toward a scarred wooden long bench.

A single man sat on the bench. Stacy thought the fellow looked harmless for the most part, but when she moved in that direction, Chance pulled at her hand, leading to the bench on the opposite wall. They took their seats, trying to find a safe distance between the perfumed prostitutes and the old men who smelled like camphor and dirt.

"There's more room over there." She nodded toward the other bench. Compared to the occupants on their bench, the darkly dressed man sitting on the opposite one looked downright inert.

Chance shook his head. "No. Don't ask me to explain it, but I don't . . . trust him."

She shrugged as she caught a withering whiff of camphorated body odor. "Okay." She glanced back at the desk sergeant. "How do you think we're doing, otherwise?"

Chance squeezed her hand. "So far, so good."

She kept her voice low. "Do you think this Lt. Harrold will believe our story?"

"No reason why he shouldn't. It sounds reasonable and that's the key to being believable."

"B-believable."

He grinned. "I know. You don't have to even say it. How can I, a ghost, pronounce the word *believable* with a straight face?"

She nodded nervously. "I just hope he buys our reasons for being concerned."

"He will." Chance glanced in the opposite direction, at the single man occupying the bench. "Don't worry," he said half to himself.

A small *ping* announced the elevator's arrival to that floor. They watched the doors slide partially open, then close. A moment later, the doors jerked again, stiff-armed apart by a powerfully built black man dressed in plainclothes. He scowled at the desk sergeant. "Brannigan, have the elevator people phoned back yet?"

"No sir."

"Then, give them another call and tell them if they don't show up soon, we'll assign a special detail to keep a close watch over their parking indiscretions."

"Think they'll fall for it, Lieutenant?"

"They will after the third ticket." The man scanned the room, then turned back to the desk officer with an inquisitive look. "So?"

The sergeant pointed at Chance and Stacy. The plainclothes lieutenant wore a guarded smile as he approached them. "I understand you have some questions about a case of mine?"

Stacy bounded to her feet, betraying her anxiety. She tugged Chance up by their laced fingers. "Yes sir. My name's Stacy Reardon. I have a store in Chapel Valley Mall, where the man . . . died."

"I see. And you, sir?"

Chance offered his right hand which the detective took in a quick greeting. "Brandon, Peter Brandon, attorney at law. I'm here at Miss Reardon's request in an . . . unofficial capacity." Chance dipped into his pocket and pulled out a business card.

Stacy held her breath as the man contemplated the piece of cardboard.

"A sort of an *amicus curiae?*"

Chance adopted a knowing look. "Something along that line."

When Lt. Harrold shoved the card in his pocket, Stacy allowed herself to breathe again. They hadn't had time to get fake cards made up so Chance ''created'' a couple while in his ghostly state. He convinced her that the detective would pay only a minimal amount of attention to the card before discarding it. Like the roses Chance had conjured up, the card had a limited life and after a few minutes, it would simply disappear. Stacy prayed the card would evaporate some place convenient, like a trash can or the man's pocket—as opposed to the palm of his hand. She gave her partner in crime a quick glance and he squeezed her hand in acknowledgment.

''Sir, Miss Reardon is here on behalf of many of the mall merchants who want to be reassured that the death was an isolated incident and not a harbinger of things to come.''

The policeman gave them a disconcerting stare, as if he almost didn't believe them. ''You're expecting a rash of suicides?''

Stacy took the opening. ''That's our question; is this going to set up a precedent? Can we expect a series of copycat suicides?''

The man crossed his arms, then glanced at the piqued faces of the other people waiting in the lobby. ''Let's go somewhere more private to talk.'' He gestured to them. ''Follow me.''

With fingers laced together, Chance and Stacy followed the detective to the elevator. Waiting by the doors, they could hear noises echoing down the shaft. A split second after the elevator dinged, the doors jerked open and a tangled ball of arms and legs tumbled out.

To his credit, Lt. Harrold stepped between his visitors and the new arrivals, shielding Stacy and Chance from the flailing fists of two police officers and their prisoner. Chance pulled her behind him as well, offering a second level of protection.

Shouting invectives which not only questioned the lineage but the species of the policemen, the prisoner continued to struggle, foiling all attempts of the officers to subdue him. The wild-eyed man lunged for Stacy, but her two protectors thwarted his initial efforts.

With a scream of rage, the man spun, warded off the lieutenant with a quick jab and grabbed Chance, pulling him into a chokehold. As Chance was jerked away, she released a muffled warning, watching his fingers slip out of hers.

Holding Chance as a hostage, the man backed toward the elevator. "Take one more step and the suit gets it!"

Despite the warning, Stacy took an involuntary step forward, but the lieutenant pushed her back. As she watched helplessly, she realized Chance's face didn't reflect the painful strength of the criminal's grip, but the agony of being torn from this world and propelled into another one.

"I'll be okay, Stace." Chance grunted between his captor's screaming threats of death and dismemberment. "Come back to the mall when you finish. Promise?"

She nodded, consumed by her own inability to help.

"I'll kill him, you hear?" the drunken man screamed. "Don't try to follow me!" He dragged a remarkably calm Chance into the elevator.

The doors jerked a few times, then slammed closed, muffling the man's dire predictions. A second later, a high-pitched scream echoed through the elevator shaft.

Harrold sprinted toward the stairs, taking each flight in just a few steps. Stacy followed behind, along with several patrolmen. The men quickly outdistanced her, leaving her to climb the stairs as best she could in heels. When she got to the second floor, Harrold and two other officers waited at the elevator door, guns drawn and pointed in anticipation.

A loud metallic groan heralded the elevator's arrival.

"Be ready," Harrold issued between clenched teeth.

The doors jerked open.

"Oh my God."

Stacy pushed forward, although she knew that nothing terrible had gone wrong. After all, the man couldn't kill someone who was already dead.

Could he?

She pushed between the men and spotted a single body on the floor of the elevator.

Harrold stood by the still form, scanning the area with a professional scowl. He nudged the lifeless form with his foot, flipping the body over. It was the drunk who flinched, throwing his hands up to protect his face. He looked as if he'd been to hell and back.

Stacy could guess what he'd witnessed.

"Get up, you scumbag," Lt. Harrold commanded.

The man trembled as he struggled to his feet. "It was horrible. Horrible!" he groaned.

Harrold grabbed him by the lapels. "Where's the lawyer?"

The man's bottom lip quivered. "He t'weren't no lawyer. He was the devil, his'self."

One patrolman nudged the other. "I've always thought that about lawyers."

"Shut up," Harrold commanded to his outspoken underling. He turned back to the shivering prisoner. "Where's your hostage?"

The man grasped Harrold's sleeve and held on tightly. "One moment I had 'im in my arms, then the next . . . he turned into a big puff o' smoke. And vanished!"

Chapter Eight

''He what?'' Lt. Harrold tried to brush away the man's clawing hands, but he was persistent.

''He vanished!'' The drunk's bleary eyes grew wider. ''Just like that Copperhead magician on TV. Poof!''

The detective released a labored sigh, then gestured to the other officers. ''Get him out of here,'' he ordered.

The drunk reached for Harrold's sleeve again, but the lieutenant pinned him down with one sharp glare.

Obeying the implicit orders, the man backed up, wringing his hands instead. ''But I see'd him . . . I mean I didn't see him—I mean . . .'' A look of confusion blanketed his features. He began to mumble to himself, counting on his fingers. ''First he was there and then he wasn't.''

Harrold stared at the man, then shook his head. ''Why me?'' he muttered to no one in particular. He turned to the nearest officer. ''What's this idiot in for . . . besides having breath bad enough to stop a charging rhinoceros in heat.''

The patrolman pulled out a pair of handcuffs and snapped them on his bewildered prisoner. ''Drunk and disorderly, sir.''

The lieutenant released a sharp bark of laughter. "Then throw him back in the tank. He hasn't sobered up, yet."

"Yes sir."

Two officers flanked the prisoner and carted him down the hall.

The man stumbled, calling back over his shoulder. "But I'm tellin' you . . . he faded away just like them dudes on *Star Trek.*"

Harrold brushed his sleeves as if trying to remove all vestiges of the drunk's touch. "Vanished. Right. Last week, we had a guy in who swore he'd been in a spaceship piloted by a two-headed lizard woman." He hesitated, giving Stacy a critical glance. "You okay, Miss Reardon?"

She nodded and wondered when her brain cells would jump-start into action. She knew she had to come up with a reasonable explanation for Chance's unscheduled disappearance, but her mind was still numb with shock.

Think, Stacy. Think!

Harrold shrugged. "The only thing I can figure is that the doors opened up again on the first floor and your lawyer friend simply walked out."

Her heart skipped a beat. It couldn't be that simple.

Nothing could be that simple.

Her imagination sprang to life after its brief vacation. "I bet you're right, Lieutenant. Chance—Chances are Peter had to go to the other appointment he had in the building. He only meant to stay here long enough with me to make sure I got hooked up with the right detective before he had to go." She'd always been a terrible liar as a child and hoped it was a skill that improved with age.

Harrold nodded. "Just as well. I'd just as soon talk to you alone about the Johnson case."

She swallowed hard. "A-alone?"

"Let's go to my office."

Unable to speak, Stacy followed him in silence as they wandered through a maze of corridors. Finally, they entered a small room which contained the necessities: a desk, chairs, a wall full of file drawers and a copier. A curious aroma filled the room, a mixture of stale coffee and copy-machine toner. Her stomach lurched at the odd combination of smells.

Before they had arrived, she and Chance had discussed their strategies on getting information out of the police, but now she felt suddenly overwhelmed by the enormity and solitary nature of her task. Her stomach jolted again.

What if the lieutenant didn't believe her?

What if he realized she had a hidden agenda?

What if . . .

"Just why do you want to know about the Chance Johnson case, Miss Reardon?" Harrold leaned back in his chair, giving her a calculated stare. "Did you know Mr. Johnson?"

She swallowed hard, again. Suddenly their well-crafted plans seemed juvenile at best. Maybe the best tactic was the truth. Or at least a slightly altered version of it.

She took a deep breath, then leaned forward, trying to ignore the mirror behind his desk, which reflected her duplicitous face. "No sir. I never met him. However I have heard it may *not* have been suicide."

He straightened in his chair. "Where did you hear something like that?"

Stacy shrugged. "You hear things at the mall. It's not necessarily gossip. More like rumors in the bathroom. Speculations. Wild tales."

He picked up a pencil and tapped a file on his desk. "What sort of wild tales?"

She mentally crossed her fingers. "That this Johnson fellow wasn't the type to commit suicide. That he had no reason to kill himself."

Harrold watched her much too intently. It made an uncomfortable sensation crawl up the back of her neck. She'd had men stare at her before, but those had been stares meant to see through her clothes, not through her brazen lies. Despite the enlarging aspect of the mirror, the walls began to close in on her.

After a few tense seconds of claustrophobic silence, Harrold slumped back in his desk chair. "That's one rumor which we can put to rest. He definitely had reason to kill himself."

She felt her heart wedged itself in her throat. "He did?" she managed to croak.

"Unfortunately."

"What . . . I mean, why?"

He lifted an eyebrow. "You're too curious, Miss Reardon. Why is that?"

She unclenched her hand which had somehow tightened itself into a fist. Drawing a deep breath, she tried to perform a careless shrug. "Rumors have a way of hurting business. After all, I understand he j-jumped right in front of my store."

Harrold said nothing. She'd hoped he'd deny it, but his silence was a damning confirmation.

She pressed her luck. "Uh . . . I've heard several other store owners voice their concern that there might be copycat suicides."

"Copycat suicides . . .?" He looked downright dubious.

Her palms started to grow damp. "You've heard of cases like that before, haven't you, Lieutenant? Where one suicide starts a whole chain of others?"

"And you think this might happen again? Six weeks after the fact?"

Stacy paused for a moment, formulating her strategy. It was sink-or-swim time. Depending on what she said, he was either going to believe her or get ready to snap the cuffs on her.

She made direct eye-contact with him, commanding herself not to waver. "No sir, I don't. However, there are some mall merchants who are still paying an inordinate amount of attention to the rumors concerning this man. According to the various stories floating around, he was everything from a troubled teenager to a mob informant. I figured if I knew the truth, I could prevent needless worry and idle speculation which could eventually hurt all of our businesses."

"Oh, so your concerns are more fiscal than philosophical?" He contemplated her for a few moments, then nodded. "I suppose—" He riffled through the pages of the manila file folder on his desk, "—I could give you some details." He shot her a knowing smile. "To forestall any undue rumors, you understand."

"Absolutely." She caught his drift—right in the solar plexus. He didn't believe a word she'd said. But for some unfathomable reason, he was cooperating.

He opened the file folder and tapped the top sheet.

"Johnson, Chance R. Single, white male. Occupation: architect. A partner with the firm of Browne, Johnson, and Associates. He was just one week short of his thirty-sixth birthday when he died."

Stacy straightened in her chair and drew in a hasty breath which sounded suspiciously to her like as gasp.

The lieutenant continued. "According to his partner, Neal Browne, Johnson had been despondent for a few weeks before his death. Apparently, he'd been accused of design irregularities."

"What are *design irregularities?*"

"Evidently, a building he designed developed severe structural flaws. According to his partner, Johnson joined in a conspiracy with the construction company to reduce costs by using substandard materials. And the money he saved went right into his pocket. Rumor has it, most of it went right up his nose."

"Cocaine?"

Harrold nodded. "And when the legal loopholes started closing around his neck, he got scared. We think the pressure and guilt got to him and he simply took the easy way out."

"Easy way out," she repeated, scarcely believing the words.

The lieutenant shrugged. "Some people break under the stress."

She stared at the papers, straining to read the upside-down

words. There *had* to be something else in the file, something which explained why the Chance Johnson who reportedly killed himself bore little resemblance to the man she had gotten to know so well.

She corrected herself.

To the *ghost* she'd gotten to know well.

"Is something wrong, Miss Reardon?"

She shook her head, dragging her attention back to the problem at hand. "Uh . . . nothing, Lieutenant." Their gazes locked for a moment. "Nothing," she repeated.

The ringing telephone provided enough distraction to draw away the man's attention. When he grabbed the receiver, it looked almost fragile in his large grip. "Yes?" His gaze cut toward her, making her push back in her seat. "She's right here. Just a moment."

Her mind raced ahead. Who knew she was there? Chance!

Harrold covered the mouthpiece with his hand. "Will you excuse me for a minute? I need to check on our friend in the elevator."

"The e-elevator?" *It is Chance!*

Harrold nodded. "The drunk. He's kicking up a fuss and if he doesn't calm down, I'll need to get a statement from you."

"A statement?"

"And one from your lawyer friend, too, if you know where he is at the moment."

It was evidently time for another burst from her unbridled imagination. "Uh . . . he didn't exactly say who his appointment was with. Lawyer-client privilege being what it is . . .

The policeman shot her a smile. "Aw, don't worry about it. It's just a little bit of insurance to put the fear of God in him. Yours will do. Give me—" He looked at his watch, "—ten minutes to break out my rubber hose and threaten him, okay?"

"Okay."

He got up, excused himself, then disappeared out the door.

Stacy waited for a full minute before she turned the file around to read it. As she thumbed through pages, she half-expected Harrold to burst through the doors and discover her in mid-indiscretion.

The first page was a daunting account entitled an "Initial Crime Scene Report." She needed a dictionary just to understand half the terms used in it. Then it hit her; even if she had an opportunity to read the material, how much information could she digest, then accurately recall when she and Chance compared notes?

Stacy stared at the efficient-looking copy machine beside the door, shifted her glance to the file folder, then back to the machine.

Do it!

In four-and-a-half minutes, she'd copied every page and was in the process of reassembling the pages in the folder when she heard heavy footsteps in the hallway. By the time the lieutenant entered the office, Stacy had replaced the file, precisely returning it to the same place on the desk.

"Sorry it took so long." His smile was just a bit too bright. "It was a false alarm. When I explained the sort of charges your friend the lawyer might make, the drunk sobered quickly enough and decided to cooperate."

"Oh . . . good." Guilt made her stomach perform a flip-flop.

"Let me reassure you, Miss Reardon, that Mr. Johnson's death has been categorically ruled a suicide. And since he wasn't a teenager, I don't think we can expect a rash of copycat problems.

She nodded numbly.

"So you can go back to the mall and assure your fellow merchants that we've run a full investigation on the situation and have everything under control."

"U-under control. Yes sir." Stacy rose stiffly, trying not to dislodge the papers which she had stuffed into her waistband and covered with her blouse. "Uh . . . well, thank you, Lieutenant." She stuck out her hand, wondering if he could read signs of conspiracy in her damp palm.

"You're welcome, Miss Reardon. Your police department is always happy to serve you."

Happy to serve me? Stacy repeated to herself as she stumbled out of the building. *Yeah, if you find out I copied the file, you'll be happy to serve me . . . on a silver platter with an apple stuffed in my mouth.*

The automatic controller in her brain drove her back to the mall without incident, allowing her to devise a thousand scenarios which involved either incarceration or institutionalization. When she pulled into the parking lot, the two halves of her brain rejoined and she was appalled that she remembered practically nothing about the return trip.

She stared at the slightly crumpled papers sitting on the passenger's seat. Should she preview them first? Read them so she'd be able to soften the blow for Chance? She reached for the top sheet but as she read the first line, tears blurred her eyes.

Who was going to soften the blow for her?

She drew in a deep breath, gathered the papers, then got out of her car. As she trudged across the parking lot, Stacy wasn't sure why she looked up at the wide expanse of windows that allowed sunlight to spill into the second-floor food court. A figure hovered in the upper right-hand corner of the window, a place where no ordinary human could reach.

The figure waved to her.

Chance.

She battled a sudden fatigue as she lifted her leaden hand, returning his greeting. By the time she reached the mall entrance, he stood by the door waiting for her.

"Well? What did Harrold say?"

She glanced around, lowering her voice. "Let's go someplace where we can talk."

A spotty-faced teenager walking nearby gave her a leering smile. "Sure, baby. C'mon."

"Not you, buster." Chance bent down, rubbed his fist across the carpet, then threw a punch at the young man. Even though his hand passed harmlessly through the teen's face, the young man's eyes widened. He sniffed as the first signs of blood dripped from his nostril. His bravado faded as his nose began to gush all over his shirt.

Stacy looked at Chance and sighed. "Did you have to hit him?"

Her ghostly companion shrugged. "Technically, I never touched him. Anyway, he's not hurt. He's just one of those guys who has a tendency to bleed when he gets fresh with a lady."

"Aw, Chance—" She propped her hands on her hips. "I could have handled him."

The young man leaned against the wall, tilting his head up and pinching his nose to stem the flow of blood. He spoke in a nasal voice. "You're crazy lady. You're ef-fing crazy!"

Stacy glared at him. "One more word out of you and I'll do it again."

The teenager flinched, shielding his face but made no effort to follow her as she strode down the hallway and headed to the elevator. Chance hesitated for a moment before entering.

She reached around him, pushed the button for the third floor, then glanced up at his clouded expression. "What's wrong?"

The doors slid shut behind him and he shoved his hands in his pockets. "I don't know." He looked past her and out through the glass panel behind her. "I have this . . . funny feeling."

Glass elevators had never bothered her before, but this time, her stomach remained on the first level of the mall as they rose. "Me, too. Do you think it's elevators in general? Or perhaps just the disconcerting view of the world growing smaller?"

He shook his head again. "I don't think that's it. I didn't feel anything . . . odd while I was in the elevator at the police precinct." Chance flexed his shoulders as if trying to shake off an uncomfortable sensation. "I think it's just *this* elevator." He blinked, then tried to smile at her. "Maybe it's just the view. Either way, I'd rather stick to the escalator next time, okay?"

"Sure."

"So did you find out anything?"

The strap of her purse suddenly burned into her shoulder. "Yeah. I did. I—"

The elevator slid to a stop. The doors slid open to reveal a harried mother waiting impatiently. Inside her twin stroller, the matching toddlers were in the midst of a joint tantrum of epic proportions. Stacy stepped out, then held the door open while the woman tried to maneuver the stroller over the uneven entrance.

When Stacy turned around, her good deed completed, she found Chance standing at the railing. Staring across the mall, he wore an expression of blank confusion.

"Chance?"

He didn't respond.

"Chance."

He leaned forward, coming dangerously close to the edge. For a wild moment, she worried that he'd lean too far out, past the railing and fall.

"Chance!" She nearly reached for him, but realized two things in succession. One: the bustling crowd wasn't ready for his sudden appearance. Two: the laws of gravity don't apply to ghosts.

Chance inclined his head to the left. "Do you see him?"

"See who?" Stacy craned to see around him.

"No, don't look!" He pivoted, effectively blocking her view. "I mean don't let him know you're looking."

"How am I supposed to do that? If he can't see you, then for all intents and appearances, I'm facing him right now."

"Turn around, then," he ordered. "Whatever you do, don't make it look as if you're staring." He glanced around, evidently searching for inspiration. His gaze settled on her purse. "You got a mirror in there?"

She zipped open her bag, pawed past the purloined police papers and found the compact mirror her oldest niece had given her for Christmas. She held it up for his inspection. "I'm armed. Now what?"

"Turn around and pretend to powder your nose or something."

"Powder my nose?" She released a sigh. "You've been reading too many mystery novels. We don't carry around powder puffs any more."

Chance tapped an impatient rhythm with his foot. "Just do something unobtrusive!"

Stacy opened the mirror, expecting to see Chance. Instead, she had a clear view as if he wasn't there. She spun around, only to discover he still stood there in all his anxiety.

"Stacy . . ."

"You're like a vampire, you know." She turned around and repositioned the mirror and pretended to be adjusting a nonexistent contact lens. "Where am I supposed to look?"

"In front of the sporting-goods store. The man over there . . . dressed in black."

Stacy squinted and the mirrored image sharpened. The man wore a black trench coat, black boots, and a black fedora. Considering it was early June, the fellow was doing a terrible job of trying to blend in with the crowd. "Tall guy? Bad tailor?"

"That's the one."

"Besides the fact he's seen too many James Bond movies, what about him?"

"He can see me."

Her heart skipped a beat. "What?" Stacy spun around.

Chance nodded. "You heard me. He can see me. He's been following me around ever since I got back. In fact, I think he could even be the same guy we saw sitting on the bench in the police precinct."

Stacy's mind jumped back to an image of the old man with the stained raincoat and the killer aroma.

"No . . . not the flasher. The man sitting on the bench by himself."

She remembered Chance's reluctance to sit on the opposite

bench. She stepped to one side to get a better view of their mysterious Mr. Black. "You're sure?"

"Don't be so obvious." He shifted back, obstructing her view. "Yes, I'm sure he can see me, and no, I'm not totally sure it's the same guy."

"So what do we do?"

Chance dragged his hand through his indeterminate-colored hair. "I don't know. I just don't know."

Stacy craned around him to take one last look and discovered the man had moved. He was striding toward them.

"He's headed this way!"

Chance glanced over his shoulder, then took a stumbling step toward Stacy, nearly making physical contact with her. "Don't ask me why . . . but we gotta get out of here."

She found herself suddenly rooted to the spot. "What do you mean? Where can we go?"

He scanned the area, his gaze shooting past her shoulder and settling on something behind her. "The elevator!"

"But I thought you said—"

"Forget that. Hurry! He's coming!" Chance zipped to the elevator door. "The button. Hit the button, Stace."

She hurried toward him, slamming the call button with the heel of her hand. Turning around, she watched the man approach. All she could distinguish about him was the darkness of his clothes, which seemed to absorb all his other characteristics, and to absorb all her attention.

Somewhere behind her, machinery whirred and a bell signaled the elevator's arrival. She felt her muscles melt and her bones fuse in place.

Chance charged through the open doors, then spun around. He was shocked to see Stacy, staring in the direction of the approaching threat. "Stacy . . . c'mon. We've got to get out of here, now!"

She took a small step backwards. "I c-can't stop staring . . ."

The man in black riveted his attention on Chance with dark eyes sending out a silent message. Chance fell under the mesmerizing spell for a moment before he tore his gaze away. "Close your eyes, honey. Don't look at him."

"C-can't . . ." Her voice trailed off.

"Just two more steps, Stace. You can do it." He hoped she heard his words of encouragement, not the sense of despair behind them. "Just two more steps into the elevator and we'll be gone."

The approaching man waved at them, mouthing words which Chance couldn't quite understand.

"Stacy . . . please."

Stacy responded by taking one small step backward.

"Just one more—" Chance looked down, appalled at the sight of a gaping black hole beneath him. He stood unsupported in midair. And Stacy was mere inches away from plunging down the empty elevator shaft.

"No . . .!"

Chapter Nine

Chance lunged toward her, hitting her as hard as he could. He prayed that forward momentum and his fleeting moment of substance would knock her to safety. He didn't care about being seen; his main mission, his only mission was to save her. Stacy crashed to the floor under his momentary weight, shielding her face with her arm as landed.

Chance stood over her, fearful to touch her, yet aching to do just that. He knelt beside her. "Stacy . . . sweetheart? Are you all right?"

Her eyes were open, but she didn't answer him.

"Stace?"

She blinked. "Whah happ'n?"

Chance started to speak, but he became instantly aware of another presence. The man in black? No, it wasn't fear he felt, but irritation. Overwhelming irritation.

"Jeez, Stacy . . . you all right?" Chuck Canton appeared out of nowhere and sidled up to Stacy to tower over her. What was it about the man that always made Chance think that Upchuck would be much more appropriate name for him?

Chance moved more out of instinct than necessity when the man finally knelt beside Stacy.

"Move over, you slimeball."

For some inexplicable reason, UpChuck shifted to her other side, allowing Chance to move back closer to Stacy.

"Stacy, honey? Wake up. People are starting to stare. You're making yourself look plenty silly all stretched out across the floor." He played up to the crowd which started forming. "Well folks, you think if I kiss Sleeping Beauty, she'll wake up?"

Chance bristled, pushing right up into UpChuck's lecherous face. "If you so much as touch her, I'll haunt you for the rest of your miserable life."

UpChuck looked as if was going to contemplate a quick liplock, then changed his mind when Stacy opened her eyes, took one look at him and shrieked in unholy terror.

The crowd, galvanized by her screams, took over. Voices blended together.

"Call an ambulance."

"Don't push me."

"The elevator doors are open but the car's not there."

"My God . . . she could have fallen down that thing."

"Help her up."

"No, don't try to move her."

"Has anyone called mall security?"

"Is she drunk?"

Chance watched helplessly as UpChuck regained his role as hero, shooing away the worst of the gossip-mongers and helping Stacy to a seated position. She seemed merely stunned, not physically harmed by their ordeal.

An ordeal which was far from over.

Chance sensed another presence again. This time, it wasn't the irritating Upchuck, but something, someone more ephemeral, threatening. Chance scanned the area and spotted the man in black working his way through the crowd toward them. Panic rose to commandeer the situation. He squatted next to Stacy.

hoping to enter her blurry range of vision. "Stace, honey . . . we have to go. Now."

She shot him a groggy look. "Go . . . with you?"

UpChuck gave her a licentious grin. "Of course you can go with me. We'll just head back to my storeroom where you can lie down and get some rest."

Chance threw an elbow into UpChuck's midsection. "I don't have time for you, scuzzball." The lecher showed no signs of having felt the attack.

Her focus appeared to sharpen and she began to struggle to her feet. "Where is he?"

"Where is who?" UpChuck asked, wrapping a too-possessive grip around Stacy's arm.

"Right there." Chance pointed to the edge of the crowd where the onlookers were fortunately impeding the man's progress. "Shake a leg, sweetie. We've got to get out of here."

"Where is *who?*" UpChuck repeated. He rubbed the heel of his hand across his stomach. "All this excitement has my stomach tied up in knots."

She glared at the man. "Who do you think? The idiot who pushed me."

A large lady standing nearby, loaded with shopping bags released a harsh volley of laughter. "Lady, you better talk nicer about the man who saved your life."

"Save my—"

The elevator dinged again, this time signaling the real arrival of the elevator car.

"Stacy! C'mon. He's almost here!" Chance gestured toward the elevator.

She pushed a strand of hair out of her face, then nodded toward her benefactors. "Uh . . . thanks for your help . . . everybody. I'm okay. Really. I just want to go collect myself. Okay?"

Chuck shook his head. "Stacy, I think you ought to wait and—"

"Thanks, Chuck." She tore out of his grasp and shot Chance a hooded glance. "Let's go!" she mouthed.

The elevator doors shut, insulating them from the curious stares of the onlookers, including one ominous one in black. Stacy sagged against the wall. "What's happening, Chance?"

"I don't know." He turned and stared out of the glass panel. A figure in black rode down the escalator almost matching their rate of speed as they descended. Chance took a protective stance between Stacy and the man's dark fathomless gaze.

"What's going on?" She stepped to the side so she too could see out the glass panel.

Chance sighed and stepped away, giving her a full view. "On the escalator. He's following us."

Stacy reached up, cradling her head between her palms. "This is too weird for me. He couldn't have gotten all the way around to the escalator. He simply hasn't had enough time to get over there."

A strained logic persevered. The man in black could see him, move like him. The answer was obvious. "He could if he's not real. Like me."

"He's a ghost, too?"

"Could be. After all, why should I think I'm the only ghost in the mall?"

She gave Chance a confused look, to which his only response could be to open his arms and invite her in. Stacy complied, wrapping her arms around his waist and resting her cheek on his shoulder.

Chance's heart sprang into action, matching her thundering tempo with his own. As life poured into him, he watched the man in black slowly fade away. He felt Stacy's grip tighten.

"Did you see that?" she asked in a hoarse whisper.

Chance swallowed hard, then nodded. "You think it's a trick? Is he only fooling us into believing he's gone?"

Stacy pulled them closer to the wall, so they could take as much cover as they could away from the glass. "I don't know."

Suddenly the elevator stopped and a shrill bell pierced the air.

He glanced up. "Stace—"

She shook head. "Don't worry, I did that. I hit the emergency-stop button." She placed one hand against the small of his back, then released his arm. "Is still he there?"

Chance scanned the escalator. "I don't see him."

A second later, she lifted her hand, breaking contact with Chance. "Now?"

As the life flowed out of Chance's veins, the ominous man faded back into existence. No one around him on the escalator seemed aware of either his departure or his rematerialization.

"They didn't notice . . ." Chance stared in dread at the figure who met his gaze with an expressionless face. Chance heard himself whisper, "Do it again, Stacy."

Although she touched him gently, the sudden change from life to death and back to life again hit him like a fist in the gut. He arched his back and his muscles knotted with their sudden flush of reality. In a fleeting moment, he wondered if the man in black suffered from a similar malady as he faded from view.

"Well, I think we have our answer for the time being." Chance reached back and grabbed Stacy's hand. "Experiment time is over. We touch; he goes away. That's all I really have to know, right now."

She nodded, then pulled out the stop button. The alarm ended in pulsating echoes which lingered in Chance's newly invigorated ears. The elevator shuddered slightly as it started moving, then jerked to a stop, signaling their arrival on the first floor. Bowing to the side of his intellect which screamed for precaution, Chance motioned for her to stay back as he scanned the first floor, searching for their mysterious observer.

The most sinister character he spotted was a lady with an armload of packages who was trying to outrun a harried mother herding her brood toward the elevator. Sidestepping the toddler hoard, he tugged Stacy into the mainstream of traffic, hoping to find a sense of anonymous safety among the other shoppers.

"Where to, now?" she asked between clenched teeth.

"Food court?" he offered.

She rubbed the heel of her free hand across her stomach. "I'm not too hungry. I'm still shook up . . . over my fall."

He skidded to a stop, suddenly aware of what she *wasn't* saying as opposed to what she *was.* "Don't be scared, Stace. I won't let anything happen to you." He pulled her into his arms, suddenly aware of how small she was compared to him.

How fragile.

How precious.

How very important to him.

"Fragile?" A small nervous smile played across her lips. "You think I'm fragile?"

He sighed, reached down and stroked her face with his fingertips. "*You* are made out of steel. It's life that's fragile. No matter how strong the body, our grasp on life is tenuous at best."

She leaned her head against his chest, an intimate gesture which made his heart beat a little harder. "This is too crazy, you know."

He looked down, overwhelmed by the sensations and senses that made up life—her floral perfume mixing with the clean smell of shampoo. The muted background noise of the mall merging with the insistent roar of life's blood in his ears. Her thoughts intermingling with his own until they were so tangled, he couldn't separate his from hers.

"Crazy," he repeated in a strangled voice. "Absolute madness."

"We're being pursued by a strange figure dressed in black who disappears when I touch you and you become real. Tell me that's not straight out of a lost episode of the *Twilight Zone.*"

Chance involuntarily lifted his gaze from her silken crown and scanned the area. Seeing, sensing no threats, he gave her a quick squeeze. "*Submitted for your approval,*" he started in a stentorian tone. "*One Chance Johnson, Esquire. Bon Vivant, Epicurean, All Around Nice Guy also known as—*" He switched to his scariest voice, "*—The Phantom of the Shopping Mall.*"

"Also known as—" Stacy suddenly pulled away from him, a new expression suffocating her halfhearted smirk. Grasping his hand tightly, she dragged him toward the wall. She drew a deep breath, then reached up and fingered the bronzed letters of a plaque embedded in a polished walnut panel. "*Chance Johnson, Architect,*" she read aloud.

Chance's heart skipped a beat.

She looked up at him with tear-choked eyes. "Part of the answer was sitting here all the time without us knowing."

He stared at the small plaque.

Chapel Valley Mall
Built 1996
Johnson, Browne, and Associates Architects
Built by Bains/Bowren Contractors
Designed by Chance Johnson, AIA

Stacy tried to coax him away from the plaque, but he seemed entranced by it. She tightened her grip as he lifted his free hand and fingered the raised letters.

"*Architect* . . ." he repeated with a bewildered sigh. "I would have never guessed. I am . . . was an architect."

She checked an urge to put her arm around his waist. "Lt. Harrold said you were an architect but he said nothing about you designing this mall."

He shrugged and turned away from the wall to scan the area. "Architecture doesn't sound like one of those high-energy, high-stress jobs that drives a man to suicide. Of course, how many people can say they designed the place where they died?" He glanced back, catching her in his solemn gaze. "You haven't said anything about what you found at the police station. It *was* suicide, wasn't it?"

Stacy knew her best weapon in the upcoming battle of wits was logic: her logic versus that of the police. She adopted her most authoritative face. "That's what the police think, but when we examine their records, I think we might come to a different conclusion.

Confusion masked his expression. "Examine their records?"

Stacy patted her purse. "We now have a copy of their reports."

"They *gave* you a copy?" He lifted his eyebrows in incredulity.

"Not . . . quite." She swallowed hard. "The lieutenant was called away for a few moments and left the folder on his desk. It was too much of a temptation." She offered Chance a small smile. "He had a copy machine sitting by the door so I was able to make copies and keep an eye out for his return at the same time." Her retrospective courage and sense of triumph built at the same rate. "I finished the copies and got the original back on his desk before he even steped back into the hallway."

Chance responded to her jubilant news with a frown.

A shiver coursed up her arm from their laced fingers. "What's wrong?"

He drew in a deep breath. "Don't you think that was a bit too convenient? Too coincidental?"

"Coincidental?" Her shiver turned into a full-fledged chill.

"Sure. You show up, expressing interest in a case. He produces the file, then conveniently leaves it on his desk when he's called away for a few minutes. At the very least, it sounds . . . suspicious."

Stacy's stomach began to sour. Chance was right. She'd been so exhilarated with the unexpected opportunity, she hadn't thought to question its timing.

His frown deepened. "Did he have a mirror in his office?"

Stacy remembered seeing a glimpse of her nervous face reflected behind the lieutenant's desk. "Y-yes," she whispered.

Chance dragged his free hand through his hair. "Damn it, Stacy! It was probably a one-way from the office next door. He was watching you. He knows you made a copy of the file." Chance turned to scan the crowd of shoppers who strolled idly through the mall, seemingly ignorant of his turmoil. Or were they? "He might send someone to watch you . . . to watch us!"

Stacy followed his gaze, first focusing on the unconcerned expressions, then imagining duplicity behind the oh-so-innocent faces of the passing people. "It could be anybody," she whispered.

"Exactly."

"The man in black?"

The muscles in Chance's hand contracted. "Not unless the police have supernatural talents we're not aware of."

"S-supernatural?"

Chance nodded. "I think Mr. Black might be after me, but I certainly don't think it was Lt. Harrold who sent him."

"Then who sent . . ." Her voice gave out.

"Death."

Chapter Ten

"Death?"

He nodded. "I'm a . . . a rogue spirit. Doing things I'm not supposed to do." His grip tightened on her hand. "Doesn't it make sense that if a mistake has been made, then someone—or something would try to correct it?"

"You consider yourself a—" She swallowed hard, "—mistake?"

"What else can I be?" Regret filled his face. "My God, Stacy, look at the facts. I can become real! Flesh and blood. How many times have you ever heard of a ghost becoming real?"

She swallowed hard. "N-none."

"Exactly. It's not supposed to happen. The dead stay dead. But I'm not." He lifted her hand, pressing it against his chest. "Feel that?"

His heart rumbled in rhythm, *a-live, a-live, a-live.* She nodded.

"And this." He shifted her hand, this time placing it against the warm bristled skin of his cheek. "When we touch, I'm as

alive as you are, Stacy, and we both know that's not right. I've got this uneasy feeling our mysterious man in black is here to rectify a slight oversight—" Chance swallowed with obvious difficulty "—namely, me."

The room tilted for a moment, taking a distinctly counterclockwise spin. Stacy gripped his fingers tighter out of instinct as well as balance.

He reached out to brace her with his other hand. "Whoa . . . Stace! You okay? Maybe I shouldn't have hit you with this so soon after your fall."

Clenching her teeth, Stacy grabbed at her equilibrium with a mental fist and held on for dear life. "Don't worry about me. I'm just d-dandy. I'm standing in the middle of a mall, talking to a ghost only I can see and hear, and learning that we're expecting a visit from some sort of cosmic bounty hunter."

Chance helped her sit on a nearby bench and knelt beside her, his hand resting lightly on her knee. "The only problem with that analogy is that I have a sneaking suspicion it's not going to be a case of *Wanted Dead or Alive.*" He paused to shrug and give the seating area around them a quick once-over. "It's more like . . . simply *Wanted Dead.*"

The part of her mind which controlled reason and rationality simply shut down. Logic had flown the coop and was a fleeting speck on the horizon. Chance didn't know anything about himself, about who he was, about why he was there. But he remembered something so trivial as some stupid television show from the sixties she barely remembered.

"Actually it started in the late fifties." He flinched, flushed then raised one hand in surrender. "Sorry . . . I didn't mean to read your mind without permission."

She shook her head, fighting the tears which formed heedless of her fervent wish to stay in complete control. After she wiped her eyes, she lifted her head to look at him. Their gazes locked, blunting out all the distractions of the mall. Stacy allowed herself to forget Lt. Harrold and his dangling paper bait, to forget the mysterious figure in deadly black. All she wanted in her life was the security of knowing Chance.

Of touching Chance.

Of never losing Chance.

He shifted, gathering both of her hands in his. A flash of electricity tingled in her palms, reminding her of how real their uncommon connection was. After several intense moments when concepts, wishes and perceptions flowed unobstructed between them, Chance pulled away. Although he didn't break their physical connection, he put up an invisible wall between them which effectively blocked his thoughts from tumbling into her mind.

''You can't . . .'' His voice trailed off.

''Can't what?''

''You can't write my name in that secret place in your heart.''

Stacy flushed. It was the exact image she'd conjured in her mind.

''I'm alive . . . for the moment, but I can't cheat Death forever.''

''But—''

''What am I supposed to do? Stay alive by holding your hand forever?''

A stray giggle of absurdity bubbled up from behind the hot tears that spilled down her cheeks. ''Would that be so bad?' Holding hands for the rest of our lives?''

''Don't do this.'' He tightened his free hand into a fist and pounded the bench beside his leg. ''Don't fool yourself into thinking I'm going to be able to exist like this indefinitely. You need to save that special place for someone who's going to be around a lot longer than me.''

She touched his cheek, hoping she could regain the ineffable sense of closeness they'd shared earlier, but the mental block remained between them. ''But, Chance—''

He lifted his hand as if to touch her lips with his forefinger, but he halted in mid-motion. ''I need to—''

''To . . .'' She supplied her own answer. *Touch me forever.*

"—use what time I have on this world to—"

Be with me, forever.

"—find answers to my questions."

"Q-questions," she echoed, barely cognizant of the meaning of the word.

"Our mission," he prompted. "The reason why we went to the police station."

She sighed. It took a few precious moments before she could tear herself away from the wishes of the heart and force her attention back to the spoken conversation. "Police station . . . of course." She squeezed his hand and glanced at the purse dangling from her shoulder. "The papers."

He stared at her for a long moment without saying anything, then he blinked. Jerking his attention away, he scanned their surroundings, then turned back to her. "The papers. Yes . . . we need to go somewhere. Private."

"My storeroom?" she offered.

He shook his head. "More private than that." He resumed his inspection of the mall and its shoppers, his gaze stopping at the plaque. "I think I remember a place. A secret place. Trust me?"

Stacy felt herself blush. "Of course."

Chance led her by the hand through a series of service corridors and doors marked Employees Only, taking her through places she'd never been before. No one followed them into the labyrinth, reassuring her that perhaps, her fears about Lt. Sherlock Harrold may have been premature. Chance pulled her through one seemingly forgotten hallway which came to a halt at the foot of a dusty metal staircase. Their shoes left fresh prints as they climbed the narrow set of treads to a doorway which refused to open.

"Maybe it's locked," Stacy offered. "Judging by the dust, no one has been here in ages."

"Just let me try . . ." Chance rammed the door with his shoulder, jerking her off her feet as he tugged her along for the ride.

She regained her balance. "You're going to hurt yourself!"

"One more—" He reared back and shouldered the door again. It emitted an ominous creak, then swung open.

"Get the light," he ordered in a strained voice.

Stacy scanned the shadows, and spotted a naked bulb hanging from the ceiling by a gnarled wire. When she reached up and thumbed the switch with her free hand, harsh light came on to reveal a small dusty room. It contained a filthy chair and a makeshift table formed by a door placed across two sawhorses.

Stacy stifled a sneeze. "How did you know this was here?"

Chance scanned the room blankly. "I . . . I have no idea. But . . . I do know it's a safe place." He grimaced and sagged against the wall. "A secret place."

"Chance!" She grabbed him, sliding under his arm for support. "What's wrong?"

The color drained out his face for a moment. Stacy looked down at their hands, expecting to discover that they had inadvertently separated, but their fingers were still intertwined.

"Chance?" She glanced up at him and watched a bright flush seep across his face. Panic flooded her at the same rate. "Answer me!"

He shook his head. "I feel so stupid."

"Why? What . . . why are you standing so . . ." Looking at she understood the source of his painful embarrassment. "Oh good God! Your shoulder or your arm?"

"C-collarbone, actually." He made a face, then glanced toward the door. "Close it, okay? And see if you can find some way to lock it."

Still clasping his hand, she closed the door and kicked over one of the chairs over to wedge beneath the doorknob. To his credit, Chance never made a sound as she performed her duties, even when she inadvertently jostled him. "There," she said, wiping her dirtied palm on her pants leg.

"Good. Now . . ." He looked down at their hands locked together. "Do you think you could please let go of me?"

After one blank moment, Stacy realized how she had inadvertently compounded her error. "Oh, Chance . . . I'm so sorry."

He drew a deep breath, then tugged his fingers out of her hand. They both paled together, Chance in color and Stacy in energy. Once he faded back into basic black and white, he stood up straight, tentatively testing his arm by extending it, then lifting it over his head.

"Everything seems to be functioning right, now." He gave her a forgiving smile which seemed just as fatally attractive in death as it was in life.

"I'm sorry." She shivered in spite of herself.

Chance stepped forward. "You okay?"

She nodded, trying to jump-start her suddenly sluggish concentration. "D-do you really think it's safe here?"

He nodded. "For two reasons. One, like you said, no one knows this room even exists. And two, as long as you and I are able to touch, he won't be able to materialize for long."

His logic seemed to have one major defect. "But we don't know how much time he needs to do whatever it is he's supposed to do. It might take nothing more than a second. And—" She shivered as she scanned the dusty room, "—just because we can't see him doesn't mean he's not here, watching us."

Chance shifted until he faced her. "Stace, I promise you he's not here. Call it instinct, ghostly intuition, whatever . . . I can simply sense he's not here. You're safe here with me."

For the first time, she felt his words flow unencumbered into her mind, without benefit of physical contact. His mouth said, "You're safe," but his mind said *"You're not safe . . ."* and she instantly realized what he meant.

They stared at each other for a moment. Then, Chance broke away, pointing to the dusty footprints which tracked their movements into the room and halted at their current position. "You were right. I mean, it's obvious no one has been in this room since they built the place." An unfocused glaze settled over his eyes. "Since . . . *I* built the place."

Breaking away, he shot her an abashed smile, then moved

across the room, not stirring a single mote of dust in his wake. "A little dirt never hurt anyone, right?" Lowering himself to a sitting position by the table, he waved his hand in the direction of the chair, indicating he'd left it for her.

"All of a sudden, you're getting mighty magnanimous with my sinuses." Stacy used a rag from the floor to gingerly brush the worst of the dust from the folding chair before opening it. She perched on the edge of the seat, fighting an urge to sneeze. "And if you want to get technical about it, as the architect, you didn't actually *build* the place."

"I realize that. But apparently, I *did* design it." His gaze sharpened. "I probably designed this room." An animated light flared in his eyes. "I wonder why . . ."

"A work space?" Stacy offered.

"A secret one? Why would I need something like that?" When Stacy failed to issue another theory, Chance crossed his arms and stared at her.

Stacy reddened. "You're staring. Why?" When he didn't answer, she began to appear uneasy. "Chance . . ."

"You."

"What about me?"

An irritating buzz echoed in the back of his head. "You know something, don't you?" When she flushed even more, his buzz increased.

"M-me?" she stuttered.

After a moment's hesitation, Chance attempted to reach out and make contact with her, mind to mind. He'd never done it deliberately and wondered if it could be controlled to such an extent. To his surprise, he actually caught fragments of her thoughts, her impressions. But without the clarification of their physical touch, the incomplete images were hopelessly tangled. However, within the confusion, he picked up definite threads of impending, unhappy revelation.

"Let's not waste any time playing games, Stacy. I know we aren't touching, but I can still read your mind." He glanced down at the purse that she instinctively pulled closer to herself.

"It's not the details in the police report that are bothering you as much as . . ." He paused, closing his eyes for a moment in order to hone his concentration. He saw a fleeting image of Lt. Harrold's face. ". . . your conversation with the lieutenant."

She swallowed hard, then nodded. Drawing a deep breath, she glanced up, catching him in a web of obvious concern. "Like the plaque said, you *were* the senior architect in charge of the mall's design. But according to Lt. Harrold, you . . ." Her voice trailed off and she ducked her head.

"Go ahead," he prompted.

Her voice echoed through the small room in cracked waves. "You killed yourself because the authorities were about to arrest you."

His nonexistent heart wedged itself in his throat. "Arrest me? For what?"

"For being am embezzler."

"An embezzler? What am I supposed to have I stolen?"

"According to the authorities, you drew up two sets of plans. You know . . . the first one showing how it should be built and the second using cheaper materials and—"

"—and pocketing the difference in material costs," he supplied automatically.

Stacy paled. "You remember?"

Chance stopped and searched his mind for the answer.

Did he?

Did he actually possess the basic skills necessary to construct what amounted to a devious financial scheme with possibly serious safety repercussions?

A sudden flash of memories made him go rigid with fear. Voices swirled in his mind, along with smirking faces and pointing fingers.

". . . if we pour the footings at eight inches instead of the usual twelve, then we'll save thirty percent . . ."

". . . cutbacks? We can make cutbacks . . . with the proper financial incentives."

". . . take care of the building inspector. Don't you worry."

"Chance?"

He heard his name and struggled to identify the voice that spoke it. The voice called out again. "Don't do this, Chance. You're scaring me."

Another voice boomed through his mind.

"Mr. Johnson, I have a search warrant here which . . ."

"Chance, listen to me!"

". . . evidence shows your signature on the blueprints, okaying the change in materials . . ."

Blueprints? Chance stared across the room at the dusty blue paper pinned to the wall behind the door. A moment later, he found himself standing in front of the plans, wondering what secrets they exposed, what proof they represented. There in the bottom right corner, he saw his hand-printed name and beside it, a signature.

His signature?

Slowly, he pulled himself away from the maelstrom of phantom accusations to concentrate on his single remaining link with reality: Stacy.

"You can't believe you're guilty, Chance."

"I believe . . ." His voice cracked.

"Chance . . . please!"

He stared at his hand . . . through his hand. Where there had been substance, there was none. He was a ghost, nothing more, nothing less.

Nothing.

The room grew dark, the lines of definition wavering as the objects in the room vanished into the shadows. Only Stacy remained visible. She was his lifeline. His life.

She stretched her arm toward him. "Chance . . . don't give up. Don't give up faith in yourself."

"Faith?" He tried to laugh but couldn't muster the energy. "Faith in what? Myself? Haven't you figured it out yet? The dearly departed give up their faith when they give up their life."

"No!" She reached out for him. "Don't say that. Please.

You're fading away and I don't want you to go. I won't *allow* you to go."

As the room darkened, the golden glow highlighting her began to grow stronger.

"I won't let you—" She lunged forward and grabbed his arms, "—go!"

The room exploded with an unearthly cacophony. Sparks flew from the places where her fingers wrapped around his arm. She arched her head back and shuddered as visible waves of electricity, of energy, perhaps of life itself, pulsed through her arms and threaded into his body.

Life boiled slowly through his veins like lava, gaining momentum as it burned a path down his arms and toward his chest. Swirling mists rushed up to encircle them, spiraling up their joined bodies and forcing them closer together. It lifted them up off the floor, turning them in a gentle circle as pulsing lights and wind combined to form a sound that Chance might, at some other time, call music. The increasing tempo of the ethereal tune matched the wind as it built to a fevered pitch.

Stacy squeezed her eyes closed and moaned, then sagged against Chance. Some inborn sense told him she wouldn't survive this onslaught for long. He had to stop it, if for no other reason than to save her.

"Stop!" he yelled, hoping to be heard above the rising winds. "This is enough!" Whether he was addressing God, the Devil or some other cosmic force, it didn't matter. This had to stop.

They spun faster. Stacy's glow dimmed.

"She can't take much more!"

The wind screamed in fury, ignoring his pleas.

"I—" The wind swallowed his words. "—believe!"

They spun so fast that centrifugal force started to pull her out of his arms.

"I believe—" he shouted, desperate to be heard above the roar of life and death, meeting like matter and antimatter in an explosive finale.

"—in me!"

Chapter Eleven

And then . . .

There were no rushing winds. No howling tornadoes.

Chance and Stacy hung suspended in midair for a moment before the law of gravity reestablished itself. As they fell, Chance twisted so he could land on the bottom and cushion their unceremonious landing. After they struggled to their feet, Stacy sagged against him and started crying. Tears prickled his own eyes, but he pushed them away.

Then, knowing his duty, Chance gently pushed Stacy away as well.

She grabbed him before he had a chance to revert. "Don't—"

"I believe, Stacy," he whispered, uncurling her fingers from around his wrist. "If for no other reason than the fact that you believe. But I have to make sure I can still believe when I don't have the luxury of your borrowed life." As she started to speak, he stopped her by placing his forefinger across her lips. "I need to be sure my sense of conviction doesn't fade when I do." The brush of her lips against his fingertip sent electrifying pulses up his arm.

Stacy reached up, captured his hand for a moment, then gave it a small squeeze. "Chance, I . . ." she paused, then drew a deep breath. "I think I understand." She made a valiant but strained effort to hide her expression of stark fear as she stepped away.

They broke contact.

Chance felt the life drain from him, the retreating emotions and sensations forming a gaping hole within him. Where there had been life and love, there was nothing to secure his tenuous existence in this world but the overwhelming need to discover the truth about himself. Without love and faith to bring him alive, all he had to cling to was hope.

He closed his eyes, waiting to see if the single thread of hope he clung to was enough to prevent the whirling dervish from arising again to claim his wayward soul.

A gentle breeze stirred the dust at his feet.

"It's not enough to simply hope," Stacy said in a choked voice. "You have to believe."

Although they didn't touch, although Stacy gave him no borrowed life to strengthen that thread, he felt his convictions build. The words of belief echoed through his mind, swirling gently then building to a whirlwind, just as ferocious as the real one which had threatened both of them. For a moment, he couldn't tell the difference between the whirlwind of the mind and the one which had threatened to tear him out of Stacy's arms forever.

But when Chance opened his eyes, he realized the eloquent scream of wind and words existed in one place only.

His mind.

The room echoed nothing in its oppressive silence. Stacy stood next to him, staring at him with staunch, but teary determination, her hands tightened into fists at her side. "I believe," she spoke in obvious resolution. "I believe in you."

Drawing an unnecessary breath, he broke the eerie silence of the room by clearing his throat. Then he spoke.

"I believe."

No wind. Not even a breeze. Not a single dust mite moved.

One cosmic test down. How many to go?

Chance looked at Stacy, trying to imagine how he should feel. Scared? Relieved? Adrenaline surging through his veins? Fear like lead, lining his stomach? After all, she'd been forced to abandon the world of logic she knew in favor of an unknown world where ghosts existed and instead of a stairway to Heaven, it'd be a short escalator ride to Hell. If she could believe in him . . .

"I believe I wasn't guilty and somewhere out there is the proof I need to exonerate myself."

Somehow resolution built in him, perhaps magnified by Stacy's faithful silence. His strength returned in full force. Feeling refortified, he allowed himself the extravagance of a small smile. "I guess you could say this is my second chance." He cocked his head toward Stacy, hoping to elicit a break in her silence and bring some color back into her whitewashed cheeks. "Second Chance—get it?"

Stacy stared at him, her expression unwavering. Then slowly, the facade cracked as a hesitant glint of amusement broke through. "S-second Chance. That's really . . . bad. You're trying too hard."

"But I'm at least trying," he offered.

"You are." She wrapped her arms around herself, trying to contain the tremor which tore through her.

He pointed to the chair. "Why don't you sit down, before you fall down?"

"No." She shifted her weight from one foot to the other. "I'd rather stand." After a moment, she added, "It's nerves," as an explanation.

"You scared?"

She shrugged. "Scared of some things. Scared about the future, the past." She glanced around the room, giving its dark corners a dubious glare. "Scared of spiders."

"Scared of ghosts?"

A lone tear trickled from her eye. "No. Not of ghosts." She

swiped her sleeve across her face, leaving a damp streak of dust on the material. She glanced at the soiled spot. "If I keep on crying, all this dust will turn to mud."

Even if in his ghostly state Chance couldn't feel emotions, he knew the tension was seeping from the room. Stacy drew a deep breath then dropped into a chair. Pawing blindly through her purse, she pulled out the rolled papers along with a wad of tissues. As she dabbed at the dust on her cheeks, they played "Your left or my left" as Chance tried to guide her to the dirty places by example. Her compact mirror had turned up missing after the elevator-shaft incident.

He smiled as Stacy gave her nose a quick blow, then settled gently in the lone chair, trying not to raise any more dust. He hovered at chair level as Stacy wiped the topmost layer of grime from the table with a dirty rag and smoothed out the first sheet of paper. Leaning together, they almost touched as they both strained to stare at the title.

"*Precinct Dispatcher's Log, February 23,*" Stacy read aloud.

The words blurred for a moment. "The day I died," Chance added.

Stacy nodded, then tried to hide her expression by reaching for her purse and bringing out a small notebook. "W-why don't we keep notes on the pertinent details?"

Chance nodded, knowing the only way he'd survive confronting his death was to keep the facts at arm's length. To stay dispassionate. Detached. "Good idea. Let's start with the first call to the police. It came at 3:32 A.M. from Mall Security."

"Who called it in?"

Chance scanned the sheet. "Rufus Bryant."

"Okay. Rufus." She wrote down the time and name. "Anything else?"

Chance studied the report. "Paramedics and police were notified at 3:34 and arrived at 3:38."

"That was fast."

Chance heard her unspoken words as clearly as her spoken ones.

For what good it did you. She glanced up and reddened, aware that Chance had "heard" her unintentional remark. "Sorry."

He shrugged. "That's okay. What's next?"

Stacy willed her hand to stay steady as she turned the page. "The *Initial Crime Report.*"

They took an hour to go through the paperwork. Stacy took notes, turned pages and paid careful attention to Chance, gauging his reactions as he studied the reports. He faded for just a flicker when they found the copy of the medical examiner's report. She couldn't blame him for his brief lapse in control. Once they studied their last page, Stacy leaned back in the chair and examined her notes.

Chance adopted a similar slouched position in midair. "Read me what you have. Let's see if anything odd or inconsistent sticks out."

Stacy nodded, cleared her throat and began. "February 23. 3:32—Accident reported. Two days later, it was officially classified as suicide. Rufus found . . ." Stacy stumbled for a moment. She couldn't personalize this by saying "Rufus found *you* . . ." The circumstances called for distance and a sense of professionalism.

She drew a deep breath. ". . . found the body and called the police. Paramedics and police arrived on the scene, but it was too late. The b-body was transported to the hospital morgue after a forensics team made its preliminary investigation. Lt. Harrold of Homicide was the detective assigned to the case and the next day, he announced it was a suicide."

"I'll play devil's—" Chance made a face, "—advocate here. Isn't that awfully quick? Do you think he'd had time to talk to everybody?"

"According to his report, he talked to your partner, Neal Browne, to the firm's accountant, Robert O. Gainey of Gainey, Ackermann, and Gage, CPAs, to the foreman of the construction site, Oscar Hames, and to your next-door neighbor, Helen Mullins." For a moment, Stacy had the mental image of a femme fatale in a black evening gown coming over to borrow a mythical cup of sugar. Then with a deliberate twist of Stacy's mental dial, ''Helen'' became a grandmotherly type delivering hot chocolate-chip cookies to that nice young man who lived next door.

Chance interrupted her with a sigh. ''Not a single name rings a bell.'' He closed his eyes. ''Chocolate chip? My favorite. Go ahead.''

Stacy swallowed hard and continued. ''Your partner said you were depressed over the impending lawsuit. The accountant denied any knowledge of a second set of books. The foreman said he was only following your orders when he substituted inferior materials and your neighbor said you had been acting strangely the past few days.''

''And because of that, it's supposed to prove I killed myself?''

Stacy shifted in her seat. ''Apparently.''

''But what proof do they have? From what it says, I left no note. Don't suicides usually leave notes?'' His eyes sprang open. ''Someone could have thrown me over that rail.''

''Without you putting up a fight?''

Chance tented his fingers. ''Maybe I did put up a fight. Or maybe I'd been drugged or hit on the head or incapacitated some other way.''

Stacy thumbed through the pages for the copy of the medical examiner's report. ''The problem is . . . if you'd been drugged, there would have been some evidence of it in your blood system and they would have caught that during the autopsy. It says here you died of—'' she squinted at the paper, ''—blunt trauma and massive internal hemorrhaging consistent with a fall in excess of forty feet.''

''Forty feet. I guess that's just about three stories.''

She nodded. ''I guess so-o-o.'' To her horror, a yawn slipped out in the middle of her recitation.

Chance shot her a strained grin. ''Am I keeping you up?''

''I'm sorry.'' Stacy rubbed her eyes, trying to regain her fleeting ability to focus. ''All of a sudden I feel so tired.''

"You've had a demanding day. Stealing police reports, almost falling down an elevator shaft, escaping Death, not to mention a whirlwind to hell. It's no wonder you're tired."

"Just another typical day in the Twilight Zone," Stacy added with a weary laugh.

Chance extended his arms out in front of him as if to stretch then stopped in mid motion. "Why am I doing this? I'm not sore." Chance rose, then leaned forward to drift free of the table and suspend himself in midair. "I'm not anything," he complained as he rotated to his back.

Stacy watched him hang effortlessly above the table, looking more like a swimmer riding a gentle ocean current, rather than a rampaging ghost looking for revenge. She groaned and closed her eyes.

"What's wrong?"

Stacy leaned down to cradle her head in the crook of her arm. "I just want to rest for a moment."

"You mean sleep for a couple of hours," Chance supplied. "Nope. Nothing doing. Get up."

"What?"

"I said get up. Sleep is good, but not here. Go home. Go to bed."

She lifted her head. "But what about that guy? The one in black? Death."

Chance waved an arm, sweeping the room with a gesture. "Do you see him here? As far as we can tell, this is a safe place. A good place to hide all this incriminating evidence as well as the criminal himself. I'll be fine, here." Chance flipped into an upright position, hovering an inch or two above the tabletop. "Tell you what you do: spread all the pages across the table, face up, and I'll spend the rest of the day going over them, looking for loopholes or inconsistencies, anything that might help us figure out whodunit. You go home and get some sleep. You look . . . terrible, you know."

Stacy pushed up from her chair. "Why, thank you," she said

with halfhearted sarcasm. She waved him away so she could fan out the pages across the table.

"You know what I mean." Chance drifted toward her, coming so close she could feel her skin prickle with something which felt suspiciously like static electricity. "It's been a rough day. Get some sleep and we'll start over in the morning." He lifted a hand to caress her cheek, but hesitated before making contact with her. "I . . . I better not."

Stacy's senses went on full alert. "Why?"

He shrugged. "I dunno. It's not that I don't want to . . . it's just that . . ." His voice trailed off and he graced her with a strained smile. "I might not want to stop." He ran his hand through his indeterminate-colored hair. "Go home, Stace. We'll talk in the morning. Okay?"

She stared at him for a moment, trying to read the expression on his face, the message between the lines. Her mind snagged on the punch line to an old joke: what was black and white and red all over?

An embarrassed ghost?

She struggled with her wandering thoughts as she straightened the last page on the table. "Where will I find you tomorrow?"

His smile brightened perceptibly. "I'll be hanging around."

Chance paced back and forth in front of the counter. "Where is she? Why is she so late?"

Peg alternated between tapping her fingers on the glass case and checking her watch.

"Don't just stand there . . . call Stacy! See what's keeping her."

As if Peg heard his pleas, she stared at the telephone.

"Call," he repeated, his hope rising. "I'll feel better—we'll both feel better if we know why she's so late."

Peg bit her lip, then, after a moment, picked up the receiver and punched the numbers.

Chance floated closer, straining to hear. "Well? Is it ringing?" He leaned closer and heard a soft rhythmic burr in the background. "Maybe she just overslept and the phone will wake her up. She did look awfully ragged out yesterday."

Peg tapped her foot impatiently.

"Well?" he prompted. "Well?"

Peg continued to listen to the receiver.

Chance paced through the counter, ignoring the odd sensation of passing through the glass and metal. "If she's not there, then where is she?"

His silent partner released a perplexed sigh.

He came to a halt in the middle of the display case. "You think maybe she left already? Or maybe she's sick and can't get to the phone? Jeez, now I'm really worried." Chance looked down, realized he stood in a pile of panties and started to pace again. "It's not like her simply to not show up without calling. So, where is she, Peg?" His voice grew louder as his sense of desperation increased. "Where *is* she?"

Peg slammed the phone down. "I don't know!"

Chance froze. Something similar to a lightning bolt started at his chest and radiated across his body. In that fleeting instant, he felt his heart thud without the luxury of a borrowed life. And inexplicably, it hurt like hell. "Y-you can hear me?" he stuttered.

For one very long, very eerie moment, Peg glared directly at him. Then as suddenly as her focus rested on him, it shifted, landing somewhere past his left shoulder.

"Oh, good Lord," she moaned. "I'm not only talking to myself, I'm answering myself as well."

The painful elation of inadvertent discovery faded as Chance realized he was no closer to knowing where or more importantly, *how* Stacy was. Frustrated, he stalked through the glass counter and made a vaporous grab at the telephone. Peg reached for the instrument at the same time and for a moment, their hands occupied the same space.

Both recoiled. Peg jumped back as if she'd been jolted by

a small electrical charge. Chance pulled back, finding the concept of dual occupation disconcerting at the very least. There was almost something fundamentally wrong about entering someone else's body, even if it *was* purely accidental.

But . . . if it was his only way to reach Stacy . . .

Chance shifted beside Peg, aligning his left shoulder behind her right. He whispered a plea for forgiveness, then merged with her.

He felt everything and nothing. Closing his eyes, he concentrated on picking up the phone. To his surprise, Peg complied. Maybe it had been her idea in the first place. Maybe not. Either way, she was doing exactly what he wanted.

They punched in the telephone number together, then Peg wedged the receiver between her ear and her shoulder. Chance hesitated. It was one thing to merge with her arm; but to merge heads, and perhaps even minds? He satisfied his need to hear by merely leaning as close as he possibly could.

The metallic echo of the ringing phone raised imaginary hackles on the back of his neck. It reminded him of something, a faded memory . . . an ominous one at that.

Then the ringing stopped and a tired voice answered.

"H'lo?"

Peg and Chance spoke in unison. "Stacy?"

She sounded half-dead. "Uh huh? Whozit?"

Chance spoke first. "Me and Peg. Are you all right?"

"Peg?" Stacy repeated in a leaden voice.

"Yeah, honey, it's Peg. I was starting to get worried. I've been trying to get you on the phone for the past hour."

"Been . . ." her voice trailed off.

Chance took advantage of the moment of silence. "Stacy, it's Chance. Are you all right?"

". . . been asleep."

Chance felt himself make Peg's hand tighten on the phone. "Stacy? Can you hear me?"

"Wha' time is it, Peg?"

"Almost eleven."

Chance released a sigh; she couldn't hear him. He withdrew his arm from Peg's. At least, he was still in a situation where he could hear her.

Stacy seemed to suddenly wake up. "Eleven? Oh my God, I overslept! I've never overslept like that before in my life!"

"I know, honey. But you know you haven't been feeling well lately and it's evidently caught up with you. Why don't you take it easy today and—"

"No!" Stacy's voice rang out with sudden clarity. "I'm supposed to meet a friend there. I'll be there in a half hour . . . er, forty-five minutes, tops. I'm so sorry Peg."

"It's okay, boss lady." Peg's look of concern faded into a smile. "These things happen."

"You're the best, Peg. I'll be there in thirty minutes."

"Don't rush. It's been dead this morning. If your friend stops by, I'll tell her you're running late."

"Him," Stacy corrected, absentmindedly.

"A man? Congratulations. It's about time."

"Peg . . ."

"Don't worry. I won't embarrass you if he comes by. Promise. And take time to get something to eat. Okay?"

"Yes 'Mother.' See ya."

Peg released a sigh as she replaced the receiver. "That girl . . ."

Chance nodded. "She works too hard."

"Don't I know it. She won't—" Peg stopped in midsentence, her eyes grew large and her face reddened.

Chance matched her expression of shock with his own look of amazement. "You *can* hear me!"

Peg leaned her elbows on the counter, rested her chin in her hands and stared across the store. "If I keep talking to myself, the little men in the white suits are going to come looking for me."

Realizing that he had again been the butt of some great cosmic joke, Chance sighed and mimicked the woman's position. "It could be worse, you know," he said as he tried to keep his elbows from sliding through the surface of the glass. "I've got little men in the *black* suits after me."

Chapter Twelve

Stacy heard the blood rushing through her ears as she climbed the last flight of stairs. After her almost-incident in the elevator shaft and the memory of the man in black watching them from the escalator, the stairs seemed the most logical, perhaps the safest way of getting to the third floor of the mall. She paused to catch her breath before opening the door which led from the service hallway to the main mall corridor.

Looking through the rectangular pane of glass, she saw a familiar dark figure leaning against the wall opposite her store.

Lieutenant Harrold?

He shifted, glared toward the store for a moment, then turned away. Stacy squinted at the small black object in his hand. *A radio. No,* she amended, *a walkie-talkie.* He looked as if he was muttering something into it, then scanning the shoppers as they strolled by.

He's watching the store. Watching for me! Guilt flared, pointing a thousand imaginary fingers toward her. A vein in her temple throbbed like a neon sign, "Guilty, guilty, guilty!"

He knows I copied the file. He knows I'm interested in Chance's case. He knows . . .

''Nothing.''

Stacy pivoted to find Chance standing at her elbow.

''Don't worry. There's no way he can connect you to me. You and I never even met each other while I was alive.''

She peeked once more through the window, then turned to search Chance's face for any sign of false bravado. ''Are you really sure?''

He sighed and grinned. ''I'm sure I never met you. And pretty sure Harrold thinks yesterday's stunt was born out of curiosity, maybe even concern, but not guilt.''

Feeling encouraged, she stepped away from corridor door. ''And being a curious, perhaps even a nosy type of person, I might even go around and question some of the other business owners and see if they knew anything or saw anything. After all, if the police thought it was suicide, they might not have been as thorough as they would have been—investigating a murder.''

Chance stroked his jaw. ''I hadn't thought about doing that.'' His pensive expression sparked into a full-fledged smile. ''When do we start?''

She returned a more faded version of his grin. ''Now, I suppose.''

''Great!'' He strode through the closed door and paused on the other side, making a face at her through the window. ''Well? What are you waiting for?''

Stacy pushed open the heavy door, drew a deep breath and followed him to her store.

It took all of her concentration to ignore Harrold, who skulked in the shadows of an empty storefront, watching her. Since he had a radio, he probably had other people keeping her under surveillance as well. She found it disconcerting to think that one or more of the shoppers who breezed past her might actually be an undercover cop, reporting her every move.

Once she stepped into her store, Stacy released the breath

she'd unconsciously held. ''I'm safe, now,'' she muttered to herself.

A woman near the robe rack glanced up at her for a brief moment before turning her attention back to the garments. Suddenly, Stacy's sense of security vanished.

''Don't worry . . . she's not a cop,'' Chance whispered, his voice buzzing in Stacy's right ear. ''I took a good look at the stuff in her bag. So far she's bought a bottle of expensive bubble bath, a sample of perfume, the latest erotic vampire video and a box of condoms.'' His grin widened. ''If you ask me, a bustier and garters are the next ingredients in her Recipe of Lo-o-o-ve.''

''Cops make love, too, you know,'' she whispered back.

After a thoughtful moment, Chance's conspiratorial smile turned into a grimace. ''Jeez . . . I could have gone all day without seeing a mental image of Lieutenant Harrold in the throes of passion.'' Chance performed a theatrical shiver.

''What about that woman?'' Stacy nodded toward a red-haired woman standing behind a rack of nightgowns.

''Nope. She's no cop either.''

''How can you tell?''

''A combination of several factors. It's a matter of great observation, intuition, inspiration, info—''

The woman stepped from around the display rack.

''Gestation?'' Stacy nodded toward to the woman's swollen stomach as she stepped into view. She felt her worst suspicions melt away. ''You're a cheat.''

He shrugged. ''Me? Cheat? Be careful. They have those fake stomach things men strap on to experience pregnancy. It's entirely possible that tummy isn't real.''

''Not real?'' Thoughts swirled through Stacy's mind as she stared at the woman. The borders between real and unreal had become muddled somewhere along the line. Her ordinary life no longer existed. Now it was a matter of talking to invisible men and scanning the shadows, expecting either to see undercover police or Death.

"Stace?"

Somewhere along the line, silk, satin, and lace had given way to conspiracy, collusion, and intrigue.

"Stace . . . you're staring."

The impossible was possible and the improbable was almost a sure thing.

"Snap out of it, Stace."

"Huh . . . what?" She felt someone grab her arm. "Chance?"

"Chance for what?" Peg dragged her toward the counter. She stopped and gave Stacy a perplexed look. "You're too young to be worrying about a biological alarm clock, yet."

"C-clock?" Stacy tried to focus her stare on her companion.

"Oh Jeez . . ." Chance complained. "Is that all women think about these days?" He trailed beside them.

"Be right with you, ma'am," Peg called to the customer. She turned back to Stacy, lowering her voice. "You know . . . approaching birthdays, thoughts turning to mortality, staring at pregnant women with a look of either wistfulness or absolute dread?"

"Dead?"

"Dread. I said *dread."* Peg gave Stacy a critical once-over. "Stay here while I help that lady. You look like you're about to fall down and *she* looks like a biological time bomb about to explode any minute now." Peg pulled out a chair and forced Stacy to sit. "And we only had the floors cleaned last month!"

Chance crossed his arms as he watched Peg hurry off and turn her ministrations to the pregnant woman. "Peg looks just like the sort of hearty, practical type of person who would be able to roll up her sleeves and deliver the baby right here and now *without* messing up the carpets."

Carpets . . . Stacy's fuzzy mind latched onto the word, for what seemed no particular reason. *Carpets.* A series of prickles formed on her arms, turning into goose bumps. "The carpet . . ."

Chance's amusement faded. "What is it? What's wrong?"

An explanation hovered in her mind, just beyond her mental

grasp. ''The carpet,'' she repeated, hoping repetition would shake loose a better answer.

''What about the carpet?'' Chance looked down at the muted rose-colored material.

''We cleaned it.''

''So I see. Now about our plans—''

''Stop'' she commanded, then lowered her voice self-consciously. ''You don't understand. We *cleaned* the carpets.'' Stacy stood, ignoring Chance's remonstrative stare and her own lightheadedness. ''Peg . . . come here for a minute.''

The saleswoman gave her a curious look, excused herself and approached the counter. ''What's wrong, Stace? You like you've seen a gho—''

''When did we get the carpets cleaned last?''

A fine flush rose on Peg's neck. ''Last month . . . no, it was more toward the end of April. Why?''

''We used the same company as last time, right?''

Peg's flush faded as quickly as it rose, leaving her distinctly pale-faced. ''Uh . . . not exactly. Can we wait until the store closes to discuss this? I think the lady—''

Stacy pushed on, despite Peg's uncharacteristic hesitation. ''If we didn't use the regular guys, then what company *did* we use?''

Peg swallowed hard. ''It wasn't exactly a company . . .'' Her voice trailed off as she shot a guilty glance over her shoulder at the departing customer.

''Peg?'' she warned.

A muscle in the woman's jaw tightened. ''If you'll remember, all you told me was to go ahead and get the carpets cleaned after that little boy spilled the grape soda over by the display window. You didn't say I had to use the *same* company and you did say we should hurry to clean it before the stain had a chance to set . . .''

Stacy nodded. ''I'm not arguing with you. You're right—I didn't insist we use the same company, just that we get it cleaned quickly. So tell me who we used and the subject will be closed. Okay?"

Peg went from pale to totally colorless. She drew a deep breath then a second one. "It was . . . Danny." She raised a hand as if to stop any tirade Stacy might turn loose. "Before you say anything, let me explain. Danny's uncle owns a professional steam cleaner and he let us use it. After all, I didn't think you'd mind if we were able to do as good of a job as the other company and since we needed the money so badly, it seemed a shame to hire someone else when we could earn it ourselves."

She wrung her hands, knotting her fingers like a guilty schoolchild. "The carpet looks good, doesn't it?" Moving toward the display window, she pointed to the floor. "I mean, look. You can't see where the kid spilled the soda, can you?"

Stacy knew Peg Sullivan as an unruffled sort of woman who kept her head in all situations. But now it was painfully evidently that Stacy didn't know her friend as well as she professed or she would have been more aware of the Sullivan family's money troubles. And in a situation where Peg could have been tempted to find a more expedient answer to their financial woes, she and Danny had taken an honorable stab at earning a few extra bucks.

If anybody should feel guilty, Stacy thought, *it ought to be me.* She placed a reassuring hand on the woman's shoulder and squeezed it gently. "You're not in trouble, Peg. The carpet looks fine—Danny did a great job with it. In fact, I'dlike for him to be our carpet cleaner from now on."

Peg managed a pale smile. "Thanks, Stace."

"But," Stacy continued, keeping her hold on Peg's shoulder, "I do need to know when—what day did he clean it?"

Guarded relief flooded the woman's face. "Uh . . . it was a Saturday night—I remember that much right off the bat because we wanted as much time as possible for the carpet to dry and of course we wouldn't open until noon on Sunday."

"Which Saturday night?"

''Lessee . . . I believe it was our bridge night, so it had to be the third Saturday of the month.''

''Of April. Right?''

Peg nodded with building enthusiasm. ''Right, the third Saturday in April.''

A solemn voice added, ''April twenty-third.''

Stacey pivoted and stared at Chance. ''The twenty-third?''

He nodded. ''The day I died.''

Peg nodded as well. ''The twenty-third. That sounds right.''

Stacy felt her heart pick up speed. ''Maybe Danny saw something.''

Peg stepped closer. ''Saw something . . . what?''

Chance nodded. ''Get him here. We have to talk to him.''

''Peg . . .'' Stacy turned to give her assistant the most unthreatening, amicable smile she could. ''Could you call Danny and ask him to come here to answer some questions for me?''

''Are we in trouble?'' Peg asked in a low voice.

''Absolutely not. I promise.'' Stacy drew a solemn cross over her thundering heart. ''How can I be mad? You did a great job. Just call him, okay? We really need to talk to him about something else. Something he may have seen that night.''

''We?''

''Chance and . . .'' She stopped short, covering her slip with a counterfeit cough. ''Uh . . . I mean we need a chance to talk—me and Danny.''

Forty-five minutes later, an uneasy-looking Danny Sullivan stood in her office, shuffling his weight from one foot to the other. He wore Guilt across his sweating forehead like the bold letter emblazoned across a collegiate sweatshirt.

Danny attempted a nervous smile. ''Uh, Peg said you wanted to ask me some questions?''

Stacy nodded. ''Sit down, Danny. You make me nervous, standing like that.'' Actually, Danny wasn't the one making her feel jittery; it was Chance who was taking advantage of his unique ability to stand inches away from the man and watch him unobserved.

"Stace, we certainly have an interesting specimen here. He's starting to sweat." Chance leaned forward for a closer examination. "He knows . . . something. I can tell."

Danny dropped into a chair, but still managed to convey his rampant uneasiness through his unnaturally stiff posture. For as long as she'd known him, Daniel Sullivan's philosophy of life was something on the order of "Hang loose," a motto he followed in almost all situations. He was an old friend from high school. He'd never yet found a business partner who seemed to appreciate his laissez-faire attitude when it came to fiscal responsibilities and other unavoidable aspects of business. Danny had been everything from a day laborer to a stockbroker to a shoe salesman and hadn't found his niche in life, yet.

"If it's about the carpet cleaning," he said, holding out an open palm, "I just want to say that we figured the important thing was to clean them the way the professionals do and—"

Stacy interrupted him, gesturing for him to be quiet. "Like I told Peg, you're not in trouble. All I want to know is what did you see that night?"

Curiosity rapidly replaced his expression of guarded relief. "See? Was I supposed to notice something?"

"You couldn't have missed me, stupid." Chance crossed his arms and glared at the man. "I fell right in front of the store."

Stacy tried to ignore Chance and his building rage. "I want to know what you saw while you were cleaning the carpets."

He thought hard for a moment, as evidenced by his wrinkled-brow expression, then he nodded and even smiled. "Oh . . . I see what you mean. First, there was the grape stain near the window, what appeared to be an ink stain by the front display rack and a lot of extra wear near the entrance which I had to pretreat and—"

Exasperation made her eyesight blur for a minute. "No . . . not about the carpet stains. What did you see in the mall? Outside in the corridor."

"Outside?" Danny gave her a puzzled stare. "Was I supposed to notice something in particular?"

"You didn't see a man out there?"

Danny waited for a moment, then nodded brightly. "Yeah sure . . . the security guard came by around one. He knocked on the glass, I cut off the steamer and he asked me how long I'd be."

"And that was the only person who came by?"

"It was the only person I saw but that doesn't mean he was the only one out there. If I hadn't looked up when I did and spotted him, I wouldn't have known he was there at all. I couldn't hear a blasted thing 'cause the vacuum motor on the steamer was pretty loud."

"You didn't notice anything . . . odd that night?"

"Well . . ." His face darkened. "Now that you mention it, it was plenty spooky, being here by myself, what with the rumors I hear about this place."

"Rumors?"

He nodded, evidently grateful to lead the subject away from the steam-cleaning debacle. "Of course, I didn't know about it then. I only learned about the ghost later on."

"Ghost?" Chance and Stacy blurted the word at the same time.

"Sure . . ." A sense of conspiracy replaced the tension in his face; his body language loosened perceptibly. "Haven't you heard about the 'vengeful Chapel Valley ghost'? Everybody's been talking about it over at the electronics store. Chuck says he even has some great footage of the ghost on his store security camera. He's trying to sell the tape to the folks from that tabloid show, *Current Copy.*"

Chance took one look at Stacy's silent accusations and threw his hands in the air. "It wasn't me, I swear it. Like I told you, first thing I did when I figured out I wasn't real was to play around with the cameras and see if I could appear. I can't. It's that simple."

She managed to adopt a strained smile. "I bet it looks suspiciously like Chuck Canton wearing a sheet. He'd do anything, say anything if he thought he'd *sell* more televisions that way, not to mention an opportunity to *get* on television."

"I thought that too, but he acted really spooked. He says he won't stay late any more, especially on Saturday nights."

Goose bumps slithered up Stacy's arms. "Why Saturday nights?"

" 'Cause that's when the ghost becomes the most active, according to Chuck. A couple of days ago he showed me the tape of the stuff that happened several nights ago. You could see the ghost or whoever—whatever floating through the store, walking through walls, displays, counters as if they we weren't there at all."

"C-could you make out any of the ghost's features?"

Danny shook his head. "Nope. It was like he was made up of shadows—he'd emerge from the darkness from one wall, float across the room then disappear through the next wall."

Chance released a sigh. "You know who he's describing, don't you?"

Stacy felt her heart give an extra beat. "M-made up of shadows?" she repeated. "With dark clothes, dark features you can't quite make out?"

Danny's eyes opened wider. "You've seen him before?"

"Not exactl—"

"Tell him yes," Chance interrupted. "Tell him that's why you were interested in what he saw while he was cleaning."

"Uh . . . well, yeah. I saw someone, something like that out in the corridor the other night. That's why I wanted to know if you saw anything unusual while you were here cleaning the carpets."

Danny nodded knowingly and leaned forward in his chair, all thoughts of interrogation evidently forgotten. "I didn't see a thing. Of course, like I said, I didn't hear about the ghost rumors until some time later. I can't say I was surprised because I had a real uneasy sense I was being watched all night long.

When Chuck told me about his ghost, it explained why I felt I wasn't alone."

"But you weren't alone," Stacy corrected. "You said the security guard dropped by."

"Yeah, but that was only once. It was that Rufus guy. After we spoke, he went off on his rounds I guess, and I never saw him again."

"Not even when you left?"

"Nope. And that was the funny part. He told me to ring the security extension when I was ready to leave and he'd escort me to the exit. Evidently there were some alarms I might set off if I used the wrong door."

"You didn't call him?"

"Sure I called him but no one ever answered."

Chance glowered at Danny. "Ask him when he left."

Stacy dutifully repeated the question.

"I got through around quarter after three and let the phone ring for a couple minutes before giving up. I locked up the store behind me, set your alarm and headed for the nearest exit. I must've lucked onto the right door or else I would have set off the mall alarms. Guess I'm just a lucky stiff, eh?"

Chance stuffed his hands in his pockets and faded slightly. "Yeah . . . and I'm the unlucky stiff."

Stacy waited until the storage-room door closed behind her before allowing her excitement to boil to the surface. "Do you know what this means?"

Chance hovered in one place a few inches above the floor, his hands still jammed in his pockets. "It just proves how truly unimportant my death was in the grand scheme of life."

Why was he so dense? Why couldn't he see the truth? She stepped closer. "No . . . it means the police report is all wrong."

He snorted in an undignified way. "Tell me something I don't know."

She sighed and out of desperation, reached forward and grabbed his arm. Life flowed with ease out of her and into him, causing him to drop heavily to his feet.

He managed a halfhearted scowl. ''I wish you'd give a guy some warning before you did that. I don't want to break something again.''

She ignored his complaint. ''Listen, Chance. You heard what Danny said. By the time he left the store, it was around 3:30 . . . at almost the exact same time they discovered your body.''

''Meaning . . .''

''Meaning Danny had all the equipment shut off. It was quiet!''

''So?''

She sighed in resignation at his sudden lack of imagination. ''If you were involved in a struggle outside of our door, Danny couldn't have missed it, even if he was on the phone.''

''Whereas he could have easily missed a man deciding to take a sudden swan dive into the fountain below.''

''No, you idiot.'' Stacy pawed through her purse and pulled out her notes from the purloined police report. ''The police said Rufus discovered your body at 3:32 which explains why he didn't answer the phone when Danny called—he was out doing a security sweep of the premises.''

Chance grew more animated, his eyes narrowing in thought. ''So if Danny was paying attention, trying to watch for Rufus to let him out, he would have seen me, one way or the other. So something's not kosher about the police report.''

Stacy nodded. ''Exactly. Either you didn't fall around 3:30 in the morning—''

''Or I didn't fall from the rail in front of your store.''

She tightened her grip on his arm. ''So how many other inconsistencies do you think are in the report?''

''Maybe we'll find that one discrepancy which will help prove I was murdered.'' Chance uncurled her fingers from around his arm and raised her hand to his lips for a quick kiss. ''So what's our next step, Ms. Holmes?''

She drew a deep breath. ''We return to the scene of the crime, Dr. Johnson.''

''Are you sure about this, Chance?'' They stood hand in hand and Stacy couldn't tell whether the unusually strong pulse she felt came from his fingers or hers. Her other hand was anchored safely around the railing.

''I guess. You know, I'm surprised I don't get any déjà vu heebie-jeebies from standing here.'' He glanced down with an affected look of mild curiosity.

Stacy knew he was lying. The driving thrum she felt emanated from him.

''Uh, what time is it, again?''

She pried her hand from the rail long enough to check her watch. ''It's twelve-forty. Rufus won't make his security check until one o'clock.''

''Okay. Well . . .'' He squeezed her hand. ''Ready?''

She nodded.

Chance climbed over the railing and balanced on the narrow ledge, still clutching her hand. ''I'm going to have to push out pretty far to miss the second floor. It's not going to be easy. You ready?''

She swallowed hard, then nodded. ''Be . . . careful.''

He smiled again, betraying a nervous tension in his smile which seemed a little too carefree. ''Aw, don't worry. This time it won't hurt.'' He drew a deep breath, then jumped into the emptiness, his fingers sliding out of hers to break contact.

Chance maintained his substance long enough to make gravity pull his weight downward. A couple of seconds later, he reverted to his ghostly status and his act of falling became more of an act of floating. But despite the change in speed, Stacy could still see what gravity had intended as his final destination.

The second floor!

He floated down as if to confirm his probable landing spot, then rushed up to hover at her eye level. ''Did you see that?

There's no way I could have reached the first floor. I would have landed on the second level. It juts out too far."

Stacy leaned over the railing to examine the ledge. "Do you think it's possible to lean out more so when you jump, you clear the second floor railing and fall to the first floor?"

He looked down and scratched his chin. "I don't think so, but I'm willing to try again . . . if you are."

She nodded and reached out to touch him. The moment her fingers closed around his arm, she'd realized her mistake; he wasn't standing on the ledge.

Instincts said that when someone is falling, you hold on to them for dear life. And that's just what she did. But Chance's weight pulled her down faster than she realized, forcing her feeble grip on the railing to break and allowing her to be dragged over the railing.

In the back of her mind, she heard him command her to let go of him, but fear blunted her ability to respond. Equilibrium gave away to confusion and she felt herself falling.

"Stacy!"

Chance clutched at the railing with one hand, trying to cope with his own sudden solidity as well as Stacy's unexpected weight. In the split second it took for him to grab the passing rail and snag Stacy before she plunged downward, she grasped the severity of their no-win situation. If she broke contact with Chance, he'd revert and be out of danger himself, but his solidity was the only thing keeping her alive. If she held onto him, they might both fall to their deaths.

Fear swallowed up her screams as she struggled to get a better hold of her temporary savior.

"Hold on, Stacy," he commanded.

She felt his hand tighten around her wrist and she responded by reaching up with her other hand and grabbing his belt.

"Good girl. I'm going to try to pull you up so you can grab the rail yourself. Okay?"

"O-okay." Her teeth chattered. Her muscles quivered in

exertion. Her skin burned where Chance's grip around her wrist tightened.

He groaned as he lifted her with almost inhuman strength until her fingers brushed against the ledge. She scrabbled for a handhold. He grunted again as he tugged her an inch higher.

"Grab the rail!"

She complied, wrapping her fingers around the cool rod of metal. It seemed insubstantial to her, unlikely to hold her weight. She found her other grip tightening on his belt for reassurance.

"Let go of me, Stace."

You'll fall. Her mind latched onto a hideous image of Chance plunging to his doom. *It happened once. It could happen again.*

"I won't fall, honey. And you won't either. Just let go of me and hold onto the rail."

"N-no." The image kept flashing through her mind in an endless loop. Letting go equaled falling; the concept was so simple. And to fall was to die. He'd proven it once. She wasn't going to let him prove it again.

"I won't die, Stace. And neither will you. Just let go." He suspended himself by one hand and used the other one to unhook her fingers from his belt and swing her closer to the railing. "Use both hands, okay? All you have to do is hold on by yourself for a couple of seconds."

She managed to nod.

Then to her dismay, he released her hand, then released his grip on the railing. "I'll be back . . ."

Even as the borrowed life trickled back into her, Stacy turned away, unable to witness his fleeting expression of fear as he fell backward, a temporary victim of gravity. He wouldn't die . . . she knew that. But her fate wasn't as secure. She felt her fingers slip, her grip on the rail weakening. She squeezed her eyes shut.

I'm going to die—

"Hold on, Stacy . . ." Something streaked past her.

She opened her eyes, but instead of looking up, she glanced down where she had sensed someone waited for her. A dark figure emerged from the shadows.

Death!

As suddenly as the specter of Death appeared, it . . . he faded away. Stacy felt a hand circling her wrist.

"I've got you, Stace!" With a groan of exertion, Chance hauled her up and across the rail. They tumbled into an unceremonious heap, crying, laughing, and hugging each other.

Chance helped her lean up against a nearby planter and ran a hand lightly over her arms and legs, checking for injuries. He leaned forward and placed a kiss on her forehead. "You okay? Do you hurt anywhere?"

She lifted a hand to caress his cheek, then finally found her voice again. "He was here. Watching. Waiting."

"He?"

She began to shake for no reason at all. "Death. I saw him. He was down there, waiting, ready to take you again."

Chance took her hands in his and began to rub them briskly. "But he didn't, sweetheart. You're safe, I'm safe. And he's gone."

"Are you s-sure?" Her teeth began to chatter.

He made a pointed effort to scan the level below them. "I don't see a thing."

"You can't see him when we touch."

"And you can bet I'm not about to let go of you in order to look for him. I'll hold you for the rest of the night if I have to." He leaned forward to place a second chaste kiss on her forehead, but Stacy lifted her face and surprised him with a new destination.

For a moment, they remained on the floor, desire building to fill the void created by fear. Her lips trembled beneath his as she thought how odd it was to find such warmth, such caring, such life in a man who wasn't supposed to exist. She wasn't sure how a passion for life could replace the fear of death, but it had. She conquered her tremors but found relief to be fleeting as a leering image of Death flooded her mind again.

Chance broke off their kiss and pulled her into his arms. "Is that how you see him?"

"See who?"

"Death . . . as a black-hooded specter beckoning to us with a bony finger?"

She nodded, shivering at the eerie but apt description.

"I don't." He shifted in order to drape his arm around her shoulder. "I see an average-looking man, dressed in black. No Grim Reaper, no apparitional figure with a scythe ready to chop me down in my prime. In some ways, he's not even scary-looking."

"But you're scared just the same."

"Sure I am." He shrugged. "Who wouldn't be? Who isn't scared of the unknown? I know I must accept my fate and I'm willing to do that if I can learn the real reason behind my death. And—" He shifted to clasp her hand, then rose to his feet, "—from what we just experienced, I'd say there's no possible way I fell from the third floor ledge and landed on the first floor."

Stacy allowed him to pull her up. "Could someone have thrown you far enough to miss the second level?"

He shook his head. "I don't think so."

They moved cautiously to the railing, neither one willing to take any more unnecessary risks. Chance leaned cautiously out to peer over the balustrade. "Even if I jumped as far as I could, I would still hit the second level, not the first."

"Which means . . ."

"Which means there's at least one error in the police report. Maybe even more."

A strong shudder rocked Stacy. "You think so?"

Chance nodded. "It would explain Lt. Harrold's sudden interest in you. He took the first shift himself, then after that, he had someone watching the store all day long."

Stacy reached up and placed a white-knuckled grasp on the railing. Her head ached with apparitions and accusations. "Do you trust him?"

Chance shrugged. "Not as far as I can throw him."

Chapter Thirteen

Stacy paused at the top of the stairs to catch her breath. Either she was getting out of condition or someone had sneaked a few more stairs somewhere around the second floor. Pushing open the heavy door leading to the third level of the mall, she found herself taking an inside track, staying near the walls and store entrances rather than the banisters that bordered the openings to the floors below.

"Lessee . . . no elevator, no escalator, and now I find myself too afraid to go near the rail. What's next? An inordinate fear of silk?" She shook her head as if to shake away ridiculous thoughts.

"I hope not."

She spun around, ready to chastise Chance for sneaking up on her. But Chuck stood there, caught in mid-smirk.

"I'd hate to think of you cowering in fear at the thought of putting on some silky underwear." He gave her a close-up of his libidinous grin. "Then on the other hand . . ."

"What do you want, Chuck?" She cringed in anticipation of his answer.

"Nothin' more than any other red-blooded American boy. Mornin,' Stacy. I haven't seen much of you, lately. You'd think you were trying to avoid your old pal Chuck."

She drew a deep breath, ready to tell the bastard off at last, to unload, to tell him just how obnoxious, how rude, crude, lewd, and socially reprehensible she thought he truly was . . . and then she remembered Danny's comment.

Stacy gathered up her flagging energy and turned it into a twenty-watt smile. "Avoid you? Of course not. It's just . . ." She allowed her voice to trail off.

"Just what?"

She ducked her head and stayed calculatingly silent for a moment. "It's just . . . the ghost."

Chuck's licentious expression faded. "You've seen it, too?"

She nodded, then gave him a mournful stare from beneath her lashes. "It scares me. If only I could see it . . ." Stacy simpered on cue.

Chuck straightened his shoulders in a renewed air of importance. "You *can* see it. I was bright enough to capture the ghost on video tape, unlike most of the other geekazoids around here. I've even got a few feelers out, hoping to sell it to one of those tabloid TV shows."

"Can I see it?" she asked in a breathless voice. "If I know what he . . . it looks like, maybe it won't be so scary."

"Sure." He wrapped his fingers around her arm and pulled her past her store and toward his. "It's in the machine, all loaded up and ready to go. You know I don't show it just to anybody. Just special people, like you."

Stacy controlled her urge to pull loose from his damp grip and forced herself to walk along with him as a volunteer, rather than as a victim. She caught sight of Chance as he zoomed toward them. Judging by the look on his face, he was determined to free her from her 'captor.' She stalled him with a small shake of her head.

"I think it's really nice of you to show me this videotape, Chuck," she said in a clear voice. "I'll feel so much better seeing the real thing for myself rather than basing my beliefs on rumors spurred on by imagination."

Chance skidded to a halt and stopped in midair, balancing his hands on his hips. "He's going to show you his ghost video?"

Chuck responded with a intimate leer. "Anything for you, doll baby."

Chance tightened each hand into a fist. "What's next? Taking her into the back room and showing her your etchings?" He flew down and took a position a few feet ahead of Chuck. "You're too busy to do anything but load the video and let her look at it, right? Too busy . . ."

Chuck continued, unaware of the spectral roadblock in front of him. "Normally I spend this time of the morning posting the previous night's deposit 'cause I don't trust the idiots who close at night but—"

Stacy closed her eyes as Chuck steered her unsuspectingly toward Chance's position. If she touched Chance as he passed through Chuck, she didn't want to see the results. It could be . . . messy.

Chuck continued, unaware. "—but since you want me so badly—" He paused to emit a short huff of laughter, "—to play you the video, I think I can change my schedule for you."

She shifted to the far side and peeked as Chuck stepped right through the belligerent Chance who continued to repeat the words, "Too busy . . ."

Chuck didn't lose a step, but a blank look dropped over his face. "—but you'll understand if I'm too busy to stay there with you . . ." He blinked, but kept on moving. "Too busy . . . that's right. I'm too busy to stay with you. You don't mind, do you?"

She turned around and watched Chance punch the air with a triumphant fist. Deep inside, she shared his sense of relief. The last place in the world she wanted to be was stuck in a storeroom with a world-class lecher.

Chance caught up with them, falling into step beside Stacy. "You aren't mad, are you?"

She made herself look forward. "No."

"Good." It was a simultaneous answer from both men.

Chuck led her through his store's gauntlet of electronic gadgetry, past the computers, the display of telephones, the table of stuffed animals with radio dials protruding from their stomachs. He guided her through a maze of peg racks loaded with bagged transistors, coils of wires and fuses, and through a back door into a cramped storeroom. Chance lagged behind, momentarily distracted by a display of computer software.

Chuck held out his chair. "Here, you sit in *my* chair and I'll pop that cassette in. Okay?"

"Thanks, Chuck." She leaned forward and watched the screen change from snow to a bird's-eye view of the electronics store. She realized belatedly that the video came from a security camera, not one of the display models on the floor.

"Here." Chuck shoved a remote control in her hand. "It starts in a minute." He leaned forward, obviously angling himself for a view down her cleavage. "I've got . . ."

Chance stepped through the closed door and leaned down to whisper something in Chuck's ear.

The man straightened, then picked up a new train of thought with only a moment of hesitation, ". . . to go out front. Will you be okay watching it by yourself, Stacy?"

She nodded and turned her attention from the departing Chuck to the approaching Chance. "Thanks," she mouthed. As soon as the storeroom door closed, she held up the remote control. "Ready?"

"As I'll ever be." Chance took his place at her side and they watched the clock on the screen tick off the seconds. At precisely 3:29 A.M., something, someone appeared in the corner of the screen and glided slowly across the room, passing easily through solid objects. It looked like a man, dressed in black, his face draped in shadows.

Stacy reached out automatically and grasped Chance's hand. "It's him."

Chance seemed not to notice his sudden reality, being transfixed by the shape on the screen. Stacy hit the pause button just as the figure turned to stare up at the camera as if he knew it had been there all along, charting, recording his progress. It was the face of a handsome man—good-looking like Mel Gibson, with a straight nose, pleasant lines around his mouth, clear eyes that looked as if they could twinkle given the proper circumstances. He looked neither threatening nor deadly, but Stacy knew it was all a facade. What was it her Great-uncle Anatole always said about attracting more flies with honey than vinegar?

"*The taker of souls on beauty relies; To gather the lost, the foolish, the wise.*" Chance spoke the words in a quiet voice as he watched the screen.

Stacy tore her attention away from the television to stare at him. "Did you just make that up?"

He shrugged. "I'm not sure. I just remember it . . . from somewhere. But it does an apt job of describing our Angel of Death, doesn't it?" He indicated the screen with a nod. "Captured in black and white for your viewing pleasure."

She studied the figure's upturned features. "Funny . . . I always thought Death would look more frightening. More *deadly* looking."

Chance released her and shifted closer to the screen, staring at the figure caught in a frozen pose. "If God can look like George Burns, then I guess it wouldn't be so unreasonable to imagine Death might look like . . ." He stopped to contemplate the television.

"Mel Gibson," she supplied.

He nodded. "Exactly."

"Mel Gibson?" Chuck stepped into the storeroom. "What did you do? Change channels to *Lethal Weapon?*"

Stacy pointed to the screen. "Don't you think this . . . ghost looks like Mel Gibson?"

Chuck glared at the screen. ''Are you kidding? If I was to compare him to some movie star, I'd say he looked more like . . . Boris Karloff. All he needs is a scythe and some rusty chains to complete the image. That guy's just damn scary-looking!''

Although Stacy didn't push any of the remote's buttons, the picture flickered and the figure finished his slow trek across the store and merged into the opposite wall.

''Now here comes the weirdest part. Three doors down, at the bank, they have a security camera like ours. I persuaded them to review the film over the last week or so. Turns out that they have a similar shot taken three nights later. See the significance?''

Stacy shook her head. ''No.''

Chance straightened up. ''I do. Three stores down, three nights later.''

Chuck held up his hand, displaying three fingers. ''Three stores down . . . three nights later. Get it? There's a pattern. This ghost is making an appearance nightly and he's going through the stores in order. Last night I set up a camera in the optician's store and we got a suspicious blur which just may be our friend the ghost. Two stores down the corridor and two nights after the appearance at the bank. It's a pattern!''

Chance rushed toward Stacy. ''Listen, when you get through with this jerk, meet me upstairs in the hidden room. We need to talk.''

''Uh sure . . .'' Stacy glanced at Chuck and added, ''Sure, I understand now. A different store each night.''

''Not just a different store. He's going through them in order. Me, the clothing store next door, the card shop, then the bank. One, two, three. One store each night in order.''

Stacy's thought became instantly entangled in one massive calculation. The optician, the florist, the dentist, the candle shop . . . she mentally ticked off the stores between the last known sighting of the ghost and her lingerie shop.

Six stores. Six days.

She swallowed hard. Death would be knocking on her door in less than a week.

Her world swam for a moment then turned black.

Chance stared at the official reports that were still spread across the sawhorse table. He knew the material almost by heart, now, having studied it several nights in a row after Stacy went home. There was little for him to do other than contemplate his own unknown life and death.

Before he had this new mission in life . . . er, death, he'd been content to wander around the mall, entertaining the kiddies and causing a little mischief now and then. Nothing vindictive, nothing damaging. But now it all seemed such a waste of time. Time he could have spent investigating his own death.

It wasn't suicide, he could now state with unusual clarity.

But was it murder?

He'd already found a few minor inconsistencies but they didn't add up to conspiracy—just sloppy police work. Chance planned to run the discrepancies past Stacy and maybe the two of them could figure out the next step. He glanced at the dusty blueprints tacked up on the wall.

But first, he had to explain his newest theory. The theory which said they had six days left to solve his murder.

Six stores . . . six days.

Death comes a-calling . . .

Stacy heard voices in the gray dawn of her awakening.

"Well, Doctor?"

"Her blood pressure is a little low and she looks like she might be a little anemic. Other than that, I suspect she's fine."

Stacy allowed herself one good groan before she tried to sit up. Someone placed a hand on her shoulder and gently pushed her back down. "Just hold on, young lady."

She knocked away the restraining hand. "Don't tell me. Let me guess. I fainted."

Chuck's face loomed into view "You sure did."

Stacy latched onto the nearest excuse. "Uh . . . I guess I'm going to have to start remembering to eat breakfast."

Her unwanted rescuer turned to address someone else beside her. "Is she going to be all right, Doc?"

The man swam into focus, stood and brushed off the knees of his pants. "No problem. Of course, there is the tartar build-up, not to mention the cavity I spotted in her second premolar on the left."

"Damn it, Greg, I wasn't talking about her teeth."

The doctor stuffed a stethoscope back into a gym bag at his side. "Then you shouldn't have called a dentist. If you'll excuse me, I have a patient with wisdom teeth that need extracting." He wagged a finger at Stacy. "And I think you need to see a medical doctor if this condition persists. However, I suspect you'll feel a whole lot better once you get something to eat." He headed for the door and paused. "And don't forget to brush afterward."

Stacy allowed Chuck to touch her long enough to help her to the chair. Once she got her equilibrium, she started to stand.

"Wait a minute." He pushed her back into the chair only a moment before her knees buckled. "You ought to take it easy, Stacy. You know . . . I could go get you something to eat at the food court and you could rest back here for a while." He did everything but lick his lips, his expression revealing his sense of anticipation. It was probably just what he wanted; a languishing lady in his back room, dependent on his generosity for her recovery. Did he honestly think it would make her grateful for his company?

"No," she blurted out, before recovering her composure. "I mean, I wouldn't want to inconvenience you."

He squatted by her chair and pawed her arm. "It wouldn't be inconvenient at all. In fact—" His sheepish smile grew suddenly wolflike, "—it would be my pleasure."

Stacy found her wits, her energy, and her purse, in that order, and escaped. Once free from Chuck's unsettling proximity, she girded her strength and took the escalator. A strange melody filled her mind and she started humming it until she remembered the name of the tune: "Stairway to Heaven."

If she'd suffered from low blood pressure when she fainted, that was no longer a problem. The blood buzzed in her ears and pressure built behind the back of her eyes. Her heart started a new tempo, strong and pounding. It lurched when she looked up and saw a darkly dressed man standing near the rail, his back turned toward her.

As Stacy rode up the escalator, the blood began to hammer her ears, muting out the quiet thrum of the shoppers, the droning music over the mall speaker system, and the sounds of crying babies. As she neared the top, her heart wedged itself in her throat, slowly cutting off her air.

No, she whispered to herself.

As if the man heard her, he hunched his shoulders and pivoted in slow motion to reveal . . . a full beard and a Grateful Dead T-shirt.

"Dennis?"

The man smiled at her. "Stacy! Long time no see. What's shakin'?"

Her fear subsided, her heart returned to its rightful place, and her blood pressure leveled off at something near normal. She forced herself to smile at her friend and shrugged. "Oh nothing. How's the record business?"

He uttered a thoroughly theatrical sigh. " 'The days of vinyl are dead, my friend; Like Jimi, Janis, and John. All we have are compact discs; to carry the memories on.' "

"Your latest poem?"

He shook his head. "Naw, that was one of my oldies. This is my latest:

Chances are we laugh today
Chances are we cry.

Chances are we live today
Chances are we die.
Chances are—

Stacy's stomach performed a magnificent flip-flop which made the room spin. She reached out for the railing for support, them recoiled, reeling when she caught sight of the multi-story view below. "Uh . . . I wish I could stay and listen to all of your poem, but I'm really late for a meeting."

Dennis's beard twitched, signifying a smile beneath. "No problem. I'm doing a reading on Thursday at the Campus Coffee House. You're always invited, you know."

"Thanks, Dennis. I . . . I'll check my calendar. Uh . . . I better get moving. I'm late."

She hurried past with a red-faced wave and headed for the service corridor. Pausing at the bottom of the metal staircase, she tapped what seemed to be last energy reserves in order to climb the stairs to the forgotten room. Once at the top, she paused to catch her breath, then although she felt silly, she knocked on the closed door. "Chance?"

"Come in."

A cloud of dust attacked her as she entered, forcing her to sneeze.

"Gesundheit," Chance responded automatically. He was sitting at the table, lacking only a chair to look completely natural.

"Thanks."

He gave her a critical look and stood. "You okay?"

She sighed and dropped into the lone chair. "No."

"What happened?" When she didn't answer, he stood, prompting her again. This time his voice grew more forceful. "Stacy?"

"Promise you won't laugh?"

Chance nodded. "Promise. What happened?"

"Or get upset?" she prompted again.

"What!?"

"I fainted."

Chance felt something inside of him twist in sympathy and concern. ''You what?'' He zipped to her side, not knowing whether to touch her or to leave her all her strength for herself.

She shrugged. ''I fainted in Chuck's back room. When I came to, he was—''

Chuck Canton alone with an unconscious woman. The implications were staggering. ''That bastard!'' Since Chance had no blood to speak of, he knew the red haze which dropped over his eyes was one of fury, anger, and the need for retribution. ''I swear I'm going to kill him!''

She raised a feeble hand to stop his tirade. ''Get a grip, Chance. Nothing happened. He didn't do anything wrong. Or uninvited. He got the dentist from a couple doors down to come and check me out.''

Chance forced himself to regain control of his galloping need for revenge. ''A dentist?''

''The nearest person with basic medical knowledge. I told him I hadn't eaten breakfast this morning so that was why I fainted.''

''And did you?''

She glanced up at him, wearing a blank look. ''Did I what?''

''Skip breakfast?''

She shook her head, rubbing her stomach with her hand. ''I wish I had. My stomach's upset now. Three doughnuts and a pot of hi-test coffee doesn't sound so good after the fact.''

''So if you ate, then why did you faint?''

''Revelation. Chuck said something which really upset me.'' Stacy reached out to touch Chance, but he dodged her hand. She gave him a perturbed look. ''What's wrong?''

''I don't think you need to share your strength at this moment. What upset you . . . did it have anything to do with our dark visitor and where he might visit in six nights from now?''

She paled visibly, making Chance's nonexistent heart lurch in sympathy. ''You figured it out, too?''

''Yep. From what I can figure, Death started on the first floor and has been systematically working his way through every store, looking for something . . . or someone. In six days, he'll come to your store and I don't want either of us anywhere near it when he does."

"Where will we go?"

"I don't know. We could hide up here, but I'd just as soon we go somewhere else entirely."

"Okay." She propped her elbows on the table and stared vacantly at the reports spread across it.

Chance watched her carefully, not liking what he saw. She looked listless, pale, devoid of the spark which drew him toward her in the first place. Something was wrong, and he had a feeling he was at the center of the problem.

"Do I really look that bad?"

Chance realized he'd adopted an equally vacuous stare which dissipated at her question. "Now who's reading whose mind?" He lifted his hand, wanting so badly to touch her, to run his fingers through her hair, to join with her, soul to soul and perhaps body to body. To his surprise, she entwined her fingers in his, allowing the passageway of life to open and spill between them.

She uttered a satisfied sigh and smiled. "That's much better."

Her energy flooded through him, making his heart beat and his blood stir. She stirred him, all right. Maybe it was a side effect of life, maybe not. Maybe it was desire, pure and simple. Either way, she brought him more than life, she brought him love.

She lifted half-lidded eyes and smiled. "I love you, too."

For a moment, he was ready to act on the desires of the heart, but with reality came consequences and a sense of responsibility. Before the passions of life could be satisfied, questions about death had to be answered.

"Look at this." He pointed to the papers on the table.

"I'd rather look at you." She reached up and nipped his ear, blowing softly to create a tornado of erotic thought to snare his attention.

"Not now, Stacy." He fought against a libido which threatened to take over.

"Later?" She traced the outline of his ear with her gentle finger.

"Later," he managed between gritted teeth. He cleared his throat. "Look at these papers. What's missing?"

She stared at them, her features initially blank, then growing more involved. "Do you mean missing as in stolen or missing as in not here to begin with?"

Chance pointed to the collection of papers. "Not here to begin with. Think for a minute. If someone dies as a result of a suicide, there might or might not be an autopsy, but wouldn't you expect to find a death certificate?"

Stacy stared at the papers, shifting some, peering under others. "You're right. There isn't one."

"Why?"

She furrowed her brows in thought. "Maybe . . . because the police aren't satisfied with their theory?"

"Exactly. They must think there's more to this than a simple suicide. Why would they be watching you?"

"Right. Why else would they be—" She stopped in midsentence. "I forgot about the police. If they've been following me, then I've led them directly here." She lowered her voice. "They could be outside at this moment, listening to us."

Chance pulled his hand from hers and streaked toward the door. Passing through it, he sped down the stairs in time to see a man pause at the foot of the stairs and speak into a small radio.

"I'm going to see if I can get any closer and hear what she's doing in there. Over."

A tinny voice replied, "Just don't get caught."

Chance flew back to the room.

"Well?"

"A cop. Coming this way. Get these papers picked up. I'll find a place to hide them." As Stacy gathered the reports, Chance examined the walls, hoping to stumble across a forgotten memory that whispered of a secret panel or some such nonsense. Lacking any other inspiration, he and Stacy slipped the papers behind the blueprint, tightening the bottom part of the paper to hold them in place.

"That was quick." She wiped a smudge of dust from her nose.

"We're not through." Chance took a moment to concentrate and change himself. There wasn't much time for him to do anything beyond lengthen his hair and add a beard and mustache, but his quick disguise would have to suffice. After he finished, he grabbed her hand.

"Stacy . . . I love it when you do that." He spoke in a loud, love-clogged voice on purpose. Stacy merely stared at him. "Oh baby . . ." He pulled her into a tight embrace. "You're up here with a man. What else would you be doing?" he whispered.

She swallowed hard. "Oh d-darling," she stuttered in a flat voice.

"Come on, Stace. Get into the spirit of things." He shot her a wincing smile, then took things into hand.

In one swift move, he backed her up to the table. Her feeble attempts to protest faded as he leaned her backward until she reclined on the table. As she began to giggle, he smothered the sound by capturing her mouth with his. Reaching down, he pulled her leg up so that it rested on his hip. He figured anyone viewing their strained position would immediately credit it to passion gone awry. *What we do for love . . .*

"I love it when you do that!" Her voice trailed to a whisper. "Shift to the right, will you? It hurts."

He complied with a hushed "Sorry." Worrying that they were still under observation, he spoke louder, panting the words as he twined his hand in her hair. "Oh babe, you're so hot . . ."

Although she might not have been much good at amateur theatrics, she responded with enough energy to be heard easily through a closed door as they passed the threshold from pretend to real. But somewhere along the line, her authentic-sounding moans changed to reflect a genuine passion. And what was even worse, she wasn't the only one. In an effort to put on an act to satisfy a snooping cop, Chance found himself caught up in a situation which suspiciously resembled the real act of making love.

Stacy ripped his shirt open, causing buttons to fly everywhere in her haste. Although she wore a dress which buttoned from the neckline all the way down to the hem, Chance denied himself the pleasure of returning the favor. Instead, he started at the top and carefully unbuttoned them, kissing each bit of exposed skin. To his delight, he discovered she wore the same style of silky blue bra that was on the mannequin in the front window of her store. Several buttons down, he revealed the matching panties and groaned in sheer unadulterated pleasure.

Stacy stifled a small cry as she arched in response to one of his more inventive acts. When he paused to make sure her reaction was one of pleasure, she dug her nails in his shoulders, and gave him an imploring, almost frenzied look. ''Don't stop!'' she demanded hoarsely. He immersed himself in the realization of their joint pleasures, pausing only when he thought he heard the door open.

It should have been nearly impossible for Chance to ignore their peeping Tom and continue with something he considered a wondrous but wholly private act. But he persevered, propelled by both the need to appear genuine and the sheer momentum of it all. He couldn't have made himself stop if his life or death depended on it.

Luckily, Stacy seemed unaware of their observer and directed all her attention and energies into their lovemaking. She worked at a frantic pace, which he matched with renewed strength after he heard the door close gently.

At that moment, he doubled his efforts. With the lurker gone, there was nothing to interfere with the culmination of pleasure. They made magnificent, inventive love, their passions perhaps even amplified by the small element of danger involved.

It didn't occur to Chance until after they climaxed that their visitor might have simply stepped into the room for a closer view and merely closed the door behind himself. But to his utter relief, Chance realized that this had not been the case; the man had evidently slunk away after learning that his quarry was simply in the midst of some down and dirty sex.

Dirty, or in this case, *dusty* being the operative word.

"I can't believe I just did . . . *it.*" Stacy paused while buttoning her dress to glance around at the room. Patting the sleeve, she sneezed at the billow of dust which rose from it. "Here, of all places."

Chance assisted her with the last few buttons, taking advantage of her tantalizing proximity to steal another kiss. "Which one surprises you more? The use of sex as a diversion or the location of the crime?"

"I'm not sure. Either one seems . . . out of character for me." Her hand tightened on Chance's, drawing him back again. She stroked his beard, an intimate gesture which made his toes curl. "And this was a nice touch," she continued. "It was . . . exhilaratingly different, but unnecessary, I guess. Looks like we were loud enough to dissuade him from opening the door."

Chance merely nodded, knowing this was one time when silence was the better part of valor. "Uh . . . sure." He decided to use a little diversionary tactic himself. "You like the beard, eh? What about whisker burn?"

Her smile deepened. "I think it might be worth the pain." She gave him another kiss, then toyed with his hair. "It could almost be like making love to a different man each night."

Chance felt his self-satisfied grin fade away. "Now wait a minute, you don't want me to—"

She giggled as she wrapped a curl of hair around her forefinger. "No, silly. In all honesty? It was disconcerting. I was uncomfortable with it until I convinced myself you were still the man beneath all this." She gave his hair a playful tug.

"Hey . . . watch out. This stuff is real—for the moment. But . . ." He untangled her from his hair and quietly broke contact with her. "You've had a hard morning. The last thing you need to do is sustain two lives."

"Two . . . right." Her expression paled a bit and then the animation dropped completely out of her eyes, replaced with a growing sense of shock. "Two?"

"Two," he repeated. "You and me."

Stacy rubbed her hand across her stomach. "Are you sure it's just you and me?" She looked down and he followed her gaze, the significance of her gesture hitting him about three seconds later.

Fainting, an upset stomach, unprotected sex between a woman and . . . a man . . .

"A baby?" he managed in a strangled voice.

Chapter Fourteen

She dropped onto her chair. ''I couldn't be—I mean, it's impossible. I'm real and you're—''

''R-real when you touch me,'' he supplied.

She swallowed hard. ''And we do a lot of touching when we make love . . .''

Chance found himself sitting in midair, stunned by an impossible possibility. For a man who wasn't supposed to feel much as a ghost, his invisible stomach was imitating a cement mixer and his imperceptible nerves were stretched a taut as telephone wires. After a moment, he found his voice. ''How do we find out?''

She placed a protective hand across her belly. ''A pregnancy home-test kit, I guess.''

''Where do we get one?''

Her face softened. ''Thanks,'' she whispered.

''For what?''

''For saying 'we.' Twice.''

Chance ached to touch her but knew he hesitated. If she was

providing life for two, she certainly didn't need to provide life for a third at the moment. He crossed his arms instead.

Stacy stood. "If you don't mind, I'd like to go now to the drugstore and get a kit. I don't think I could stand the wait."

"Sure." Chance rose quickly, fighting the overwhelming instinct to help her up because it involved physical contact. As they made their way down the stairs and into the mall, he couldn't help noticing her pale, drawn features. He'd been so damn cocksure about his own insubstantiality after their discussion in the car that he'd given little thought to consequences after that. Yet, everything had consequences—some you could see, some you couldn't. But they existed nonetheless. Just like him.

He hovered as close to Stacy as he dared, sharing her look of panicked support as they entered the drugstore and searched for the right aisle. Stacy reached up blindly, selected a kit, and carried it toward the front of the store without saying a word. When the pimply teenager behind the checkout counter glanced at her purchase then looked up at her, Chance found the youth's sneering grin more than he could tolerate. Reaching through the sales register, Chance grabbed the boy's leather necktie and pulled him forward so that the material was caught in the closing cash drawer.

They left the drugstore with the register buzzing, the young cashier stunned into silence and the manager berating his employee for his general ineptitude. Although his initial intent had been born in anger, Chance realized his deed had inadvertently helped to lighten their mood a bit as Stacy tried to cover her brief smile with her hand. Chance took advantage of the situation to encourage her even more.

"So what do we do with it? Does it have vials and beakers and stuff? I always wanted a chemistry set so I could play mad scientist."

Stacy reached into the paper bag and pulled out the box to stare at it. "From what I understand, it basically comes with everything I need except one basic ingredient."

"What? We need to go find a rabbit?" He pretended to pull her toward the pet store.

She shook her head, "No."

"A blood sample?" He hunched his shoulders up in shivering sympathy. "Jeez I hope not. I can't stand the sight of blood."

Chance dutifully followed her down the hallway. When she came to a sudden halt in the doorway of the ladies' rest room, he almost plowed into her.

"Wait out here."

"But I want to know—"

"Chance . . ."

He waited. And waited.

After a few unbearable minutes, Chance realized the police reports never listed his middle name, but somehow he knew "Patience" wasn't it.

After another minute straggled by, he gave in to his restlessness. "Stacy?" he called out. "What's going on?"

There was no reply.

"Stacy, if you don't answer me, I'm coming in. I swear it."

"Hold on," a small voice called.

He strained to find hidden meaning in those two words. Did she sound . . . pregnant? Was she happy? Disappointed? In shock? Was she—

"I'm not pregnant." Stacy stood beside him with her arms folded tightly across her body. "The test was negative."

He glanced around, discovered they were alone in the hallway, then allowed himself the latitude to touch her. To hold her. To comfort her. He wrapped his arms around her, knowing even before he touched her that she felt both relief and disappointment. She buried her head in his shoulder and her tears seeped into his shirt. "It's okay," he crooned. "It's over."

"I know," she said between sniffs. "It's just that during the time it took to walk from the room upstairs to the drugstore, I started thinking that maybe . . . just maybe I could handle being pregnant with your child. That maybe this was a way I could help pay you back since your life was taken so terribly early."

He pulled her into tighter embrace, feeling her pain, her confusion, her love all rolled into one single piercing emotion. He felt her hair brush across his face, smelled the mingling aromas of her perfume and shampoo, and heard her soft sigh between sniffs. He pulled back to cradle her damp cheeks in both hands.

"Sweetheart, you've given me life already. I can see, feel, hear, touch . . . What I am, right now, is all because of your generosity, your giving spirit." He paused long enough to kiss her nose. "But look at what we've been doing . . . playing with laws of nature we don't understand, taking risks we can't even define at the moment. I'm not sure whether we could have taken the responsibility to bring a child into all this. A child you most probably would have to raise alone unless you decided to live here in the mall."

She nodded. "I realized that." She burrowed against his chest, heaving one final sigh. "But still . . ."

"Just think," he whispered, "what sort of holy terror a half-human, half-ghost baby would be. And imagine what it'd be like when he grew up to be a teenager. He'd always disappear when there were chores to be done."

For an uneasy moment, Chance couldn't interpret the sounds she made, her mouth muffled by his shirt. Then he realized it was laughter. Sweet, tension-releasing laughter. Once she regained control, she pulled back, wiped her eyes and gave him a kiss.

"Thanks."

"For what?"

"For reminding me it's too easy to imagine yourself holding a picture-perfect diaper-box baby who never cries. In reality, we both know that those not-so-quiet babies do tend to grow up to become incredible disappearing teenagers."

"And mad scientist wannabes," he added.

She started laughing again.

He pulled back, still clasping her hand. "What?"

"Speaking of teenagers, do you think our friend at the drugstore has gotten loose yet?"

Chance spent the rest of the day hanging around Stacy's store, making her feel self-conscious. He found a comfortable out-of-the-way perch on the top of the wooden wall case behind the register. From his position, he could observe the mall traffic through the front windows and also had a good view of practically every corner of the store.

"You know if you ever decide to install a security camera, I know the exact place to put it."

"Really," Stacy muttered under her breath.

"Yep, I can see everything from up here, including those two teenage girls who are trying to shoplift a set of white lace garters."

Stacy wandered over to the garter display, and gave the girls a disapproving look that said, "I-know-what-you're-really-after-and-do-you-really-want-to-flirt-with-another-black-mark-on-your-juvenile-record." And she watched them slink out of the store empty-handed.

She marched back to the counter and shook her head. "Some kids . . ." She glanced up and shot her guardian ghost a grateful smile. "Thanks. Can you see which store they're headed for?"

Chance leaned over, stuck his head through the wall and pulled back after a minute. "They made a beeline next door."

Stacy dialed the bookstore number, give the manager a brief description of the potential thieves, then listened to his tirade about how all teenagers look alike.

"In my day, we fought to be independent," he droned, "to have the freedom to choose whatever style we wanted. We didn't wear a uniform like these kids today with their cookie-cutter baggy pants, their identical sloppy plaid shirts and that gawd-awful hair."

Stacy found a graceful place to interrupt his diatribe and hung up.

"What's wrong?" Chance floated down to her level.

She sighed, nodded toward the store next door. "The manager of the bookstore is a nice guy but he gets wound up on occasions. He gets on this kick about teenagers. It's the same old complaint one generation always seems to have about the following one—'They all look alike and I don't like their clothes, their hair, their music . . .'"

"So the teenagers aren't as original as a man who wears a black suit, a white shirt and a red tie every day at work?"

"Oh . . . so you *do* know who I'm talking about." She grinned. "He does wear a blue shirt on Sundays, you know."

Chance affected a look of shock. "How reckless of him! You wouldn't catch me dead in a blue shirt and . . ." His voice trailed off and a pensive look replaced his mock dismay.

"Oh come on . . ." Stacy punched him in the shoulder, her brief contact lasting long enough to drop him several inches in altitude. "You're not getting squeamish on me when it comes to vocabulary, are you? I think you've used every alive or dead metaphor in the English language."

Chance crossed his legs Indian-style and propped his chin on his templed fingers. "The shirt . . ." he muttered after a few seconds.

"What about the shirt?"

He bobbed like a cork in the air, his concentration evidently redirected to something other than his relative elevation. "I'm not sure. There's something about a shirt, but I don't remember exactly what."

She tried to get a good look at his face, to read whatever emotion he was hiding, but he drifted around so much that she was starting to get seasick. "I-I don't understand."

"The reports didn't mention what I was wearing when I died, did they?"

Stacy closed her eyes, sifting through her memory for the missing details, but coming up empty-handed. "I don't . . .

think so." When she tried to focus on him, a queasy wave hit her stomach. "Do you think you could stay still for a minute? I'm getting motion sick just watching you."

"Sorry." Chance straightened out and floated down to her level. "Do you know if Rufus is on day shift today?"

She drew a deep, centering breath. "I have no idea. Do we need to talk to him?"

Chance nodded. "According to the reports, he's the one who found my body. I think he's the right man we ought to ask about some details."

Fifteen minutes later, Stacy had not only determined that Rufus was on duty, but that he could swing by in a few minutes on his lunch break if she didn't mind him eating while they talked.

She turned to her ghostly partner in crime. "So what am I going to ask him?"

Chance paced, creating an unsettling path back and forth through the counter. "First, we ask him what I was wearing when he found my body."

"Then?" she prompted.

"Then everything else depends on his answer. We'll simply play it by ear."

"We?"

He held out his hand. "I can either be here in person or just a friendly voice in your ear."

She reached out for his hand, then hesitated. "Do you think he might recognize you?"

Chance raised an eyebrow. "It's a possibility. I can change my appearance but we'll have to stay joined at the hip, so to speak if I do. Why don't I simply remain the embodied voice of reason this time?"

"Okay." Stacy looked up and saw Rufus striding their way. "Here he comes." She drew a deep breath, then gave the security guard her best smile. "Thanks for coming, Rufus."

He stopped a few feet away and gave her a very uncomfortable once-over.

Guilt crept up her face in a hot flush. "What?" she asked, afraid to know exactly why he seemed so critical.

Chance floated closer to the man and gave her a perplexed stare from approximately the same vantage point. "I don't see anything unusual."

Rufus raised one grayed eyebrow, gave her one more stem-to-stern glare, then shook his head. "You ain't."

Stacy tried to smile through her embarrassment. "I ain't what?"

"Preggers." Before she could comment, he continued. "I'm an old hand at this, you know. Never had a child of my own, but I'm the uncle of twelve and I knew every time when one of my sisters was pregnant. All I have to do is look at a woman and I can tell."

Total shock robbed her of the ability to say anything but a few words. "How . . . who . . ."

He nodded. "I could have saved you the cost of one of them kits, had I known. They're damn expensive." He reached into his pocket and pulled out a handful of coins. "Mr. Greeley from the drugstore asked me to give you your change. Evidently their cash register screwed up while you were there." He reached down for her hand and pressed a few coins into her palm. He gave her a fatherly pat on the shoulder. "I know things're different than from my day, but it's still hard for a young lady like you to raise a young'un by herself. You might think twice before letting someone like Chuck Canton quite so near again."

"Chuck?" Her embarrassment made a leap directly into full-blown rage. "Chuck Canton? Oh good Lord . . . people don't think he and I . . . that we . . ." She gulped. "Together?" She shuddered in spite of herself.

Chance stared at the man, slack-jawed.

She raised a hand, surprised to see it clenched into a fist. "Rufus Bryant, you know very well I'd kill myself before I'd let a creep like Chuck touch me."

Rufus's concerned expression melted into a grin. "Of course

I know that. I had more faith in your taste in men than what the rumor mill was saying, but I figured you needed to know what sort of trash was being slung behind your back." He pushed his hat back and scratched his head. "Hell, I suspect Canton's the one who started the rumor in the first place."

Chance raised a forefinger. "I'll be back in one minute."

She'd never seen him move quite so fast. One moment he was standing there, the next he was gone. So was her composure, a victim of Rufus's revelations. She tried to improvise past her sense of discomfort. She pointed to the storeroom. "Why don't you sit in here and you can sit and eat lunch while we talk." She led him to the back room.

A few moments later, Rufus had the contents of a greasy lunch bag spread across her worktable. He bit into a drippy, unappetizing sandwich, then wiped his mouth. "Now what seems to be the problem, missy?"

Stacy stayed in the doorway so she could watch the sales floor. "Do you remember the fellow who killed himself a month or two ago?"

"The jumper? Sure."

"Can you tell me about him?"

Rufus eyed her with growing suspicion. "Can't say much about it. I didn't know him at all."

The hackles on the back her neck started to rise for some unfathomable reason. She glanced out, hoping it signaled Chance's return, but it didn't. "Um . . . I don't mean something about him. I was wondering . . ." She hesitated. Exactly how did you bring up a corpse's fashion sense in polite company?

"I suspect you're curious, too, eh? You're probably the only person around here who hasn't grilled me for all the grisly details. So, you want the long-drawn-out story or the quick-and-the-dead version?"

She glanced around the store, checking to see if Chance had reappeared. No sign. The mind's eye offered an unsettling image of Chuck Canton being given the full haunted-house treatment with headless apparitions rattling their chains. Swallowing hard, she managed to smile. "Tell me everything."

Rufus pushed back in the chair, laced his fingers behind his head and drew a deep breath. "Well, it was a Saturday night. Actually Sunday morning around three-thirty if you want to get technical about it. Derrick was on the cameras and I'd just come inside from my outdoor rounds when I spotted the guy."

"Was it messy?"

Stacy jumped at the sound of Chance's voice.

"Ask him," he urged.

"Uh . . . was it m-messy?"

Rufus crossed his arms and almost smirked. "My goodness. You never struck me as a gore lover. No . . . it wasn't particularly messy. He landed in the fountain, which kept him from being splatted all over the mall floor."

"Fountain?" she and Chance blurted simultaneously.

"Uh-huh. Soon as I saw him, I rushed over, pulled him out of the drink and started CPR. He was still warm, so he hadn't been there long."

Stacy covered her gaping mouth with her hand. Up to now, dead had meant dead—instanteously dead—no-hopes-of-revival dead—no-lingering-to-the-last-shred-of-warm-life dead.

Just simple dead.

Chance spoke first, his form wavering for a moment. "Do you know what this means, Stace?"

She had to forced herself not to respond to his obvious anguish, but she managed a quick nod, acknowledging his observation.

Picking up his sandwich, Rufus paused to admire it for a moment. "Of course, it didn't do the poor bastard any good. The paramedics said he never started breathing on his own. He had a chance and croaked before they could get out of the parking lot. And me? Damn near caught pneumonia, wading into the water like that, then waiting outside for the police to come."

Stacy tried to split her attention between the two men, balancing her concern between Chance's growing dismay and Rufus's smug satisfaction. The guard expected to be the center of attention and if Stacy wanted to get more details out of him, she was going to have to give him her total attention, no matter how difficult that might be.

She leaned forward, trying to create a more confidential air. "The cops didn't get there before the paramedics?"

Rufus contemplated his sandwich, extracting a wilted piece of lettuce. "The patrolman did, but he couldn't do much until the detectives arrived. Made me go out and watch for them while he 'secured the crime scene' or some poppycock like that."

"W-what did they . . . the detectives do once they got here?"

"The usual stuff." Rufus shrugged and took a big bite of his sandwich, sensing he had a captive audience. "Fingerprints, measurements, looking for a suicide note."

"Did they find one?"

"Not there." He uncapped his thermos and poured out a steaming cup of coffee. "Want some?"

She declined with a terse smile and a shake of her head. "Didn't they think it was unusual that the man didn't leave a suicide note?"

"I didn't say they never found one—just not one at the mall. Turns out he'd sent some sort of computer message to someone he worked with, talking about feeling guilty or some such thing. All I know is he took a header from the third floor right outside your store."

"And landed in the fountain? Give me a break!" Chance thundered. "It's physically impossible."

It took all of Stacy's concentration not to respond to Chance and to direct her remark to Rufus. "They couldn't have been mistaken, could they? Could he have fallen from the second floor?"

Rufus shook his head. "They examined the railing there at the clock shop on the second floor, but concentrated more up here. For a while there was talk of removing the railing for evidence but the management people came and talked them out of it. After all, we had to open the next day and the last thing they wanted was lots of publicity about a suicide at the mall."

"Oh . . ." There was little else Stacy could say. Rufus's story made Chance's painful death all that more real and unavoidable. She shuddered.

Rufus wiped his hands on a paper napkin and reached over and patted her shoulder. "Now don't you worry, little lady. Something like that won't happen again. Ol' Rufus will see to that."

Grateful for his misinterpretation, she nodded and smiled. "I know you'll make sure no one else—"

A beep interrupted her. Rufus reached with one hand to turn on his radio and with the other to readjust his ear piece. "Say again? This damn thing's acting up. What? How in th' hell did he manage that? Don't tell me . . . I don't want to know. I'm on three and I'll need to go to the storeroom to get a grease gun and some bolt-cutters. Just tell him to . . . hang loose, okay? I'll be there as soon as I can."

Stacy read his unmistakable look of disgust. "What's wrong?"

"It's that fool Canton at the Electro Shack. Somehow he got his hand caught in a drain hole in his back room. I gotta go pry him out." Rufus gathered up his lunch things and packed them back into the tattered brown bag.

Chance, who had been sitting silently after his first outburst, content to scowl into the distance, didn't seem to notice Rufus's departure until the man was almost gone. "Wait!" He streaked out of the back room. "Ask him about my clothes. What was I wearing?"

"Uh, Rufus. One last question. Just out of curiosity, what was the man . . . wearing when he jumped?"

Pivoting, Rufus's expression changed from knowing to perturbed. "You know, no one's asked me that and it's probably the oddest fact about this whole situation. The guy had on a really nice suit which really fit him well. Expensive, like those custom Eye-talian ones they sell at Sandori's. And nice shoes, too. He didn't take them off like they say a lot of jumpers do. But the strangest part was his shirt." He paused for emphasis, then leaned forward to complete the illusion of conspiracy. "It was too big for him."

"Too big?"

He nodded. "He was a good-sized man, a six-footer, probably wore the same size shirt I do, but the shirt he was wearing that night had to be a couple sizes too big. The sleeves were so long they dangled out from beyond his coat cuffs. And I figured a man like that would wear a shirt as tailored as his suit. You know what I mean? Sort of a package deal?" His radio beeped again. "Well I better get going. I suspect our good friend Chuck is getting tired of being stuck in a hole in the floor. See ya later." Rufus waved and trotted out into the mall corridor, nodding in greeting to the three ladies who passed by him and entered Stacy's store.

Although she was frustrated by the interruption, Stacy's sense of commerce rose feebly to surface as she attempted to play a suitable hostess to the ladies' giggly requests. When Chance learned of their quest, he retreated into the storeroom. A half hour later, the three bridesmaids-to-be walked out with an inspired wardrobe, guaranteed to heat up a wedding night between—as the woman had said—the last two virgins in America. As soon as the coast was clear, Stacy rushed into the back room.

She expected to find Chance, sullen, arms crossed, doing his best impression of a disgruntled spirit. Instead, he wore a pensive, almost expectant look.

"Good you're through. I thought they'd never leave. So . . . what do you think?"

His change in attitude caught her off guard and Stacy didn't know what to say in response. She offered him a helpless shrug.

''Don't you see? I was right about the shirt.'' His expectancy turned to triumph. ''I was right all along.''

''I don't understand.''

Chance motioned for her to come closer. He stood, closed his eyes, then slowly transformed from his polo shirt and jeans to a suit similar to the one Rufus had described. ''What do you see?'' Chance asked, displaying his outfit like a model posing for *GQ*.

''A man dressed in a nice suit.''

''Nice?'' He affect a brief look of disappointment. ''It's another suit from Sandori's window. Expensive, tailored. A complete package, right? And it looks good, doesn't it?''

Yes indeed, Stacy thought. Dressed like that, she could imagine him as a successful professional, a big-time architect at ease in the corporate boardroom. With equal clarity, she could imagine him sitting at an elegant dinner table, staring at her from over a glass of red wine, an enticing smile on his lips. Candlelight would add just the right atmosphere. And music . . . a piano in the background, playing some soft jazz which would tempt them to the dance floor where they would find the music an aphrodisiac leading to something more—

''Stacy?''

''She shook herself out of her daydream, embarrassed at the speed and depth she attained in her unbridled fantasies. *Damage control,* she demanded of herself. ''Just what I need. A vain ghost.''

He raised an eyebrow and gave her a brief smile which matched the one she'd imagined only a moment earlier. ''Not vain. But thorough.'' He took off his jacket and slung it over his arm. ''I think I tend to manifest my clothes in the same style I wore in real life. I don't see why death would make me want to dress any different. So look at this.'' He pointed to his silk shirt which accentuated broad shoulders and tapered to an impressively narrow waist. He straightened his red tie then pulled the double-breasted jacket back on, buttoning it. He straightened his cuffs, allowing just the right amount of sleeve to appear. ''Can you imagine me . . . or any man for that matter, wearing this suit with a shirt that was undeniably too big for him?''

She eyed him, flashing only for a brief moment on the two of them swaying to a forgotten tune. He was right. It was a package deal. Suit, shirt, tie.

''Try this. Close your eyes.''

She complied.

''Now open them.''

Stacy open her eyes and focused on Chance, instantly seeing the large shirt peeking out at his wrists and blousing around his neck.

''Your first reaction,'' he commanded.

Her reply was automatic. ''You look like you're wearing someone else's shirt.''

''Bingo! The lady wins a kewpie doll!''

She stared at him, her own words slowly sinking into the dark crevasse she called a logical mind. ''So you think you traded shirts with someone before you were pushed? Why?''

''Maybe there was something on my shirt which might prove I was pushed rather than jumped.''

''Like what?'' Something close to excitement began to build inside her as possible answers began to float into her mind. ''Maybe you were in a fight before you were pushed and you bled all over your shirt.''

He shook his head. ''Who would be able to tell what bloodstains came from before the fall and what came after.''

She picked up his thread of thought. ''Of course, it might not be your blood on the shirt. Maybe you fought with someone else and it's their blood on the shirt. And if the police did a DNA test on the blood,they would have known it wasn't yours.''

Chance stroked his chin in thought. ''That's pretty high-tech for goons who throw unsuspecting architects off balconies.''

''Maybe it's something as simple as you pulled off a button during the fight.''

Animation sharpened his features. ''Or tore my shirt pocket.

Maybe I was wearing the killer's shirt when I fell because he couldn't take any chance that the police would mistake the signs of a fight as damage that occurred when I fell. My God, Stace, you're brilliant!" He reached forward and grabbed Stacy by the shoulders, his happiness flowing into her as his mouth closed over hers. "We need to find that shirt if it still exists."

It was a heady experience, this sense of sharing they had. She could feel not only her passion for him, but through the courtesy of their unearthly connection, she could feel him, hear his thoughts, understand without question how and what Chance felt for her. The prospect of being wanted, loved, admired, desired that badly, was almost frightening. But she understood it because it mimicked exactly how she felt about him. Logic be damned and reality disregarded, as her senses described in intricate detail the sensation of loving being loved in a way that transcended the rules of the known universe.

She knew what she could see, feel, and taste, and she could do all those things with Chance. She heard the words he murmured in her ear as he trailed kisses down her neck. She felt his hands reaching inside her blouse, teasing her breasts. She used all her senses together to recognize the sweet essence of desire, the indescribable combination of actions, reactions, instincts, and intuitions which defined the concept of love.

She loved him. She'd always love him, be he spirit or flesh.

However, it was the needs of the flesh which they were serving at the moment.

Stacy struggled with the buttons of the too-large shirt, forcing them open and splaying her hands across the warmth of his chest. He muttered something in her ear and though she missed the words, she couldn't misconstrue their meaning. She pulled him back toward the worktable.

"Chance . . ."

A small voice answered her. "Excuse me . . . do you work here?"

Stacy stiffened, suddenly feeling the edge of the table gouge into her back. She pulled her shirt closed with one hand, keeping the other twined around Chance's neck. Turning around, she saw a figure standing in the doorway.

Clutching her purse in front of her like a shield, the young woman looked as if she didn't know whether to run or to take notes.

"M-may I help you?" Stacy stuttered.

"I need some . . . help picking out lingerie." The woman's voice dropped to almost a whisper. "I'm getting married and I'm not . . . sure what I need." She swallowed visibly, evidently trying to avoid making eye contact with Chance. "F-for my honeymoon."

After gaping at the young woman for an impolite moment, Stacy turned and locked gazes with Chance. "Please go ahead and take a look around," she called over her shoulder. "I'll be right with you.

Chance nodded in encouragement and helped to straighten and button her clothes. When he gave her a chaste kiss on the cheek, it did nothing to extinguish the flames of desire which continued to lick at her libido.

"Go." He nodded toward the sales area. "The last virgin in America needs your help. We'll . . . help each other, later."

Stacy thought to switch off the table lamp before she broke contact with Chance, allowing him to fade away into the shadows rather than thin air. Somehow she didn't think the young woman could handle something like the incredible vanishing mall ghost at the moment. Running a hand through her mussed hair, Stacy tried to adopt a professional air as she stumbled onto the sales floor and plunged into sales mode.

"There are several types of lingerie styles to choose from," she started brightly. "Do you have a starting place in mind?"

"Well, I usually . . . er, I mean . . ." The girl's voice trailed off as she ducked her head. Glancing up, she focused beyond Stacy toward the darkened storeroom door. "Uh . . . I mean . . ." She turned her gaze back toward Stacy, the look growing more speculative.

"W-what kind do you wear?"

Chapter Fifteen

An hour later, Stacy knew someone was watching her. Some inborn instinct told her it wasn't Chance. He'd gone to check on Chuck and his mysterious imprisonment. As she stapled the credit card slip to the receipt, a man in a dark suit entered the store.

Stacy flinched when she first saw him, but quickly realized it wasn't Madmax, the Bogeyman of Doom, but an ordinary-looking man who appeared just a little ill at ease. Stacy had learned some time ago that men often acted that way around large amounts of lingerie.

''May I help you?''

''Are you the owner or manager of this store?''

A salesman, she thought. ''Yes, I'm Stacy Reardon. If you're selling something—''

''No, ma'am. My name is John Boyd.'' He placed his briefcase on the counter and pulled out a black wallet. When he flipped it open, a small gold badge gleamed in the overhead fluorescent lights.

Stacy wondered if the handcuffs and a warrant were the next things he'd produce from his briefcase.

''I'm a county building inspector. I'm here to do a cursory examination of your store. We're looking for unusual signs of settlement and stress in the walls, ceiling, and flooring.''

''Stress?'' she managed to say once her heart crawled out of her throat. ''Are we talking about a possibly dangerous situation here?'' The words *Design irregularities* echoed through her mind.

''I'm not at liberty to speculate at the moment. Right now we're simply gathering data. I'd like to inspect your storeroom, first.''

''Uh . . . sure.'' She led him to the back room where he made a beeline to the cracks in the concrete flooring.

''Just as I expected,'' he said almost to himself. Reaching in his briefcase, he pulled out a folding rule and a camera. ''This is going to take a while. If I have to move any of your boxed merchandise, I'll make sure to put it back where I found it.''

''Thanks.'' Stacy intended to stand in the doorway and split her attention between the empty sales floor and the back room, but the door chime heralded a visitor.

The young women who strolled into the store peppered Stacy with questions which kept her busy. After twenty minutes of being a polite shopkeeper, Stacy felt her control slipping. Finally, the young woman heaped her merchandise on the counter and reached into her purse.

''It's here, somewhere, I know it is.'' She fished around in the bottom of her purse. ''I'm so embarrassed!''

The first problem was the young lady didn't look embarrassed at all. There was no telltale color in her face, no tight-lipped expression of discomposure. She didn't perform the customary act of hauling handfuls of items out of her purse onto the counter in search of the elusive checkbook or credit card.

''Is there a problem?'' Stacy asked, knowing full well there was one.

''I can't find my checkbook.'' It was more a statement of fact than an apology.

"We take Visa, MasterCard, American Express, and Discover." *And I bet you have conveniently forgotten them, too.*

"I'm . . . I'm afraid I don't have any of those." She pawed halfheartedly through her purse, then looked up with a facade of expectancy. "Do you think you could hold these items for me? I'm here shopping with a friend and I'm sure she'll let me borrow the money."

Stacy agreed, knowing the young lady would never return. They never did. She didn't mind people trying on items but she hated it when they carried the delusion all the way to the counter, effectively wasting Stacy's time. She stared, sighing at the pile of lingerie to be hung up, folded, and returned to the sales floor.

"Excuse me?"

Stacy jumped, spun around, and stared at the building inspector who stood in the storeroom doorway. She'd almost forgotten the man was back there.

"I'm through now, but I may have to come back later. Okay?"

She nodded, quickly regaining her composure. "Sure. Is there anything I should worry about? I mean . . . is it safe in there?"

Chance zipped into the storeroom and gave the inspector a close once-over. "Who's the suit?"

The man shrugged. "You got the same problems everybody else around here does. We call it a post-pouring separation of the cement in reaction to an oblique foundational shift and compounded by an inferior grade of cast-iron reinforcement rods. I wouldn't say it's a dangerous situation . . . yet, but it may likely develop into one."

Chance glared at the man. "Whatever you do, *don't* ask him to explain."

"Thanks. It sounds like a serious problem."

"Indeed." The man shifted his briefcase from one hand to the other and examined his watch. "If you'll excuse me, I have several more stores to inspect." He nodded in greeting and headed for the door.

Chance gave the man a scathing once-over. "Who was that bozo?"

Stacy wrapped her arms around herself. "The building inspector. He says there might be some problems with stress and cracks and stuff all throughout the mall."

"The building inspector?" Chance started laughing. "That's the biggest load of horse manure I've heard in a long time. What was that he was babbling about? Cast-iron reinforced cement?"

Denial. It had to be Chance's sense of denial which was keeping him from recognizing the truth. And it was up to her to break the news to him. "Don't you see? This proves someone really did used substandard materials to build the mall. And I'm afraid the implications will help them strengthen their case against you."

Instead of reacting to the harsh truth, he laughed even harder. "I'd be petrified if it weren't for one little problem with his story."

"What problem?"

"The floors and walls of this mall are made of *steel*-reinforced *concrete*. Not cast iron and cement. No self-respecting person with an ounce of building experience would make a mistake like that. If that man's a building inspector, then I'm the President of the United States." He raised his hand to his ear. "And I don't hear anybody playing 'Hail To The Chief.'"

Stacy shivered at the thought of her world being so easily invaded by an impostor. "What do you think he was he doing here?"

"Maybe casing the joint?" Chance pointed to her desk. "Looks like he was also examining your accounting books for possible structural faults." He stuffed his hands in his pockets and leaned back as if propping himself against a wall.

Stacy stormed over to her desk and spotted the not-too-subtle signs of the "inspector's" search. The more evidence she found of his snooping, the madder she got. "Why that lying son of a—"

"Police officer?"

She stopped cold, a shiver making goose bumps erupt across her arms. "You think he was . . . a cop? But wouldn't he need a warrant to search the premises?"

"Only if he's an honest cop." Chance's gaze narrowed. "I've been thinking about the police report. All those discrepancies? I think they add up to more than sloppy police work."

"You think they're covering something up?"

He straightened up. "Yes I do. And I think I found a clue. Remember Rufus said something about him doing inside/outside duty and Derrick being on the cameras?"

She nodded. "But there's no camera in that area."

"No, but they do have cameras on all the exits. If anybody went in or out of the mall, it had to have been caught on the video. But even if the police thought it was a suicide, they should have checked the tape to see who exited from the building. But evidently, they didn't."

She felt excitement bubble through her from forgotten depths. "Then all we have to do is find those tapes! It'll be the proof we need!" To her surprise, Chance didn't react with equal enthusiasm. "What's wrong?"

"They keep those surveillance tapes for two weeks, then record over them. If there had been any evidence, it's been long since destroyed."

She sighed, seeing elusive victory slipping through their fingers one more time. "Are you sure?"

"Yeah. I went up to the surveillance room last night and watched how it works. Rufus was on duty and I watched him change the tapes and listened to him cuss about a guy named Derrick Bains who I guess is the fellow in charge of it. It's a thorough system which involves numbered tapes and color-coded schedules and—"

"Bains?" Stacy felt an uncomfortable sensation start at the

base of her spine and pickax its way upward. "We ran into somebody else named Bains, recently."

"In the police report?"

Stacy combed through her memories, trying to remember where she'd seen the name before. She closed her eyes, trying to picture the name. She saw raised letters. "The plaque!"

"The one downstairs?"

She nodded. "I'm sure I saw that name on there, somewhere."

He grabbed her hand and nearly jerked her off her feet as he lunged for the door. "Then let's go!"

Stacy allowed herself to be pulled several feet before a sense of duty kicked in. "But the store. I can't leave the store unattended."

Chance heaved a sigh of disappointment, then nodded in reluctance. "Okay . . . I understand." He dropped her hand, then closed his eyes and sank through the floorboards until just his head emerged from the cracked concrete. "Just wait right here, okay?"

She stared at his disembodied head and managed to emit a strangled noise which at least sounded to her like an agreement. Feeling light-headed, she sagged into the seat, praying the door chime wouldn't make a peep. It was hard to instantaneously switch gears from dutiful saleswoman to partner in crime with the Super Spectral Sleuth doing his best impression of being buried to his neck in beach sand.

She leaned forward, resting her chin on her crossed arms and praying the stupor of exhaustion would pass with a few indulgent moments of rest. But before she could close her eyes, Chance zoomed out of the floor.

He wore a tight smile of triumph mixed with unsettling revelation. "The mall was built by Bains & Bowren Contracting. Looks like our friend Derrick has some family members in the building business. It's too damn convenient, don't you think?"

"Absolutely." She fought to shake off her lethargy. "Since you were supposed to have killed yourself over building irregularities, then I think we ought to take a very close look at Bains & Bowren Contracting, don't you?"

He nodded. "Where do we start?"

"Where else? The phone book."

They worked out a system. Stacy stayed behind the counter with one foot hooked around Chance's, allowing her to operate the cash register and him to use the phone. The few times when she had to help a customer on the sales floor, they found an excuse to duck into the storeroom first, where Chance dematerialized, allowing Stacy to emerge alone and render whatever service required of her.

Luckily, Chance looked up and spotted Peg heading their way. He barely managed to drag Stacy into the storeroom in time to escape a sticky assortment of questions. When Stacy stepped back onto the sales floor, alone, Peg opened her eyes in alarm.

At first, Chance thought he'd been seen, but Peg flew around the counter and grabbed Stacy by the elbow. "Good Lord, you look terrible. Are you coming down with the flu or something?"

"Or something," Stacy echoed dully.

Chance took a long look at his companion in crime, shocked to discover that the only color in her face came from the dark circles under her eyes. She *did* look terrible.

Peg charged toward the spot where he stood and he moved, out of habit. She glanced down at the scrawled notes Chance had left by the phone book. "You looking for a builder or something?"

Stacy shot him a panicked look which he shrugged away. "Heck . . . ask her. She seems to know everything that happens around here, anyway."

"Uh . . . no, I don't need a contractor, but someone asked me to recommend one." Stacy stabbed the Yellow Pages with a shaky index finger. "Do you know anything about this Bains & Bowren Contracting? They're the ones who built the mall."

"Danny worked for them for a while, but he didn't like the job."

Chance lifted both his hands. "What did I tell ya? She knows everybody. Ask her why?"

"Why didn't he like the job?"

Visions of conspiracies danced in Chance's head. Maybe they asked the guy to do something illegal, unethical, immoral, unscrupu—"

"They made him work too hard." Peg reddened slightly. "You know Danny's allergic to sweat. But they were nice; they moved him into the office where he worked as a gofer, but he quit after two weeks."

Chance's imagination flared again, seeing conspiracy within the shadows of the company office.

"Why?" Stacy probed.

Peg developed a full flush. "He didn't like driving that far to work. Their offices are across town."

"There was nothing sinister about the organization? They never asked Danny to do something he thought was suspicious or wrong?"

Peg balanced her fists on her hips. "How come this is starting to look more like the Spanish Inquisition than an idle conversation?"

Stacy motioned the woman closer. Chance complied as well. "The building inspector was just here and he said there were some problems with the foundation of the building. From what he implied, someone had used inferior building materials and I figure that reflects back on the construction firm who built it in the first place."

Peg nodded sagely. "I heard the same thing. I even heard some guy was caught doing it and he killed himself."

Stacy shot Chance a quick glance, then redirected her attention. "I heard that, too, but I'm not sure I believe it. That's why I wanted to know about the construction company. Did Danny ever say anything else about it?"

Peg knitted her brows for a moment in deep thought. "He

said he really liked the Bowren guy, that he was a regular Joe, but he never said anything about . . . wait." A hint of expectancy lit her face. "It was the Bains guy he liked. He had a wimpy first name—something like Irby or Irlin or Irwin. That's it Irwin Bains. The Bowren guy was the one no one ever saw."

"No one?"

The woman shrugged. "Danny said they described him as an invisible partner but since no one was sure the man even existed, it was more like a ghost partner."

"Ghost?" Chance and Stacy said simultaneously.

Peg raised her hands in mock surrender. "I know. I know . . . a bad choice of words considering the haunting scares going around here. But you know what I think? I think all this ghost stuff is nothing more than some stupid trick Chuck Canton is trying to play on all of us. I think he manufactured that tape of his and he's only trying to stir up trouble." Her gaze narrowed again. "And speaking of trouble, you don't need any. Why don't you go home? You look like you could really use the rest."

Stacy started to protest but Chance took a menacing step forward, hoping he could forestall any argument. She conceded and uttered a halfhearted promise to go right home. He trailed her into the storeroom and almost plowed into her when she stopped short to stare at her desk.

"I want to get to the bottom of this. Now."

Peg stepped into the doorway. "C'mon, Stacy. The books will wait for you. You can come in tomorrow and catch up. But for right now, I prescribe a long hot soak, a good book, and a good night's sleep. Oops . . ." The door chimed. "Duty calls."

Evidently afraid to say anything else aloud, Stacy waited until Peg left, then glanced up and mouthed the words, "Upstairs."

Chance nodded. "I'll meet you up there, but first I want to go check something out, okay?"

After having studied the blueprints of the building, Chance found he could navigate through it more easily. Not confined to hallways and staircase, he personally confirmed that the shortest distance between two points was indeed a straight line, despite such obstacles as walls, ceilings, or floors. Yet he still found it necessary to close his eyes when his head passed through objects.

He moved with so much speed that he initially overshot the Security Surveillance room. As he barreled through the opposite wall, he instinctively closed his eyes again. When he opened them, he discovered he was standing in their secret hiding place.

"Wait a minute. How'd I get in here?" He moved gingerly to the wall he'd just come through and stuck his head into the brightly lit room next door.

Since the hidden room hadn't been included on the blueprints, Chance didn't realized the two rooms backed up to each other. The first time he had gone up to check on the videotapes, he'd used the regular method of getting there, coming up the staircase which originated on the other side of the building. Somehow, the distance between the two staircases had misled him into thinking the rooms were further apart and certainly not adjacent.

Stepping completely into the surveillance room, he noticed two things initially. There were an impressive number of monitors which represented the camera view covering each mall exit as well as various corridors including the ones in front of the mall office, the three banks, and the four jewelry stores. The biggest difference between Chance's late-night visit and this one was the amount of shopper traffic on each screen.

Looking closer, he discovered there was even a camera pulled up in a tight, angled focus on the front display window of Lacy Lady. But it didn't take a genius to realize that the security guard was more interested in getting a glimpse of who was using the dressing room than who came in and out of the store.

The guard.

That was the second thing Chance noticed. The young man sitting behind the desk and eyeing the wall of monitors was, in a word, huge. Had he stood, Chance would have guessed the man would have topped six feet eight or nine in his stocking feet. And this was the sort of guy no one would ever laugh at for wearing stockings.

Leaning back in his chair, the man paid more attention to the coin he was flipping with his thumb than paying attention to the monitors. Yet, when he caught the coin, he never checked to see if it was heads or tails.

Chance moved closer to get a good look at the name badge pinned to the man's dark blue uniform jacket. "*Bains.*" So this was the elusive Derrick Bains.

Suddenly, something on one of the monitors piqued Derrick's interest. He tossed the coin one last time, caught it in a beefy fist, then leaned forward to adjust a dial on the control panel in front of him. Wondering if the man had spotted a shoplifter, chance moved closer to get a good look at the screens.

Stacy.

The Jolly Blue Giant pushed a couple of buttons and smiled. "Well hello, Lacy Stacy. Bet you got on something mighty silky fine underneath that Miss Prim and Proper outfit, don't you? So where are you off to, today, my love?"

He tracked her progress with a series of cameras. As soon as she stepped out of the range of one camera, another camera picked her up. The closer Stacy got to the hidden room, the more steamed Chance got. But he tempered his anger with the realization that, judging by the inordinate attention the guard paid to her cleavage, his interest in her was based more on puerile satisfaction than suspicion.

To Chance's relief, Stacy walked out of range of the last camera before it became evident where she was headed. Evidently, their location was still a secret. Losing interest, the guard slumped back into his chair and started flipping his coin again. Although Chance didn't burn for retribution, he figured he deserved a chance to complicate the lumbering giant's life a little. As Derrick flicked the coin in the air again, Chance reached out and batted it away. As it fell soundlessly to the floor, Chance realized it wasn't a coin; it wasn't metal at all.

A look of horror dropped over Derrick's face. "Jeez, I'll be up shit creek if I lose this baby.'' He scrambled after the object, snatching it from the killer dust bunnies under the monitor stand. He held it up for inspection, a relieved smile draping his face. ''Whew!''

Chance leaned down and examined it as well.

It was two round pieces of clear plastic sealed together to make a protective round envelope around a small white button. A few threads of rust-colored fabric still clung to one side of the button.

Derrick gave the button a sappy look which reminded Chance of a man gazing at a million-dollar cashier's check. ''I better take real good care of you. You're going to be my ticket to fame and fortune in Cousin Irwin's building business as soon as I find the shirt you came off of.'' He tucked the button in his pocket, patted it, and leaned back to admire his collection of monitors. ''Yep, nothing gets past Derrick 'Eagle-Eye' Bains. Nothin'!''

Wanna bet?

Chance tumbled through the wall and landed in the hidden room, causing an unsuspecting Stacy to shriek in alarm.

''Quit doing that!'' she complained after regaining her breath. ''You scare the dickens out of me when you pop out of nowhere like that.''

He grabbed her arms, forced her to twirl in a circle as he performed a few left-footed dance steps. ''You won't believe what I found!''

''What?''

''I didn't realize that the surveillance room is next door. And Derrick Bains is in there gloating over a small white button he found somewhere. He has it all sealed up in plastic to protect what I might guess are fingerprints.''

''Fingerpri—''

''And . . .'' He held up a finger. ''That's not all. He seems to think this button represents his—quote, 'ticket to fame and fortune in Cousin Irwin's building business.' But he realizes he first has to find the shirt the button came off of.''

''The shirt?'' A little bit of color flooded her whitewashed face. ''Then you were right all along about the shirt you were wearing when you fell. It wasn't yours. And I bet this button is from—''

He interrupted her with a big kiss. ''Exactly what I think.'' He slid his grasp down, locking his hands behind her waist. ''And to prove it, we need to find my shirt!''

Instead of reflecting his enthusiasm, she seemed strangely bereft.

''What's wrong, Stacy?'' He searched for the spot on her neck which he knew always made her shiver in delight. ''Don't you see? It's all starting to come together, now. We're slowly finding the proof we need.''

She pushed back and he watched a far-away look wash over her face. ''And then what?'' She cocked her head. ''Do you simply bid me a fond farewell and ride off into the sunset with Death?''

The future? Didn't he have enough to contend with, discovering the Ghost of Christmas Past and Present? Somehow he didn't think this was going to turn into a non-seasonal production of *A Christmas Carol* and Bobby Ewing was going to wake up and discover it had all been nothing more than a dream.

She shuddered in his arms and what he thought was a precursor to a cry turned out to be smothered laughter. ''Only you, Chance. Only you could equate a classic Dickens tale with an episode from *Dallas.*'' She buried her face against his shoulder. ''How am I going to live without you?''

''Simple. We'll just have to learn how to cheat. If there's a way to cheat death, I'm going to figure out how to do it. Okay?''

''Uh-huh.''

The warm moisture of her whispered agreement penetrated his shirt, reminding him of the glorious sensations of renewed life as it poured through his veins, warm, flowing, circulating through him like blood.

Blood?

Bloodstains?

The shirt!

Stacy lifted her head to give him a bleary but inquisitive stare. "What's wrong?"

"The button. I bet you wouldn't catch me dead wearing a rust-colored shirt with a business suit. It wasn't pulled off of a rust-colored shirt." He gripped her tighter. "Those were bloodstains!"

She caught the thread of his story. "And if they can prove it's from your shirt but it's not your blood—"

"Then their suicide theory is shot to hell and maybe someone starts a new investigation to find my killer."

Instead of jumping for joy, Stacy sagged against him. "That's so wonderful . . ." Her words died out at the same moment her knees gave out.

He grabbed her as she started going limp in his arms. "Stacy? My God . . . what's wrong?" His heart wedged itself in his throat as he gently lowered her to the chair.

"I feel so . . . funny. So tired."

He placed his palm against her head, measuring her elevated temperature. "You're burning up. I think Peg's right. You're catching the flu." She tried to bat away his hands, but he kept one hand braced on her shoulder.

"I never get sick." A moment later, she groaned and tried to rest her head on the dusty table.

"Hold it, Stace. Let me wipe that before you lie down." Keeping his hand on her shoulder, he stretched and picked up a dusty rag from the floor. Swiping it across the table, he removed an additional layer of dust and helped her get in a comfortable position.

"If I can stay here for a moment, I'll feel better. I'm just tired. I haven't been getting much sleep lately."

"You've been so busy worrying about me that you've neglected yourself. What I want you to do is rest here for a while, then we'll work our way very slowly downstairs, and see if Danny can't come get you and drive you home. Now will you promise me you'll stay right here and take a little nap?"

"Where are you going?"

He pointed to the room next door. "I want to see if perhaps Derrick has any more ghoulish mementos of my death. You're going to nap. Promise?"

She managed to nod despite her awkward position.

"Good. I'll come back and check on you every now and then, okay?"

" 'Kay." She started to close her eyes, but she rallied for a moment. "Chance?"

"Yeah?"

"I don't want you to go." Her drowsy consternation turned into a sleepy smile. "I love you."

He lifted his hand from her shoulder and life drained from him, taking everything from him except his love which seemed able to withstand any obstacle. Even death itself.

"I love you too, Stacy."

He tiptoed out of instinct rather than necessity as he headed toward the common wall between the two rooms. Hesitating for a moment before thrusting his way through the wall, he turned back to sneak a fleeting look at the only woman in the world who could make him feel they way he did, whether they were touching or not.

But she wasn't asleep.

She wasn't resting on the table any more.

She sat straight in the chair and was staring with a mixture of shock and dread at the dusty rag which he'd used to wipe the table.

"Stacy? What's wrong?"

Her bottom lip quivered as she held up the grayed fabric in one hand. Unfolding the material, it started looking less like an anonymous rag and more like . . .

A shirt.

Chapter Sixteen

Stacy pushed her finger through the gaping hole where evidently there had once been a button. ''Your shirt,'' she said in a choked voice. She slumped in the general vicinity of the metal folding chair.

Chance streaked to her side, more concerned with her failing health than their momentous discovery. ''Stacy—''

She waved off his solicitude. ''No, I'm okay. This is more important at the moment.'' She spread the shirt out across the table. ''Not only is there a button and some of the fabric missing, but this dark streak.'' She pointed to dark smear across the front of the shirt. ''I think it's blood. Either yours or that of the man who killed you.''

Chance stared at the wrinkled shirt, trying to see beyond the dust and filth, trying to imagine the stain when it was a vivid red instead of a rusty gray. The pocket had been torn loose and hung by a few threads. Chance stared at it for a few minutes, then reached up to push it back into place. His hand passed through the material. He stared at his fingers, trying not to feel a sense of betrayal.

Stacy drew a deep breath, then placed her trembling hand on top of his. Instead of a quickening of life, the energy that moved between them melted through his veins like lava. Burning hot, sluggish. Destructive. Together, they pushed the loose flap of material into place, revealing three embroidered initials. *C.E.J.*

After a moment of oppressive silence, Chance found the strength and inspiration to speak. "Edward."

A tear trickled down Stacy's face.

"My middle name is Edward." He pulled his hand from hers, unwilling to face the revelations of the dead with borrowed life.

"It's a lovely name," she managed between sniffs.

"I was named after . . . my father." A fleeting flash of memory provided him with an image of an old man. His father? Had his father outlived his own son? Some inner voice said no.

Chance closed his eyes, wondering if this new memory would start a flood of other recollections; would the answers to a thousand questions inundate him in the next few moments?

His mind went blank.

But as suddenly as ignorance swelled, another sensation crept into his consciousness. He sensed a second presence in the room. Chance opened his eyes at the same time Stacy gasped. Together, they watched an apparitional form materialize slowly in front of them.

Rather than face down the specter of dusty death, Chance grabbed Stacy's hand. As he expected, the physical contact forced the figure to fade out of view. But Chance decided not to push their luck. "Run!" He dragged her toward the door.

"Wait!" She lurched out of his grasp and stretched across the table, trying to reach the stained shirt. The mysterious figure in black started forming again.

"Hurry!" He snatched her hand again and jerked her toward the door. They barely controlled their thundering trip down the steps to the first landing. Seeing no one behind them, he signaled for them to pause in order to get their breath and collect their thoughts. Stacy sagged against him and he braced her. "You okay?"

"F-for the moment. How about—oh no . . . Chance!" She pointed over his shoulder as she gasped his name.

The unwanted visitor began to materialize beside them on the landing. Chance adopted a protective stance between Stacy and their deadly visitor, but a few seconds later, he found himself mesmerized by a familiar face that wavered into focus.

Stacy felt his hand slip out of hers, all thoughts of maintaining contact forgotten at the moment. To her dismay, he took a half step toward the figure.

"Dad?"

The man smiled and nodded. "Chance, Son, it's time to go."

Stacy compared the two faces, seeing the obvious similarity between father and son. But something didn't ring true. Something wasn't right.

"Chance . . ." she called, taking a stumbling step toward him. When she tripped and fell against him, it brought him to life. The image of his father flickered, then faded away.

"Dad!" Chance reached out toward the disappearing figure. "Don't go."

Stacy clutched Chance for support, unwilling to let him break contact again.

"No . . . let go! That was my father, Stacy." A sense of supreme wonderment filled his face. "Don't you understand? My father! My way home . . ."

Despite his efforts to break her grip, Stacy hung onto him. "Stop, Chance. It's a trick. It's got to be a trick!"

Chance spun around, wearing his sense of betrayal like a badge. "How can you say that, Stace? Don't you understand? He died when I was a kid and I've missed him ever since." He jerked out of her grasp and pivoted, facing the unknown with blind expectation.

The figure wavered into sight again. "It's time to go home, Son. You can rest easy because the truth has been revealed.

Your killer will get his just due and your spirit can rest easy now." He reached out his hand and gave Chance a paternal, beckoning smile.

"Truth?" Stacy rushed toward the figure, blocking his passage to Chance. "Try telling the truth yourself. You're not his father." Her accusation rang out clear in the empty hallway.

"But Stacy . . ."

She pivoted and grabbed Chance by the shoulders, hoping their physical contact would drive the accursed demon back to whatever pit he sprang from. "Think, Chance. How old were you when your father died?"

He looked past her shoulder, his face still registering a look of bemused satisfaction at the prospect of joining his father. Stacy turned around long enough to see that the figure, although faded, had not gone away completely as he had before. Whatever power her touch represented, was weakening. She had to fill the gap in her defenses with logic.

She demanded his attention with a steely-eyed stare and a voice of authority. "Chance Edward Johnson, answer the question, now! How old were you when your father died."

He had a hard time turning his gaze back to her, his attention drawn elsewhere like iron filings to a magnet. She moved quickly, pulling him around until his back was to the omnipresent figure.

Chance slowly focused his blank stare her direction. "I was—was . . . ten when he died." He looked over his shoulder like a small child seeking assurance from a parent. "Right, Dad?"

Stacy watched the specter's face tighten in disapproval. Logic scored its first hit. "Chance, if you were ten, then how old was your father?"

Logical reasoning began to gain a foothold in his thoughts. His mesmerized look sharpened as he began to calculate an answer. His voice lost its sound of passive acceptance. "Thirty-five. He was only thirty-five when he died."

Stacy jerked him around before the damage could be rectified.

"Look at this impostor. He's an old man because that's what he thought your father ought to be. A kind, old gray-haired gentleman, but your father wasn't old, was he?"

A look of fiery comprehension replaced the blind certainty. "You're right. Dad didn't have gray hair. He was a young man, my age when he died. Like father, like son." A new rage fueled the fire in his eyes. "But nothing like *you!*"

Robbed of the support of false conviction, the figure began to transform before it faded away. The gentle smile turned into a grimace and the caring hand, a bony claw. A moment later, he was gone.

Chance turned and pulled her into his arms, crushing her in an iron grip. "How could I do something that stupid? How could I believe him? Over you?" Chance held on for dear life. "I'm so sorry . . ."

Suddenly, she was a dead weight in his arms. "Stace?" There was no answer. "Stacy?" He braced her with one hand around her waist and one supporting her lolling head.

"S-so tired," she spoke, barely moving her lips. "S-sleepy."

Rising panic took over, whispering that this unearthly lethargy was as unnatural for her as living was for him. He hoisted her into his arms and moved as quickly down the stairs as caution would allow him. At the foot of the stairs, he adjusted her limp body more securely in his arms and started down the long corridor toward the mall.

Suddenly, in the hallway, a black silhouette of a man filled the hallway. Chance skidded to a stop and retreated, realizing that there were no other routes of escape other than the stairs leading back to the hidden room.

Stacy began to gasp for breath. Knowing that her health, her safety was his primary concern, he lowered her gently to the floor. After all, Death was after Chance's wayward soul, not her earthbound one.

"Sssh . . . calm down, sweetheart. Everything's going to be fine." He brushed her hair out of her face. The moment he broke contact, her breathing grew easier. Chance suddenly realized the lethal implications of his touch.

The dark figure approached.

Stacy roused enough to see their unwanted visitor and her protective instinct was to reach out and take Chance's hand. The moment she touched Chance's wrist, the image flickered, but kept coming in their direction.

The figure stepped into a revealing pool of overhead light. He was no hollow-cheeked specter, no apparition of doom, but an ordinary-looking man. He wore a hooded black sweatshirt, a pair of matching sweat pants, and an almost angelic smile.

"You . . . can't . . . have . . . him," she croaked between gasps for breath.

His smile dimmed a bit. "But it's my job."

Chance pried her fingers from his arm. "Stacy, what you're doing is wrong. When we touch, you're giving me your life." He pushed her hand away.

The man nodded. "And right now, you don't have too much of that to spare, Miss Reardon."

She leaned up on one elbow. "Y-you know my name?"

"Sure. You're Stacy Reardon and this gentleman is the very elusive Chance Edward Johnson. Now, how did that go? 'Chance Johnson, Bon Vivant, Epicurean, All-Around Nice Guy also known as . . .' " The lights flashed and the sound of thunder echoed down the corridor. "The Phantom of the Shopping Mall," the man announced in a shaky, spook-house voice. The lights returned to normal to highlight his slightly flushed face. "Uh . . . sorry. That was a little overboard, wasn't it? But it seems appropriate at the moment."

Theatrical? Chance thought. Somehow it did seem like an appropriate special-effect scene out of their macabre comedy of the absurd. "It seems unfair that you know our names, but we don't know yours."

The man scratched his chin. "True . . . true. However, I'm afraid you couldn't pronounce my name."

Chance shrugged. If their bantering was buying Stacy time

to recover, then he'd keep it up forever if necessary. "Just as long as your name's not Lucifer or Beelzebub."

The man drew a solemn cross across his heart. "It's not. Scout's honor." He snapped his fingers. "That's it! That's a good name for me—Scout." He crossed his arms and sighed. "You've led me on a merry chase, sir. But I'm afraid it's time to go."

"No!" Stacy lunged at Chance, throwing her arms around him.

As her life flooded into him, there was with it a sense of solace, of incomparable unity of mind, body, soul. It was unlike any other sensation he had ever experienced.

"Most people call it love," Scout supplied. "Quite frankly, we don't often run into love that's this strong. This connection you two have . . . it's pretty impressive."

Chance looked down at the pale woman who clung to him, giving him her life so he could exist at a time and in a place where he shouldn't.

"I won't let you go, Chance." She managed a weak smile as she laced her cold fingers with his. "I'll hold your hand forever if I have to."

"I'm afraid that's not an option at this point." Scout took another step toward them. "Let me make it easy on you. I'm here to collect a soul." He held out his hands as if cradling an invisible treasure in them. The look he gave Chance was dark, yet not foreboding. "It can be yours." There was a brief flicker in Scout's fathomless eyes as he shifted his gaze from Chance to Stacy. "Or it can be hers."

Alarm bells went off in Chance as his protective instincts went on full alert. But how could he best protect Stacy? The very act of holding her and protecting her from this taker of souls might be the same act that killed her. He felt only the thinnest thread of life trickling out of her and into him. She wouldn't be able to keep it up much longer.

Scout moved even closer, squatting down beside them on the floor. "You see there was a mistake made when your soul, your essence of being was allowed to stay here and it's upsetting the balance of power in this area."

"Power?"

"Sure. The Presence who tried to fool you by pretending to be your father? He's one of the more unsavory denizens of the unseen world. Nasty guy—I've run into him before. He wouldn't have been able to enter the realm here if it weren't for the imbalance you're causing. Lucky for you, the power of love was strong and it prevented him from taking you where you really don't want to go. But . . ."

Scout stood and held out his hand. "This is no time for theological discussions. I'm required to bring back one soul and one soul only. My instructions aren't specific about whose soul. It's more of an accounting situation, I suppose. If you come with me now, Stacy lives. If you wait, Stacy dies because you would have literally sucked all of the life out of her."

"D-don't listen to him." Stacy held a trembling hand to Chance's cheek. "I have faith."

Faith. Faith to move mountains. Infinite faith.

Scout nodded. "Yes you do, Stacy. It's one of your greatest strengths. But faith isn't enough to provide sustenance for both of you. Give him up. Let him go back to where he belongs. This is his only chance."

"He's my only Chance, too."

Scout sighed and ran his hand through his hair. "I forgot how exasperating mortals can be!" He turned his back to them and for one shining moment, Chance thought the man just might leave. But instead, Scout pivoted.

"I can be patient. Pretty soon her energy will give out and she will most certainly die long before her scheduled time. And because I can only take one soul with me, I'm going to leave one of you behind. Either you go with me now, voluntarily, and we leave Stacy behind alive and able to live the rest of her natural life, or I take her and leave you behind to contend with the darker forces by yourself. You won't have her love to protect you."

"I don't want—" Her body convulsed as she gasped for breath.

Chance placed a kiss on her forehead. "Don't try to talk." He lifted her gently, sliding out from beneath her. It pained him to lower her head carefully to the hard floor. As soon as he broke contact, she drew in another shuddering gasp and opened her eyes.

"I don't want to live without you." She reached for him, but Chance dodged her weak attempt.

It wasn't a difficult choice. He was already dead and Stacy didn't deserve to die on his account. And he could never sentence her to such a lonesome fate as haunting the mall forever.

"Please . . . don't leave me."

Her words cut through him with the precision of a surgeon's scalpel. But despite the break in their physical contact, the link was still there. He felt every fragment of her fear, every shard of her shattered hopes, every shred of her broken dreams. And in the midst of all that, was her love, strengthened by adversity and tempered by tragedy. Her love, her faith were both more than he could take.

More than he should take.

Chance faced the sympathetic figure standing next to him. "Take me."

"No . . . don't leave me." Stacy struggled to touch him but Chance moved out of the way.

"Don't make this any harder than it already is, Stacy." He took refuge in the fact that in a few moments, the ability to feel emotion would fade away, but to his dismay, the desire to touch her one more time, to kiss her, to love her still remained. He pivoted and glared at Scout. "Why can I still feel the pain? We're not touching." He turned back to Stacy, finding himself ravaged by the mere sight of her tear-streaked face.

Scout offered his hand, palm open. "It wouldn't be fair for her to share the burden, the grief alone. It always hurts when you say good-bye and this time should be no different for you as well."

Good-bye? Stacy gathered all her strength to hold out her hand, but when she saw the look of determination and sorrow on Chance's face, she surrendered to the onslaught of true love which whispered that even if Chance left, their love would stay alive for an eternity.

She shifted her hand, stretching her fingers out as if placing her hand against a simple pane of glass which separated two lovers. "I love you, Chance."

Tears brimmed in his eyes and he mirrored her gesture. "I love you, Stacy."

"And someday I'll find you, wherever you are and tell you I love you again. Will you wait for me?"

"Forever. Good-bye, Stacy."

"Good-bye Chance."

Scout gave her a solemn nod and put his arm around Chance's shoulders, leading him to the stairs.

With each step up, their image dimmed a bit. The sounds of their footfalls on the metal treads subsided until Stacy couldn't hear it over the sound of blood rushing in her ears. As they reached the first landing, they didn't turn and instead an image of another staircase appeared on the wall. Stepping onto the first step, Chance turned around. Stacy struggled to focus on his wavering image.

Forever.

The room darkened, the images faded.

Chapter Seventeen

"Start a drip with ten percent Ringer's Lactate."

Voices rang out in the darkness.

"Oh my God, oh my God . . ."

Am I dead?

"Get me two units of O negative and clear out Trauma One!"

"Vitals?"

"BP ninety over sixty and shocky. Pulse thirty-two and dropping."

"Run a strip."

"We haven't lost one all day, folks. Let's not lose this one. C'mon . . ."

"BP's going down. Seventy-five over forty. Pulse twenty-four thin and thready. We have respiratory distress."

"C'mon, damn you. Breathe! Breathe!"

In the darkness, there was no pain. No desire. No longing. But there was still love. A slender silver thread of love which bound two souls together across an infinite universe. A thread which could become a ladder given the proper circumstances and the proper need for rescue.

Stacy clung to that silvery ladder, climbing out of the depths of unconsciousness and back into a world of light.

Bright light.

Harsh light from machines that bleeped and buzzed.

"A hospital?"

Stacy fought to make sense of what she saw. Finally, the pieces sorted themselves out in a logical manner. She was in a bed, in a hospital, hooked up to God-only-knew how many machines. She fumbled with the wires that had been taped to her finger and an unholy howl pierced the air.

A nurse skidded into the room, stethoscope in hand. Her look of determination faded into a relaxed smile. "You're awake! What a relief. We've been worried about you. It was touch and go for a while there."

"Where am I?"

"St. Margaret's. ICU." The nurse started to examine her, looking into Stacy's eyes and listening to her heart. "You were found lying unconscious in one of the service corridors of Chapel Valley Mall. Do you remember what happened?"

Stacy remembered it all too well, but knew that any admission of the truth would have her shifted from the ICU directly to the psychiatric ward. "Uh . . . no. I only remember feeling faint. I guess I passed out. How long have I been here?"

The woman patted her hand. "I know it may seem like yesterday to you, but you've been here two weeks."

"Two weeks, Peg! How in the world have you been able to keep things going without me?"

Peg nudged the box of candy nearer Stacy. "Eat another one. You look like you could use the calories."

"The store," Stacy prompted. "How did you keep the store running?"

Peg leaned forward and dropped her voice to a whisper. Promise not to tell the police?"

"The p-police? What do they have to do with it?"

"Nothing with the store. It's just that Raymond Kellogg, the bank manager, could get into trouble if anybody knew how we fudged the rules. We opened a new account for the store in your name and mine and I started to put all our deposits in the new account. That way I could access that money and write checks to pay the bills. We avoided the legal hassle of needing a court order and all that which would have kept the store closed for a couple of days and quite frankly, we needed the revenue. Ray's been keeping the books balanced down to the last penny and he countersigned every check I wrote just to make sure we were protecting your investment. And I did hire some temporary part-time help."

"Who?"

"Remember Evie from the music store? She needed some more hours but Dennis couldn't up her work schedule until another employee finished the semester. This way Evie gets more work, Dennis is happy because it's not like we're stealing his employee because it's only temporary. And we have someone basically trustworthy and pretty sharp working for us."

"That was brilliant. Did you give yourself a raise?"

Peg looked shocked at the notion. "Of course not!"

Stacy smiled, knowing her friend had fallen for the bait. "Then you should have. You're the best buddy and employee a girl could have. Thanks, Peg."

Peg stuffed another coconut candy in her mouth. "The person we really need to thank is your guardian angel."

Stacy's stomach performed a flip-flop. "My—my what?"

"Guardian angel. What other explanation can there be? What else can explain a wiring malfunction in the fire alarm that led the security guards right to you? Good Lord, you could've been there for hours and nobody would have even thought to look for you in that hallway. It's almost never used. Anyway, I think when you get out of here, we ought to—"

She stopped, interrupted by a rap on the door.

"Come in," Stacy replied.

An orderly from ICU named Randy slipped into the room. Stacy had made quick friends with him as he wheeled her from intensive care to a normal room. All it had taken was a promise of twenty dollars and an important request.

"Did you find it?" she asked anxiously.

He shook his head. "Nope. I asked everybody about it. All we can figure out is that it got thrown away. No one realized it might be important since it was torn and dirty."

Peg shot her a quizzical look. "Something missing?"

Stacy drew a deep breath. "Nothing really. I guess I don't need it now."

In some ways, the shirt had already served its purpose. Chance was the one who really needed to know that he hadn't killed himself. But without the proof substantiating a case of murder rather than suicide, she wouldn't be able to help the police find the real criminal. That is, if the police would be likely to listen to her at all. After the stunt she pulled in Lieutenant Harrold's office, she didn't have a ghost of a chance of being believed.

But as long as Chance knew the truth . . .

The nurse gave Stacy a big smile. "Ready to check out?"

It had been a long torturous week of recovery, more so because the doctors still wanted to understand why she'd been sick in the first place. They poked, prodded, and made absolute nuisances of themselves as she became a medical anomaly rather than a person who desperately wanted to get out of an expensive hospital and use what was left of her life's savings for living. One astute doctor described her as being totally drained. She wondered if he realized how close he was to the truth.

"I'm very anxious to get out of here. But can we swing by

Intensive Care first? I want to find Randy and thank him for doing something special for me."

"Sure." The nurse pushed the wheelchair toward the elevator and it took all of Stacy's strength and determination to control her moment of overwhelming panic as the doors slid open. She released her grip on the chair arms only after seeing the car had arrived safely.

Once they got to the Intensive Care Ward, the nurse parked Stacy by the monitoring station while she went off to find the orderly. Stacy glanced around at all the equipment, knowing that technology had saved her life. Yet, the doctors finally admitted they couldn't figure out why she'd almost died in the first place.

She knew they'd never believe her story about a ghost named Chance and a soul-taker named Scout.

Chance. Every time she thought of him, she pictured him standing on his stairway to heaven, making a promise which would stand the tests of eternity.

Forever.

A simple word.

Such a difficult concept to grasp. Nothing could last forever.

Except love.

She knew she only imagined his voice responding to her. But she still took solace from the thought that he existed somewhere, in a great timeless beyond, waiting for her.

I'll always love you, Chance, she told her mental image of him.

A shrill alarm pierced the air. A flashing light pulsed over one of the units beyond the glass wall. Nurses sprang from everywhere, converging on one bed on the far end. Equipment was wheeled in. Voices shouted orders.

"Clear!"

She recognized the static sound of the electrical discharge. Someone was being shocked back to life. Successfully, she hoped. Perhaps it was the same principle that had given Chance his life. After all, that was what a pacemaker did on a more limited scope—providing an outside stimulus to keep the heart beating.

The nurse appeared, pushing Stacy's wheelchair toward the door. "C'mon we better get you out of here. Randy's going to be busy."

Stacy looked up at the passing monitor and watched the doctors pour over their patient. A white figure shifted past the camera and then Stacy got a clear view of the patient's face.

Chance?

"Wait!" She grabbed the door frame and the nurse stumbled into the back of the wheelchair.

"What is it?"

Stacy stood up and raised a hand to touch the monitor. Someone stood in front of the camera, blocking her view. "Move, damn you! I've got to see!"

The nurse placed a firm hand on Stacy's shoulder. "Calm down. This isn't good for you. I'm sure they're going to save the patient. Our ICU team is one of the best in the state. Just calm down."

Stacy felt electrical prickles flow down her arms. "Move," she whispered, "Just let me get one more look."

One more look.

One more . . .

"One more night, eh?"

Stacy gave the nurse a sullen nod as the woman tucked the sheets around her. "Now you get a good night's sleep so you can go home tomorrow for real!"

Stacy's heart rocked her chest, marking time in milliseconds. She'd have to wait for the activity level outside to subside before she tried to sneak out. Once she had woken up from her faint in the ICU ward, she'd found herself back in the same room as before, listening to the same doctors puzzle over her condition. But this time, they proclaimed it merely a result of overexertion and told her they wanted to keep her one more night for observation.

After they left, she'd conned one of the nurses into finding Randy, her helpful orderly. When she described Chance to him, Randy gave her a blank stare.

"We don't have anybody who sounds like that in the ICU right now. A couple of old geezers with heart problems, but nobody young like that."

Later on, Stacy decided that anybody who could profess to having had prolonged discussions with both a ghost and the Angel of Death, had a perfect right to believe in conspiracies. And she was going to prove that Randy was mistaken, the hospital admissions people were lying, that *everybody* was wrong and that Chance Johnson was alive somewhere in that hospital.

A half hour later, she crept out of bed and wrapped the faded striped hospital robe around her thin gown. The paper slippers did little to cut the cold from the tile floor. She had a lovely thick green terry-cloth robe Peg had brought her from the store, but this mission required stealth, cunning, and hospital camouflage, which meant worn, faded, and unfortunately, thin attire.

Luckily, her room was right across from the stairwell and she made it from her room to the stairs without being seen. Although her energy level had risen, it still took a lot out of her to climb three flights of stairs to the ICU. By the time she reached the exit door, her heart was racing almost as fast as her mind.

She shuffled toward the monitoring area, hoping to have time to examine each screen before being discovered. She made it to the glassed-in area, careful not to make any noise which would alert the nurse sitting in front of all the monitors. Stacy pressed her forehead against the smooth glass, willing her tired eyes to focus on the screens beyond the window.

"You didn't believe me, Miss Reardon?"

Stacy pivoted and found Randy looming over her. Before

she could offer a rebuttal, he sighed and crooked his finger, pointing to a seat just inside the door.

When the monitoring nurse turned around, he waved away her attention. "No problem. I've got this under control." He faced Stacy. "You can see all the screens and readouts from here without being in the way. Anyway, you look as if you're about to drop. Maybe this is the ward where you still need to be."

"I always look like that. Haven't you noticed?" She started at the screen where she had last seen Chance's slack face. "This one. This is where I saw him." There was a middle-aged man on the screen with wires sticking out from beneath the bandage wrapped around his head.

"That's Mr. Beeton. He's been here three weeks. Boating accident. He has a wife, three kids, and an 'oops' baby on the way."

Stacy remembered the pregnancy home-test kit. Her voice cracked. "I hope he gets better. The children need their father." She skipped to the next monitor, wondering if she could have simply wanted so badly for it to be Chance that she fooled herself for a few important seconds.

Randy nodded. "They're a nice family. They don't deserve this crap. Nobody does."

She examined each of the other monitors, but found no one remotely resembling Chance. She pushed herself up from the chair, resigned to the fact that imagination in the hands of the wrong person could be a dangerous weapon.

"Thanks, Randy. I'm sorry I doubted you."

He gave her a sheepish smile. "You didn't doubt me. You simply had to see for yourself. I understand." He scuffed his shoe on the floor. "You want some help sneaking back to your room?"

"Thanks. I would."

They talked, even laughed a little as Randy returned her to her room without alerting the night staff. He helped her into bed, folding her robe neatly and placing it at the bottom of the bed. ''There. Get some sleep and maybe you can escape this madhouse tomorrow.''

''Randy?''

He paused on his way to the door. ''Thanks. I guess I just needed a—'' She stumbled over the word, ''—chance to separate fact from fantasy.''

''You're welcome.''

After the door closed, she allowed the threatening tears to escape.

''Yep.'' She sniffed, wiping her eyes with the stiff white sheet. ''I just need a Chance . . .''

''Welcome Back!''

The sign drooped a little in the middle, but Stacy didn't mind. Peg had cooked up the entire party, inviting all the mall merchants who had rallied selflessly to help save Lacy Lady during Stacy's six-week hiatus.

Stacy made sure the credit was given where it was due, on Peg's capable shoulders.

''Ladies and Gentlemen,'' she'd called out in her strongest voice. ''I'd like to propose a toast.'' Coffee cups had been held high. ''To Peg Sullivan, my new assistant manager.'' The cheers were deafening, almost drowning out Peg's murmur of thanks as they hugged.

Now that the celebration was over, life would go back to normal, or at least as normal as it could be, considering she had a gaping hole where her heart used to be. Stacy was glad to send Peg out on errands while she stayed behind, sitting on the stool that several of the merchants had given her. The ladies from the fabric store had made her a cushion for the stool, color-coordinated to match the store's decor.

Perched on her new throne, Stacy sipped her tea and watched the world pass nonchalantly by, heedless of heartache and oblivious to grief. She doodled on the morning paper, eventually turning to the puzzle section and idly filling out the crossword puzzle.

"Stacy?"

She jumped, looking up into Chuck Canton's smiling face.

"Sorry I missed the party this morning. I was out kind of late, last night."

Although she knew not to fall for his "ask me about my new girlfriend" routine, it had been almost a month since she'd seen his smirking face and she almost missed him. "Got a new girlfriend, Chuck?"

His next reaction took her entirely by surprise. He ducked his head, his face reddened, and he nodded. "Yeah . . . I do."

Chuck Canton? Embarrassed? She checked her calendar. Yep, it was July, all right. Perhaps Hell had indeed frozen over. She cleared her throat. "A new girl? You've been busy while I was gone." With a deep sigh of regret, she managed a smile and uttered the words she never thought she'd hear herself say. "Tell me about her."

Chuck drew circles on the glass counter with his forefinger. "Her name is Mildred."

Stacy heard the echo of Chance's cackle. *"Mildred? Mildread?"*

"Uh . . . she wouldn't be one of Rufus Bryant's nieces, would she?"

He looked up with expectation. "You know Mildred?"

Stacy's forced smile became genuine. "Uh . . . no, but I've heard Rufus bragging about her. She sounds like a lovely girl."

Chuck nodded eagerly. "She is! And I really would like to buy her a present."

Oh boy . . . "What kind of present, Chuck?" Visions of garter belts and G-strings floated through Stacy's mind, followed closely by irate uncles carrying loaded shotguns.

"I'm not sure. I was thinking of—"

A see-through peignoir set? A leather bustier? Her mind pushed to new heights or depths as the case might be. *Edible panties?*

"—one of these sachet things. You know the lace hearts with potpourri inside? Or maybe I ought to stick to the scented soaps. I mean that's a nice gift without appearing too intimate, isn't it?"

"A s-sachet would be . . . lovely. I'm sure she'd appreciate the thought behind it as well."

He beamed. "Fantastic." He pulled out his checkbook, consulted the balance, and shrugged. "Heck . . . you only go around once in life, right? Let me get the sachet *and* the soaps."

Despite feeling totally stunned by their conversation, Stacy managed to tally his purchase. "That'll be $14.38."

"Oh . . . and gift-wrapping. What's your charge for gift-wrapping?"

She gave him almost an indulgent look. "For you, Chuck, absolutely nothing."

He grinned. "Thanks. I'll pick it up at lunch, if that's okay."

Stacy watched him depart, wondering if aliens had landed and kidnapped the Electro Shack manager, replacing him with a clone. But as Chuck left, he gave the silk-clad mannequin a fond look and a little bit of wolf replaced the sheepishness in his smile.

Maybe some things would never change.

Several other clerks and managers dropped in to check on Stacy. Dennis of the RecordRak called her to say that their joint employee, Evie, was available to pinch-hit if Stacy started feeling tired. Stacy thanked her friend for his generosity and promised to call if she felt like she needed a break.

A parade of potential customers dropped in, evidently wondering if the sign and crepe paper celebrated a sale as well. After a brief downtime, her next customer was a large man with broad shoulders and an impressive weightlifter's build. He declined any help, saying he was just browsing, but when he started to have the glazed look of a man overwhelmed by the medium, suffering from what Peg always called "Silk Overload," Stacy came to his rescue.

"You look overwhelmed."

He nodded. ''I had no idea there were so many . . . styles. I figured women's lingerie was . . . lingerie.''

It was a typical response and she knew how to help him narrow his focus. ''Are you buying for a particular occasion?''

''Yes.'' He seemed relieved. ''We're going to Brazil on . . . vacation and I want to surprise my wife with some lounging wear.''

''Follow me.'' Stacy led him away from the nightgowns and pulled out a three-piece matching silk outfit. ''How about something like this?''

He nodded. ''Much nicer. Do you have something like this in aqua?''

Stacy found the same style in aqua and was pleased to discover that the man knew his wife's size. ''Will there be anything else?''

He selected three more outfits and to Stacy's delight, pulled out a Gold MasterCard to pay for everything. Totaling up the purchase, she ran his card through the machine for authorization. Unfortunately, the lines were busy.

''Are you in a hurry sir?''

He shook his head. ''Not really.''

''I thought I'd wait a minute for the lines to clear up to the credit card company. But, since these are gifts, would you like me to gift-wrap them?''

''Sure. That'll be great.''

While Stacy lined gift boxes with tissue paper, the man leaned against the counter, eventually pulling her newspaper toward him. ''You mind?''

''No. Go right ahead.''

''Are you a crossword fan?''

She glanced at the half-filled puzzle consisting of more erasures than answers. ''I like them, but they don't like me.''

''Me either. I like those anagram puzzles better. The answers always jump put at me. Like this one. *Nego Whti Eth Dinw.*''

She selected a ribbon to match the paper. ''It sounds like Greek to me.''

"More like Greek Revival. If you scramble it, it's *Gone With The Wind.*"

Stacy turned and glared at the letters. "If you say so. I can never see those. But what's with the Greek Revival stuff?"

"Remember Tara? Scarlett's home? That type of architecture is called Greek Revival."

"Oh." Stacy ran his card through the machine which responded with the appropriate code numbers. Writing the authorization code on the slip, she handed him the pen. "Name and telephone number, please."

He signed with a flourish.

After comparing signatures, she handed him his receipts, the card, and the bag containing his wrapped packages. "Thanks, Mr. Browne. I hope you enjoy your vacation."

"Vacation?" He looked confused for a moment. "Oh . . . yes. Thank you."

After he left, Stacy turned back to her paper. He had filled out several key clues in the crossword puzzle and every one of the anagrams. At the bottom of the page, he'd doodled the words, *Rive, ripa, river.*

She started laughing. Now she knew exactly where Mr. Neal L. Browne, the Anagram King was headed for his vacation: Rio de Janeiro. *Lucky stiff.*

She pushed the paper out of the way and allowed herself to daydream about exotic trips to foreign ports. But somehow a certain spectral architect kept popping into her thoughts.

Peg returned from her errand in time for Stacy to have a leisurely lunch. But once she stepped into the Food Court, the appeal of fast food faded as she remembered watching Chance happily grimace away the effects of brain freeze. After buying a milk shake in his honor, she found herself doing a Chance Johnson Memorial Tour, visiting the places where they had spent time together. For one wild moment, she thought about visiting the hidden room, but dismissed the notion quickly. She was too recently out of the hospital to deliberately place herself under that kind of stress.

Instead, she headed for the bench by the ferns, hoping to remember some of their calmer moments. As she headed toward the fountain, she spotted the bronze plaque. Would it hurt so much to see his name again?

She ran her fingers over the letters of his name. *Designed by Chance Johnson.* Other words snagged her attention for the first time. *Johnson, Browne, and Associates.*

Browne?

Was it merely coincidence that he had the same name as her affluent customer that morning?

Stacy heard echoes of their conversation, suddenly finding significant meaning in his innocent remarks. Of course he was an architect; who else would see things in terms of architectural concepts, like Greek Revival?

An architect going on an extended vacation to Brazil, . . . *where there are no extradition agreements with the United States.* Whether the voice originated in her head or not, she started lining up the mental dominoes.

Was her customer Chance's partner?

She headed for the escalator, finding herself impatient with the customers who blocked her way. She almost ran into her store, ignoring Peg's admonishment to save her energy. Stacy opened the register and pawed through the credit card receipts.

''*Neal L. Browne.*'' The King of Anagrams. A sneaking suspicion added a few more dominoes to the hypothetical lineup.

''What's gotten into you, girl?''

''Peg, what was the name of the company that built this mall? The ones Danny worked for?''

''Bains & Bowren Contracting.''

Bowren. It took no Queen of Anagrams to mentally scramble Browne into Bowren.

''Peg, do you remember Bowren's first name?''

The woman twisted her mouth in concentration. ''Irby? Or something like that?''

''No, that was Irwin Bains. The other one, Bowren. What's his name?''

Peg shrugged. "I don't know. You want me to find out?"

"How?"

Peg pulled the Yellow Pages from beneath the countertop, flipped through the pages, then reached over and dialed a telephone number.

"Yes, this is Ivy Greenblatt's secretary. She's got me sending your Mr. Bowren a letter, but she's too embarrassed to admit she doesn't remember his first name . . . Yes . . . with two L's? Thanks, hon." She shot Stacy a smile. "His first name is Allen."

Stacy copied it down, watching how *Allen* became *Neal L.* with little effort. "Why that bastard . . ."

"Someone you know well?" Peg inquired.

"Someone who made life miserable for a friend of mine. I think it's time someone returned the favor." Stacy took the credit slip back to her desk and used the phone there. She blessed the day that the phone-company saleswoman convinced her to buy Caller ID. It allowed her to eliminate her own number from someone else's Caller ID. Like that of the police department.

"May I speak to Lt. Harrold in Homicide?"

After a few transferring clicks, she heard a familiar voice. "This is Harrold."

She belatedly thought she should have covered the receiver with material, but it was too late for that. She drew a deep breath. "Consider this an anonymous tip. Chance Johnson didn't commit suicide. His partner, Neal L. Browne who also goes under the name of Allen Bowren either killed him or had him killed."

"How do you know this?"

She ignored his question and continued. "That means Browne is actually the silent partner in the construction company that built the mall. His partner, Irwin Bains, has a cousin who works on the mall's security force and very likely that person was responsible for destroying or hiding the tapes that showed Mr. Johnson being thrown from the second floor of the mall, not the third."

"I need proof."

"Most of it has been inadvertently destroyed. The guard has a button from Johnson's shirt with incriminating fingerprints."

"But Johnson's shirt wasn't missing a button."

"That wasn't his shirt. Surely you realized it didn't fit. It was someone else's. Perhaps the murderer's."

"Why are you telling us all this now?"

"I only just put it together. I found out today that Browne is planning a trip to Rio de Janeiro. You can't get him back from Brazil, can you?"

Harrold sighed. "No. But I sure as hell can stop him from going. This is the break we needed."

She heard papers rustling in the background.

"Let me give you a code name and a number to call. Check in every few days. If we need to talk to you, you'll hear your code name on the announcement. Then you call me and we'll compare notes. Okay?"

Stacy dutifully copied down the telephone number.

"And your code name will be *Amicus Curiae,* okay?"

He knew.

He knew exactly who she was but he was giving her an opportunity to protect her identity. Or was it merely a warning? Chance had said something about wondering if the police work had merely been sloppy or if they were covering up something.

Had she just given them ammunition to catch a killer or to eliminate the person who had put it all together?

She hung up the phone.

And began to cry.

Chapter Eighteen

Stacy waited for a harried twenty-four hours before calling the special number the lieutenant had given her. To her relief, there was no message for *Amicus Curiae.* But it didn't mean they hadn't acted on the information.

Stacy squirted glass cleaner on the countertop and rubbed it with more vigor than necessary. It squeaked as if in protest and she doubled her efforts, trying to wipe out the inner voice which reminded her that at the moment, the police could either be arresting Neal Browne for the murder of his partner or perhaps, someone was simply waiting for an opportune time to gun her down.

"Stacy?"

She jumped.

"Good Lord, girl." Chuck grabbed her by the elbow, steadying her. "You're scareder than a turkey in November. What's going on?"

"Nothing." She pulled back and stared at him. " 'Scareder than a turkey in November'? You've been hanging around Rufus too much. You're starting to sound like him."

He released her to perform an elegant shrug. "What can I say? He's Mildred's favorite uncle and man, can he cook!" Chuck crossed his arms and gave her a critical once-over. It used to be, that sort of overt attention from him made her nervous. Now, somewhere along the line, true love had mellowed him; Mildred had worked wonders, shaving off his rough edges and giving him a sense of purpose.

Of course, Chuck wasn't the only one who'd changed. Stacy had transformed as well. The uninformed attributed it to her near brush with death. However, she attributed it to her near brush with life. And love.

"You're a million miles away today, aren't you?"

She looked up and managed a halfhearted smile. Somewhere in those six long weeks since Chance's final death, Chuck had simply become her friend.

"So what's really wrong with you?" he continued.

She shrugged away his concern. "I'm just a little jumpy today. That's all."

"Well, you're not the only one." He thumbed over his shoulder toward the windows. "This whole mall is turning inside out and unraveling at the seams!"

She scanned the usual throng of summertime shoppers, dressed in shorts, T-shirts, and sunburns. They strolled the mall with their usual air of nonchalance, driven indoors by the unusually high heat combined with the worst drought of the decade. Sales had improved marginally. She watched two mothers across the way stop and greet each other while their brood swarmed around them. "Everything looks normal from here."

Chuck shrugged toward the teeming masses. "What would they know? They never see the undercurrents, the behind-the-scenes drama, the shopkeeper's agony of—"

"Can it Chuck. I'm in no mood for theatrics today."

He shook his head. "It's not theatrics. Can't you feel the erratic pulse of an area about to suffer a major coronary? Don't you sense that ineffable quality of something about to go incredibly wrong?"

"Enough!" She grabbed her damp paper towel, wadded it, and hurled it at him. "If this is more of your structural default theory, I don't want to hear about it."

He crossed his arms and lifted one eyebrow as if he possessed all the secrets of the universe.

She held up the trigger spray bottle. "Are you going to tell me what's going on or am I going to have to shoot you? Or better yet, ask Rufus to explain to me again exactly how you got your hand caught in the drainpipe?"

Chuck flushed a lovely shade of red which faded quickly as pending revelation appeared to be much more topical at the moment. He propped on the counter, ignoring her threats of Windexing him to death. "Did you hear about Derrick?"

The mere mention of the name made her heart start a frantic tempo in her chest. A thousand scenarios popped into her mind: Derrick quitting his job for a prestigious new position in his cousin's construction company, Derrick caught smuggling an assault rifle into the building, Derrick caught planting a bomb—

"He was arrested this morning."

Her heart moved up into her throat. "Arrested? Are you sure?"

Chuck leaned forward, his eyes gleaming with the light of revelation. "I watched the police slap the cuffs on him, read him his rights, and haul him away."

She sagged backward, grateful to find the stool before losing her balance. The last few dominoes were lining up. Just a few more and she'd be finished. She cleared her throat. "Did they say what the charges were?"

Chuck nodded, his excitement evidently giving away to the true seriousness of the situation. "Accessory to murder, extortion, and withholding evidence." He crossed his arms and sighed. "And he seemed like such a normal guy, too. Who would have guessed?" He glanced at his watch. "Oops, I better go. I only have a fifteen-minute break this morning. If I hear anything else, I'll give you a call. Okay?"

"Thanks."

She watched him walk out without tripping the doorchime. So much for Danny's repair job. Ironically, the thing had never worked right since Chance walked through it. He had a way of causing a permanent change in things. In people. He'd changed her life, teaching her an important lesson about the power of love. But as powerful and as lasting as love could be, it couldn't cure everything. It wouldn't repair a broken heart. Maybe someday she'd love again with such ferocity, with such completeness. But the pieces of her heart would always belong to Chance Johnson.

She leaned over the counter, watching her tears form blurry circles on the glass. The droplets helped to distort the image of the items in the case, giving them a wavering, ghostlike appearance.

The door chime interrupted her self-pity party. She looked up, expecting to see a customer. But no one was there.

It rang again.

A sudden chill dropped over her shoulders.

Ding.

She drew in a shaky breath. Was this a sign?

Ding.

Was Chance trying to reach her?

Ding.

Was it truly over? Did the arrests mean his soul was completely free from the burden of guilt?

Ding. Ding. Ding.

She rushed toward the door, half expecting to see his Cheshire-cat grin appear with the rest of him following behind. She stood expectantly in the doorway . . .

. . . and saw the piece of paper fluttering across the reflector that triggered the door chime. As a customer walked by, the resulting breeze made the paper break the beam of light and set off the chime. She snatched the paper and crumpled it into a ball, hurling across her store. She leaned against the glass wall, burying her face in her arms.

Who was she trying to fool?

A young plaintive voice penetrated her misery.

"Mommy . . . why is that lady crying?"

Stacy didn't wait to hear the explanation. She wiped away the tears as best as she could, and straightened up. Her blurred gaze noticed a figure in black coming her way from the far end of the mall. She flinched, having honed an understandable prejudice concerning ominous men dressed in black.

Her eyesight wavered as the tears sharpened her focus then blurred it again. He wore black. A tuxedo? She rubbed her eyes and squinted. He had a familiar walk, a hurried stride with hands pushed in his pockets. He moved with a speed untypical of a shopper trying to escape the heat.

He wore a tuxedo.

And a red tie.

As he approached, her heart recognized what her mind could not accept. Her body responded by propelling her into the crowd of shoppers, dodging them, dodging their bags, their strollers, their children.

He started running as well, and to her utter shock, he dashed around obstacles rather than going through them. The revelation made her come to a complete standstill and she clutched the rail for support.

Chance?

By the time he reached her, he was breathing so hard he couldn't speak. He panted as he bent over, grabbing the rail with one hand and bracing his other palm against his knee.

She found her voice first. "It's really you, isn't it?"

Chance struggled to regain his breath. "Yes . . . me," he squeezed out between gasps. He looked up and his strained smile blossomed into a look that melted her heart. He released the rail and held his hand out to her. "Really me."

She laced her fingers in his. The strong electricity that flowed between them was different this time. It contained their hopes, their thoughts, and their dreams, but no borrowed life.

Chance didn't need it.

His hand was cold, his skin pale, and a perceivable tremor coursed through him, but he was undoubtedly alive.

The worries of the world disappeared as they allowed their passions to blot out all other sensations and thoughts. His lips were just as fiercely gentle as she remembered, his simple touch even more thrilling than recollection allowed. He muttered reassurances which bypassed her ears and went straight to her heart.

In the midst of their frantic reunion, she felt him falter, sagging against her for a moment before he regained his balance. Her skewed sense of logic screamed a warning. *He's not here for good. He's only come back to say good-bye.*

"A Chance to say good-bye? Nothing doing. I'm here for good." He graced her with a pale smile as he tightened his grip around her waist. "Did you miss me while I was gone?"

"But why . . . how?"

He scanned the crowd of curious onlookers who had gathered to cheer on the two lovers. "Kiss her again!" someone called out.

Chance blushed and leaned down, nuzzling her ear. "Let's go somewhere private."

Their gazes locked for a moment, then he shook his head. "I don't ever want to go back to that staircase again. How about your back room?"

Clutching each other, they stumbled back to the store where Stacy released him only long enough to lock the front door. Chance sagged against the door frame as she fumbled with the key.

Concerned by the glazed look on his face, she helped him into the back room and seated him at her desk. Panic bubbled up through her, threatening her tentative control.

"What's wrong?" she asked, dropping to her knees beside him.

He propped his elbows on his knees and cradled his head in his palms. "I've had a helluva day." Another tremor rocked through him.

She felt a nervous smile quirk her lips. She squatted next to him. "Resurrection must take a lot out of guy."

"Not resurrection."

She remembered the fleeting image of a comatose face on a monitor. "Then I didn't imagine it when I saw you in the hospital."

He reached over and cupped her hand to her cheek. "Later, one of the security guards told me they moved me right after you identified me. They were afraid you'd blow the case."

"The case?"

He shot her a pale grin. "It feels so weird . . . having had a part of me here with you while my body was in the hospital. And for me not to have any memory of the fight with Neal. The doctors say I may never get those memories back."

"But you remembered me."

He grabbed her hands. "How could I forget? You were, are my lifeline. But I had no idea that by loaning me life, you were killing yourself. Scout said that if we had maintained contact much longer, you would have died for certain."

She rested her head on his knees. "I . . . I thought he was taking you to heaven."

"Me too. It was a real shock to find out he was taking me back to the hospital."

"But how . . . why . . ." She struggled to find the words.

"How did I become two separate entities? One in the hospital and one here? Scout said that when I fell, that for a moment I was clinically dead, then the paramedics brought me back. He didn't use the word 'soul,' but I think that's what he meant when he said my 'essence' escaped during the moment of my death. And it was his job to reunite me."

"We made it hard on him, didn't we?"

"I think he understood after a while." His smile gained more strength. "You and I . . . we had a life-or-death mission."

Stacy suddenly realized she had news to impart. "Oh! Maybe you haven't heard . . . Derrick Bains was arrested this morning."

"Along with Neal L. Browne, a.k.a. Allen Bowren. They caught Neal at the airport as he was trying to skip the country with his girlfriend."

"I thought he was going with his wife."

Chance smiled and pulled her into an embrace. "Lt. Harrold said he thought you were our informant. He could never figure out your connection to the case."

She pulled back to gape at him. "*Our* informant? You've been working with the police?"

"Only after I woke up, which was four weeks, two days—" He consulted his watch, "—three hours and twenty-six minutes ago. According to our friend, Randy, the orderly, I came out of my coma after suffering cardiac arrest." He took her face in his hands. "I heard you, Stacy," he said in a low voice. "I heard you say you loved me. And from that moment on, I started fighting my way back."

Stacy rose from her position on the floor, wrapping her arms around him. She held him, knowing she wanted to be with him for eternity. She heard him sniff and his embrace tightened.

"I wanted to call you as soon as I could manage to dial a phone, but Harrold wouldn't let me. I was a protected witness, their hidden weapon. Unfortunately, I knew why someone wanted to kill me, I even knew who likely wanted me dead, but I couldn't testify about who tried to murder me because I simply didn't remember."

Stacy shuddered, remembering how tall and strong Neal Browne appeared. He had most likely been a formidable foe.

"But, because of your tip," Chance continued, "the police raided Derrick's collection of home movies and found the tape of my death he was using as blackmail against his cousin. It sealed the case against Neal. They arrested him and I'm a free man. I checked out of the hospital, stopped home long enough to put on my tuxedo, and came here."

He nudged her back a bit and motioned for her to stand. Shifting out of the chair, he stood stiffly, his hands clutching hers.

"I'm real. Flesh and blood. I'm not as talented as a real man as I was as a ghost. I can't fly, I can't walk through walls, maybe I can't even read your mind any more. But I do love you. With all my heart, body, mind, and soul. And I'd like a chance to prove it."

A chance?

My Chance?

His serious expression melt into a grin. "But I'll warn you. I tire out more easily than I used to."

She grinned back. "Prove it."

Epilogue

Pavlachek "Scout" Strylezewski watched from a carefully planned distance, knowing that Stacy and Chance might feel his presence if he came much closer. Their emotions made the air crackle and dance, stirring an uneasy reaction in Scout.

Joy and jealousy.

It had been a long time since he'd felt sentiments such as those. Separately, they posed no threat to him, but when combined, they made for an unbearably bittersweet moment. Memories, dreams, experiences all blended together to such an extent he could barely remember which was which.

He chastised himself. He had neither the luxury of time nor the necessity of the spirit to worry about the lives and times of two mortals or even his brief dabble with a mortal existence. He had other worries.

Although Chance had peacefully returned to his rightful plane of existence, the scars of his initial penetration into Scout's world were still fresh. And the Denizens knew that scars were the best place for new assaults.

Scout would have to remain ever vigilant to guard this portal between worlds. He couldn't ever let himself be distracted again by the follies and fancies of those very beings whose existence he protected. He needed his strength, his attention, and most importantly, his cunning all devoted to his single duty.

Scout watched the two lovers kiss.

The Veil turned faster, the bright colors sparkling in the fountain below. It was the Veil which had separated Chance's body and soul when he fell through it and the Veil, as well, that allowed him to be reunited. All Scout really had to do was lead Chance through once last time. It only took one passage to unravel his life into separate strands but three trips through to braid them back up again. One by design, one by accident, and one by choice.

They kissed again and their unspoken pledges filled the air.

Bittersweet, Scout muttered to himself. A balloon floated toward him on the waves of a child's cry. He willed it back into the little boy's hands and the Veil pulsed with the power of the child's teary smile.

Bittersweet.

Dear readers,

First, thanks for all the cards and letters. I never expected so many!

Many of the letters have a common question. Where in the heck do your ideas come from? (which I think is a polite way to say "My goodness, <cough> you have a wild imagination!)

This book, like A MARGIN IN TIME, has a variety of inspirations as its source. I'll be the first to admit that QUANTUM LEAP pioneered the "how to talk to an invisible man without looking like you're crazy" concept and I stole liberally from it. My rationale? How could I improve on perfection? Thanks, Sam, Al, and Mr. Bellisario.

Stacy even mentioned my second inspiration when she likened their predicament to an episode of TWILIGHT ZONE. There was a marvelous episode of TWILIGHT ZONE that has haunted me for years. It was called "Nothing in the Dark," written by George Clayton Johnson, first aired in January 1962. (No I didn't see the original broadcast and incidentally, since the show's been aired off and on for over thirty years, I'll take a chance of spoiling the ending for you.) An old woman refuses to leave her building, even though it's slated for demolition, because she's afraid of death. But she takes pity on an injured policeman (played by a very young and very blond Robert Redford) who, as it turns out, is actually the Angel of Death, come to show her that she need not fear her trip to the afterlife. It was a touching episode and helped to shape the ending to CHANCE OF A LIFETIME. (My biggest change was to recast Mel Gibson in the role. He did so well as the new MAVERICK, I thought he'd excel equally as well in my story.)

But the big surprise is what sources didn't influence me; somehow, down the line, I never saw GHOST. I've certainly seen clips from it, viewed the trailers, read the reviews, but never saw the complete film. In fact, after this story started percolating in my mind, I deliberately stayed away from the movie, fearing that it might influence me to go in a different direction.

This is probably more than you'd ever want to know about how my mind works. However, be assured that I do try to research every book thoroughly and in this case, it meant many trips to the mall. What a sacrifice we writers make . . .

Incidentally, for those of you who enjoyed A MARGIN IN TIME and wrote about my cryptic message about "seeing you in Margin again . . ." It was cryptic because the contract wasn't finalized. But I'm pleased to say that my next DLP will be A MARGIN OF ERROR. Harvey Kirk is missing in time and it's up to his daughter, Darys, and her new-found friend, Ford Nolan (an all grown-up Ford!) to find him.

Again, thanks for the letters. And for you computer types, check out my webpage!

http://www.erols.com/lhayden
or e-mail me at lhayden@erols.com

Laura Hayden